DRAW THE DARK

Ilsa J. Bick

carolrhoda LAB
MINNEAPOLIS

Text copyright © 2010 by Ilsa J. Bick

Carolrhoda Lab™ is a trademark of Lerner Publishing Group, Inc.

Carolrhoda Lab™
An imprint of Carolrhoda Books
A division of Lerner Publishing Group, Inc.
241 First Avenue North
Minneapolis, MN 55401 U.S.A.

Website address: www.lernerbooks.com

Cover and interior photographs © John B. Mueller.

Library of Congress Cataloging-in-Publication Data

Bick, Ilsa J.
        Draw the dark / by Ilsa J. Bick.
            p.   cm.
        Summary: Seventeen-year-old Christian Cage lives with his uncle in Winter, Wisconsin, where his nightmares, visions, and strange paintings draw him into a mystery involving German prisoners of war, a mysterious corpse, and Winter's last surviving Jew.
        ISBN: 978–0–7613–5686–8 (trade hard cover : alk. paper)
        [1. Supernatural—Fiction. 2. Artists—Fiction. 3. Crime—Fiction. 4. Emotional problems—Fiction. 5. Jews—United States—Fiction. 6. Wisconsin—History— 20th century—Fiction.] I. Title.

PZ7.B47234Dr 2010
[Fic]—dc22   2009051612

Manufactured in the United States of America
2 – SB – 1/15/11

FOR DAVID.

HISTORY IS A

NIGHTMARE

FROM WHICH

I AM TRYING TO

AWAKE.

—JAMES JOYCE

NOVEMBER 1: LATE MORNING

WINTER, WISCONSIN

So. Everything I need to leave is here: My brushes. Paint. The wall.

Actually, not really the wall—my bedroom wall—but the *pictures* of the sideways place, which I copied from the cover of this really old book my mom kept on her nightstand after my father disappeared. I was only a year old when Dad went away, so I never knew him. Uncle Hank is my dad's brother, and he says Dad was a really good man and loved my mom more than was good for either of them because my mom wasn't quite right after my father vanished. Uncle Hank says Mom would stare at this old book for hours, and when he asked about it, she'd say, "He's there, Hank. He's gone sideways and he can't find his way out and he needs me. If I can just find the way . . . "

Uncle Hank figured she was crazy with grief. Most everybody else thought she was just crazy because she couldn't accept that my dad had found someone else. (Not that anyone knew that for a fact, they were just saying. People here say a lot of things when they don't have a clue what they're talking about.) Anyway, no one was surprised when, two years after my dad went away, my mom disappeared too.

That was fourteen years ago, and I've been looking for my mom ever since.

People in Winter say either she did the same as my dad, found someone else, or killed herself someplace far away to spare us. Uncle Hank doesn't believe any of that, and neither do I, because the only important thing she left behind—well, besides me, I guess—was the cover from that book, with her good-bye note to Uncle Hank written on the reverse, telling him to make sure that cover went to me. So I know that cover's the clue, if I can just figure out how to *see* into it the right way.

Which might explain why the only things I really remember about my mom are her eyes. They were . . . stormy. Gray, like mine. So maybe that's why I have this . . . well, I guess you'd call it an obsession with trying to see the world *through* her eyes. Because if I can just *do* that, I think I'll find her again. See, *I* think she figured out a way to slip into the sideways place, and that's where she is now, with my dad, and neither one of them can get back. That's why they need me. That's why, among other things, I have to leave.

The cover is . . . well, it's strange. There's this freaky, bombed, blasted-looking landscape, with craggy coal-black trees that claw at a sky that's gone the color of a bruise, a deep swirling purple streaked orange and yellow and bloodred. A spiky mountain stabs the sky. There are creatures there too: half dragon, half wolf, with drippy fangs and slitty, gold eyes. Everything on that cover is weird and scary—and somehow very, very familiar, as if I really have seen this place before. Or, maybe, just belong there.

That's the sideways place. That's what I've painted on my walls, every detail, right down to the mountain, everything the same as the cover.

Except that *door.*

I'm not talking about a real door with hinges, the one that will take me back downstairs to where it's warm and safe and familiar. No, I painted *this* door in my sleep. Twice, actually. The first time I was so freaked out, I painted over it. The second time, only a month or so ago, I let it stay on what I guess you'd call a personal dare. Because the door's incomplete. There's no knob, so there's been no way to get through. I've thought about this a lot lately, especially after what happened last night, and I think that last step, painting the knob, has to be a conscious choice and not something I do in a dream. I just haven't been brave enough and that's been fine—until now.

Because after last night, I know I have to leave. I can't stay here anymore. It's not safe for the people I care about with me still in this world.

See, I draw—and what I draw *out* comes alive. Sometimes I draw nightmares, what people want to forget except their minds won't let them. So sometimes that means I'm pulling out the past. Other times, well, I guess you could say I draw destiny because I pull out their worst nightmares of the future, what they're afraid will happen. Or maybe I do both because my shrink says the person you are is who you were, all your

3

memories and experiences and all the dreams and hopes everyone put into you, so you sometimes can't tell where they leave off and you begin. In a way, who you were is what you will be.

I think that's right because sometimes when I *paint*—when what I am comes out of my head and down through my fingers—I kill people. Or get them killed, which is pretty much the same thing, even if I don't do it on purpose. Like last night . . .

So. Whatever's really living in the sideways place is *in* me *and* behind that door. All I've got to do is draw the knob and give it a turn. And I will, I *will* . . . but if my shrink is right, if you can't know where you're going unless you understand where you've been, then I need to understand how I got here so I can keep going and make it through and, maybe, get us all back in one piece.

So I have to start at the beginning: the Wednesday morning I woke up from a nightmare. The morning after I saw the murder for the very first time.

I

The morning I got arrested, I had a headache, the worst I'd ever had, like someone hammering nails into my eyes. Waking up was like clawing through cobwebs, and I swear I smelled hay and manure. I knew I'd been having a nightmare

blood . . . no Papa no no . . .

with lots of blood and horses screaming and men shouting *Papa no . . .*

and . . . had there been a knife? No, it was . . . it was . . . *Grant Wood*, I thought. That's the painter who popped into my head when I tried to remember what I'd seen in my dream. Even if you don't know who Grant Wood is, you probably know *American Gothic*, the painting he did of this small, white Gothic farmhouse, the one with the guy and the pitchfork. The guy's really Grant Wood's dentist and the woman is Wood's sister, but that's not important, not what my brain snagged on when I tried to remember the dream.

What I thought was: *Not a knife, but*
(blood on my hands)
a pitchfork . . .

My head killed. My legs were all sore and my knees ached like when I ride my bike a long time. My right arm hurt and my fingers were all cramped up, like I'd taken a million PSATs and filled in all those circles just right. And there was crud under my nails, like dried blood only bright like I'd cut myself, which I hadn't.

And one last thing: there was this weird, well, *muttering* in my head, like the growl of motorcycles or the rumble of far-off thunder. My head felt . . . crowded.

So yeah. Weird.

This was September, the second week of school, a Wednesday. It was hot and my sheets were sticky and my mouth was gummy. We don't have air-conditioning because we're only a couple of blocks off the lake and we get by with fans. So I lay there, the fan going like a jet engine, the sweat wicking away, until I started getting cold and the smell of fried eggs told me I'd better get moving. So I sat up—and that's when I noticed that my wall was a little different.

I've been drawing and painting on my walls since forever. Uncle Hank and Aunt Jean didn't care, said creativity shouldn't be stifled. Or maybe they were remembering my mom and figured they couldn't stop me. That's about right because I couldn't stop myself if my life depended on it. First, I did kid stuff: mostly rockets and stars and things like that. The stuff with Mom—her face and eyes . . . that didn't start until maybe I was five, six. There are things I paint over, either I can't look at them anymore or they aren't important. But I never paint over my mother or her eyes. You know how when a peacock unfurls its tail, the feathers all have those cobalt blue eyes and so there are hundreds of eyes staring from that tail? Well, I did that on one of my walls, made this peacock fan of my mother's eyes. Only you see things in her eyes, the way you would if my mother's eyes were mirrors or stuffed with memories. So in her eyes, there's me when I was little and then Uncle Hank and Aunt Jean and other eyes with real-place buildings, things I recognize from around the town.

The sideways place, though, that didn't start up until after Aunt Jean died. I think that's because the afternoon *before* she died was the first time I let myself get really, really mad—so mad I reached through to the sideways place or it shot out of me, I'm not sure. All I *do* know is that by that night, Aunt Jean was dead, her car spinning off black ice and into the water, and I knew that was because of me.

Anyway... *that* Wednesday morning in September there were two things on the wall with the sideways place that hadn't been there before.

The first was a pair of eyes I didn't recognize. Not my mom's. Not mine. More like... a wolf's: slanted, the color of molten gold.

The second was a door. No knob, just a black rectangle painted a little to the right of that spiked mountain. Somehow I knew that the muttering in my head was from the things squatting just *behind* that door.

That really gave me the creeps. So I got out of bed pretty fast. Did the shower, dug out clothes from under a pile of books on Dali and Picasso, and hurried downstairs. Because I just didn't want to think about it. Not the muttering or the dream

(blood and horses screaming . . . no Papa no)

or things waiting on the other side of that door. Or the eyes, especially those weird golden eyes. I didn't know whose they were, and I sure as hell didn't want to find out.

Uncle Hank doled out a plate of eggs and sausage like usual for a Wednesday. (We have this system: Cereal on Mondays and Thursdays, oatmeal Tuesdays, eggs and sausage on Wednesdays, and pancakes on Friday. Trade cooking duties every other week. Saturday and Sunday we sleep late, only I sometimes get up early on Saturday and bike on downtown to Gina Pederson's Bakery for cinnamon rolls, especially if I know that Uncle Hank's working third shift on Friday.)

That morning Uncle Hank did a double take, gave me the squinty cop eye, like the Marlboro man without the lung cancer. "You look like you've been carjacked and drug about ten miles." His voice sounded like tires on gravel, and he leaned in a little closer and frowned. "There're smudges under your eyes. You worried about something? School?"

I mumbled I was fine and just tired, which should've satisfied him because that's about all I ever *do* say, and I'm comfortable with Uncle Hank. Only I don't think Uncle Hank would've let it go, if he hadn't gotten a call from the dispatcher. Then he was jamming on his Stetson while I shoveled his eggs and sausage onto bread and wrapped that up with waxed paper. I practically had to throw the sandwich at him, he was out of there so fast. Didn't say what the call was about, but you get used to stuff like that when your uncle's the sheriff.

Tugging on my shoes, I noticed that my new Chucks were wet, which was weird because my shoes were on the mat inside the back door. So there was no way they should be wet, but they were and smelled like grass too. So I had to hunt for an old pair because I didn't want to stink up my Chucks.

I biked in. We live south of town, which is right on the lake, and the school's about four blocks west of Eisenmann Ironworks and Ceramics Plant. If the wind's blowing the wrong way, you smell the factory before you see it. I don't know how many acres the factory takes up, but it's pretty much half the size of the town, what with the foundry and ceramics buildings, the warehouses, water towers, and all. The plant even has its own railroad.

To hear most people, you'd think the Eisenmanns are gods or something, which I guess they kind of are, considering that just about everyone works for them. (Me, I'd known for a long time there was no way I'd ever stay in this town one second longer than I had to. It's not just that I've never been very popular or had much to say. People here have known each other all their lives; they probably know things about you that you've forgotten. To them, Milwaukee and Madison are like foreign countries.)

The Eisenmanns are the American Dream. In fifth grade, we had this special civics unit on the Eisenmanns, how they were dirt-poor and came over from Germany before World War I, made the trip all the way into iron country and built up the factory, put the town on the map . . . blah, blah, blah. The second Eisenmann was the one who actually created the town when you get right down to it. Being one of the first German immigrants to come out this way and a guy who knew iron, he decided he wanted other skilled Germans to be his workforce. So he built a couple of big dormitory-style buildings about a block away from the plant and then paid for all these workers to make the trip from Germany and Austria to Wisconsin. Living in the dormitories, all they had to do was walk across the street to work. Eisenmann even paid for these guys to go to school when they weren't working their shifts. Learn about America, the language, all that. Even now, most everyone works for the Eisenmanns in one way or another. So, yeah. The Eisenmanns are gods.

School was school. Less than five hundred kids, all grades. Small. Everyone knows everything about everyone.

I was in second-period U.S. History after World War I, and the teacher was talking about our independent projects for the semester when the principal came to the door and asked to see the teacher a couple of seconds. My chair was on the right side of the room, same as the door, and in the back, so I had no idea if anyone was with the principal. Everyone else kind of started in talking, though no one talked to me. Which is okay because I'm used to it. There was my mother leaving the way she did that made other mothers tell their kids to stay away from me. Then there was that business with my first-grade teacher, Miss Stefancyzk, how she had this breakdown and put her head through a noose not an hour after she yelled at me, but I was little and I'm still not sure I did that. And then there was Aunt Jean, which I do know about—although nobody else does, especially not Uncle Hank. If he knew, he'd hate me for life. He might even kill me himself.

Anyway, it was okay that no one talked to me. Not like I have a lot to say. Probably safer that way.

Instead, I doodled an idea I had about a charcoal I was working on in art. I'd found this old picture of a lady trying on

10

a hat in front of this four-paneled mirror. The woman's back faced you—like a Magritte painting—and *her* face was reflected in each panel of the mirror at four different angles. I took a look at the Magritte and that old picture, and I thought, yeah, this is a way of seeing my mom from, like, all around. So I'd recognize her no matter what and then . . . and then . . .

And then I was *drawing*, my head growing hollow as a gourd, the knuckles of my clenched brain relaxing and fingers unfurling and filling me like skinning on a glove. I love this feeling. I'm not very good with words, but I know there's what you do with a pencil or brush and then there's *drawing*, like hauling up water from a well, sometimes so deep you wonder there's anything there at all. Michelangelo used to say that the statues he created were trapped in the stone; the stone already *was* David or the Pietà, and all he had to do was, well, free them.

I guess you could say that's what I do when I draw. I . . . draw out something just as I channel something else. Like if I draw a tree: I'll pull out what the tree is from what I see, but I'm also drawing *from* the tree, its energy. I know that sounds weird, but . . . I don't know any other words to say it. I think that's why artists say they're tapped out, nothing more in the well. For them, there's no more water, nothing left to *draw* from or out.

But for me, when I draw, when I'm at my best, there's this tiny click, the flick of an inner light switch, and then I'm pulling, *drawing* from this hidden place in my head and the drawing swells and grows larger and *is* me. When I draw, there is nothing between me and the pencil and the paper because we're all one unit, with a single purpose.

So as I drew out my idea for my mother, the world thinned, then shushed to a whisper, then simply went away, and I was at once diamond bright and formless as a nebula, floaty and yet so concentrated with purpose, and it was the best feeling. It was like I wasn't there, and still, I was most *intensely* there, in the smell of graphite that filled my nose and the sturdy feel of the pencil between my fingers and how my vision sharpened so the weave of paper was hills and valleys and threads all connecting together, and it was a real high, the best, and I loved that, I would kill to stay in that place—

"Christian."

My name dropped like a hammer. I blinked away from my drawing. The teacher and the principal stood together at the front. Every single pair of eyes from every other person in the class was on me—like they'd been calling my name for a while and I hadn't heard, which was very likely. I felt myself, all those great expansive feelings, shrivel, collapse, and go black as a lump of coal.

The principal said, "Christian, would you come with me, please? Bring your books."

"Sure." My stomach was a little fluttery. When this happened at school, it was either somebody's relative was sick or something bad at home. The only thing I could think of was something had happened to Uncle Hank.

Heads swiveled as I walked to the front of the class. A couple of people started whispering. About the only one to look as worried as I felt was Sarah Schoenberg. We used to hang around a lot when we were kids. Her parents and my aunt and uncle were good friends. Then Aunt Jean died and Sarah started getting popular, and since that was never one of my problems, we didn't see much of each other except every couple of Sundays for dinner and to say hi and how are you, that kind of stuff. Sarah's eyes are warm, buttery caramel. Da Vinci eyes. She's not beautiful, but you can tell she's a nice person when she smiles. Only this time, she wasn't smiling.

At the front, the teacher wouldn't look me in the eye and I thought: *uh-oh*. Uncle Hank was the only family I had, and if he was hurt or . . .

But when I stepped into the hall, Uncle Hank was there. He didn't smile. "Christian, we need to talk a couple minutes."

I looked from Uncle Hank to the principal and back. "Okay."

"Not here," said the principal. He led the way to the office. All the secretaries stopped talking when we pushed inside. They watched us go down the hall, looking at me like I was an animal in a zoo. We filed into the principal's office, me sandwiched between the principal and Uncle Hank. The principal said, "Have a seat, Christian."

I sat. He didn't. Neither did Uncle Hank. The principal leaned his butt against his desk, and Uncle Hank stood at my right elbow. I felt like a suspect getting sweated by the police. Maybe I was.

"What?" I asked.

Uncle Hank said, "Christian, that call I got this morning was from Mr. Eisenmann." He paused like that was supposed to mean something.

"Okay," I said.

"Someone took red spray paint to that barn on his property, the old farm about ten miles outside town. Not graffiti, either. It got reported by some of the workers coming in for first shift."

"Yeah?"

"You know anything about it?"

"*Me?*" I blinked. "No."

"You sure about that?"

"Yeah, I'm sure."

"What if I was to tell you that when I saw what was painted on that barn, I didn't think of anyone else *but* you?"

I was going to say, *Well then, I don't know what to tell you*, but I didn't because I thought about my Chucks being wet and how my arm hurt, about that nightmare, and all that blood . . .

Uncle Hank gave me that cop eye. "What?"

I didn't say anything. After a few more seconds, the principal said, "So you won't mind if we open your locker."

I shook my head. Actually, I was a little relieved, to tell the truth. I mean, how stupid would you be if you hid cans of spray paint in your locker or at the bottom of your backpack or something?

Three guesses how stupid.

There were two drippy cans in my backpack that I somehow hadn't noticed even though I'd dug around that sack that very morning. Of course, the paint was still tacky.

"I didn't put those there." I turned to Uncle Hank. "I didn't do that."

The principal said, "Who else would have access to your locker? Who would do that to you?"

Everyone. Anyone. "How should I know? I mean, you can test these for fingerprints, right?" I looked at Uncle Hank again. "Right?"

Uncle Hank put a hand on my shoulder. His hand felt like it was weighed down with lead shot. "Let me see your hands, Christian." He studied the rust crescents under my nails, and then he pulled out a little penknife and scraped out a bit of the crud. I think he and I realized what that stuff was on the blade at just about the same moment. I was stunned, but he only looked sad.

"All right then," he said to the principal. "We'll be going now."

Uncle Hank drove. He made me sit in back. We didn't talk.

We headed southwest, the road cutting through hills and farmland. The corn had petered out two weeks back and the stalks had been cut back, leaving the fields covered with brown stubble. Seven miles out, Uncle Hank hung a left onto a dirt track, and we clattered due south another couple of miles, spewing dust clouds. The farmland here hadn't been cultivated in a long time.

I was certain I'd never been here, but a weird swell of déjà vu crashed against my mind. Then, after hours of nothing, that weird muttering started up in my head again . . .

The barn perched alone on a rise coming up on the right. The barn might've been white once, but this eastern face was weathered gray, the soot black trim of its shutters mottled and looking moth-eaten. The barn was maybe a hundred feet long and fifty feet wide. A weedy ramp curled away to the northwest, probably to hay doors. All the windows were long gone, just blank sockets.

Far off to my right, I saw what remained of a house, reduced now to a foundation and rubble where there was once a chimney. As we ground up the rise, a dozen crows rose in a cloud from the bare spindles of a weeping willow bowed over the ratty ruin of a well.

I swung my head back to the barn—and then I got a good look at that northwest face. That's when my stomach kind of bottomed out.

There, just below a broken-out window, were three words in big splashy red letters:

I SEE YOU.

These were bracketed by two swastikas, one on either side. Sprayed above the words was a pair of bloodred eyes, and those eyes . . .

Dread whispered up and down my spine.

Those eyes were not my mother's. They weren't mine.

They were the eyes of a wolf.

They were the eyes of someone new.

II

"Lord knows, Hank, everyone thinks you and Jean did the right thing, taking in your brother's boy." Mr. Eisenmann frowned down at me then, the tears dribbling from his droopy left eye. "I hope you appreciate the sacrifices your uncle's made on your behalf."

"I appreciate it," I said. We were sitting in Uncle Hank's office, with Mr. Eisenmann in the one comfortable chair and me on a metal folding chair from the roll-call room. Uncle Hank was behind his desk, his face a chunk of granite. My head hurt like there were a million knives stabbing my brain, and I worried I might puke. "But I didn't do it."

Mr. Eisenmann waved my words away. His fingers were skeletal and twiglike, and he had the face of a gargoyle: creased with scars from some kind of accident almost sixty years ago. A pink seam slashed a diagonal through the outer third of his left eyebrow, bisected his left eyelid and tracked over his cheek and the knob of his nose. Another scar carved a half moon over his right cheek. A deep horizontal gash cut his chin like a second mouth. The cuts had done something to the tear duct of his left eye, so he was always crying crocodile tears.

"I think we've established, beyond a shadow of a doubt, that you did indeed do this, young man. The issue now is what is to be done about it." Dabbing at his eye with a folded white kerchief, Eisenmann swung his gargoyle's head back at Uncle Hank. Eisenmann was eighty at least, and I'd never seen him in anything but a three-piece suit and a gold watch chain with heavy gold fobs. He always carried a redwood cane topped with a gold wolf's head. "Hank, this boy isn't right and never has been. You know that, I know that. Hell, everyone in town knows it, and now he's getting violent, vandalizing—"

"Wait a minute," I said, but Uncle Hank held up a hand, and I knew better than to go on.

"Violent and *morbidly* preoccupied." Eisenmann held open the history notebook I'd been doodling in earlier that morning. "Cemeteries? *Tombstones?* It's ghoulish, Hank. It's disturbed."

For the record, I hadn't remembered doing a single headstone—I was drawing my *mother*. But there they all were, marching across the page like fence posts. The tombstones were weird, too: not singleton stones but doubles shaped like the Ten Commandments and not a cross in sight. Three steep-roofed mausoleums loomed in the background, like something out of New Orleans. But I didn't *remember* drawing on th—

blood on my hands and Papa no no . . . the horses are screaming

The thought was sudden and violent like a bolt of lightning in my brain and so sharp, I gasped. What?

blood . . . no Papa no . . .

The nightmare, again, but I wasn't asleep, I was awake, how . . . ?

watch out . . . watch . . .

Oh my God. I squeezed my head between my hands. My pulse thumped in my head, and the same muttering I'd noticed when I woke up was back now and louder, a grumble that was the sound of many voices all balled together. Not my thoughts, these were not mine, so who—

"Christian?" Uncle Hank said.

"I don't remember." I screwed my eyes shut and thought at the chaos in my brain: *Go away, be quiet, leave me alone, leave me **alone**.* I said, way too loudly, "I don't *remember!*"

Eisenmann started in again. "Hank, this boy needs help. You know it, I know it. Next thing you know, he'll be shooting up the place like those Columbine kids—"

"That's enough." Uncle Hank's voice was low, soft, and deadly. "That's *my* nephew. So I'll thank you to watch your goddamned mouth."

Eisenmann gawped for a second, then spluttered, "Do you know who you're talking to? One word from me, and I could get your tenure as sheriff revoked."

Uncle Hank's lips thinned like the gash on Eisenmann's chin. He said nothing.

"That's right." Eisenmann nodded as if Uncle Hank had agreed. "That's right. So don't think I won't press charges. Don't even *consider* that we aren't going to court."

"It's Christian's first offense." I could tell that cost Uncle Hank. He wasn't pleading exactly, but it was close. "I'll take the boy to counseling. We'll make restitution. For God's sake, that barn's seen nothing but trouble, needed to come down years ago. It's not as if we're talking something you actually use."

"That's my concern, Sheriff, not yours and property is property. As for a first offense, I remind you of that business with Ms. Stefancyzk. . . . "

"She had a nervous breakdown. Christian had nothing to do with that."

"Believe that if it brings you comfort." Using his wolf-headed cane, Mr. Eisenmann levered himself to his feet. "You're up for reelection come April. I'd keep that in mind if I were you. See you in court."

After he left, I couldn't think of anything worth saying, so I didn't. Uncle Hank didn't say anything either, just stared at that stupid cemetery drawing. Why had I drawn that? Why *today* of all days? At least the muttering in my head was just a murmur now and fuzzy, like static from an old radio.

There was a soft rap, and then Marjorie, the office manager, poked her head in the door. "I've got Madison on the line for you, Sheriff. What would you like me to tell Deputy Brandt?"

Uncle Hank passed a weary hand before his eyes. "Tell Brandt to secure the house as best he can. If the owner won't leave . . ."

"She's staying. Says she won't go near the third story, though why anyone would want to stay in a virtual crime scene, I don't know."

"Got me." Uncle Hank's ice-blue eyes clicked to me. "Go with Marjorie and wait in the roll-call room. I'll be out in a few minutes."

I stood. "I'm sorry, Uncle Hank."

"I know," he said, but he was already picking up the phone as I headed for the door.

On the way, I asked Marjorie, "What's going on? What crime scene? Who's in Madison?"

She took the last question first. "The forensic anthropologist. She'd be here sooner only they've got some sort of horrible multiple murder in a condominium right outside Milwaukee, in Brookfield. Some poor woman was having her basement extended, and one of the workmen broke through the concrete and found a body. Relatively fresh too; I hear they think it was put there when the foundation was poured, about six months ago. Now they've brought in ground-penetrating radar to check all the other condominiums. So far, they've found a body in every single basement, like a graveyard." She nodded sagely. "That's the problem; you get too big, people all piled up on each other like rats. People turn violent."

"Wow." I knew what a forensic anthropologist was from television. "So why do we need the anthropologist up *here*?"

Marjorie hesitated, her mouth puckering to a rosebud. She was office manager back when Uncle Hank's dad was sheriff and looks the way you think a woman who's run a bunch of guys with more efficiency than a drill sergeant should look: a helmet of silver-gray hair, sharp brown eyes behind steel-rimmed glasses on a holder chain. There were a few people in Winter who either weren't leery of me or who tolerated me because of Uncle Hank. Marjorie was in a separate category. We genuinely got along. When I was a little kid, she used to filch pop out of the deputies' icebox. Over the years, I'd had so much Orange Crush, I could probably float a boat.

me with me." She shooed me into the roll-call room, door, and said, "You know the old Ziegler place on ... th side? That old brownstone mansion?" (I didn't, but I didn't want to derail her by asking about it.) "Well, the new owner was having work done on the third story—the servants' quarters—and I guess the workmen were tearing out an old hearth. Only when they did, they found a *body*." She paused. "A *mummy*, actually."

"Whoa. Who?"

"Nobody knows. The coroner says it's not recent—been there for years and years. That also means there's no hurry, so we're low down on Madison's list, I guess. It happens. Your uncle says there aren't very good records, like maybe none at all since the place has been vacant so long. The Zieglers weren't even the original owners, and then they rented for years, so . . . they might never know."

"How do you put a whole person into a hearth?"

"Well," Marjorie said, "that gets a whole lot easier when it's a baby."

Something changed in my head after that. Maybe it was the day finally catching up to me, or perhaps my subconscious picked up on yet another tumbler falling into place. But when I heard about that dead baby, there was this sensation of something going *click* in my mind, almost the same as when I drew, only not as nice. I knew, without knowing how, that the baby and the weirdness I'd done at Mr. Eisenmann's barn were somehow connected. Winter was too small, the history too intertwined for all of this not to be. I had no idea *how* these two things could be connected, but they were. My problem was I couldn't talk to anyone about my feelings. Heck, I wasn't even sure what they were. Even if I had, I'd probably have sounded pretty crazy. Considering that's how most people saw me anyway, maybe that would've been par for the course and there'd have been no harm done.

But. Even now, I wonder what would've happened if I'd spoken up just a little sooner. If I had, maybe a couple other people wouldn't have gotten killed. I don't know that for sure, but I think so.

I didn't go back to school, but Uncle Hank didn't take me home right away either. He got tied up and eventually had one of the deputies drive me out. The deputy was new, and I didn't know him.

"What about my bike?" I asked as we walked to his cruiser. "It's still at school."

"Sorry, kiddo, I got my orders," said the deputy.

After that, we didn't have anything to talk about. He stared straight ahead, and I looked out the side window. People on the sidewalks turned to watch as the cruiser went past, and some elbowed each other and pointed or started nodding and chattering to each other.

By then, I was getting really scared. Eisenmann said I was crazy. Worse, I was deranged, I would go postal. But was he right? My idea of crazy was like Renfield in *Dracula*. You know, eating flies and talking to people who aren't there and spouting gobbledygook. But I wasn't like that at all. I mean, yeah, I was strange and different and people looked at me funny or made excuses not to hang around when I walked into a room . . . but it wasn't the same thing.

Only what if it was?

I thought about the muttering in my head. Was that the way voices started up, the ones that schizophrenics got? So maybe I was already way far gone. . . .

When I got home, I couldn't go to my room. I was too restless to sit still. For once, I didn't want to draw. Maybe I was afraid to. But I had to keep moving, pacing a circle around and around the living room the way caged tigers do in the zoo. I found my iPod and tried listening, but after maybe five minutes, the music was irritating and I shut it off.

It occurred to me that this was what it would be like in jail, pacing miles and miles in my cell. For years and years and years . . .

My chest got all tight, and my face flushed so hot I started to sweat, and I burst into tears. I just stood there, shoulders heaving and tears streaming down my face, gulping sobs in the middle of the living room—which we don't use except for company. There are a lot of Aunt Jean's things in here, and her pictures are everywhere, like some kind of creepy mausoleum. I could feel her eyes on me then from those pictures, and I got all limp. My legs wobbled and my knees gave out, and I sort of flopped to the floor. I groveled and sobbed the way a truly evil person does in all those movies when everyone knows he's going to hell and there isn't a damn thing he can do about it. I deserved everything bad that was going to happen because Eisenmann was right. I was nuts and I had gotten my aunt killed and made my teacher go insane, and weird shit was coming like thunderheads on the horizon, and if my mother had gone away, it was for a good reason—and probably on account of me.

I woke up in a sweaty ball on the living room carpet, drool on my right cheek. My clothes were moist and I could smell myself. At least, the muttering was gone.

I stood under a shower so hot my skin got boiled-looking and steam hazed the bathroom. Padding out of the bathroom in a towel, I dumped my clothes in the hamper, thought about doing a load. Only the laundry room reminded me of movies about prison laundries and then I felt the tears start up, and so I got out of there before I could start bawling again.

Usually Uncle Hank gets home for dinner round about seven, but it was eight thirty now, so I knew it was going to be another late night for him. Or maybe he didn't want to see me. I made myself a peanut butter sandwich, took a bite, chewed, and then my throat balled, and I had to spit it out. I tossed the sandwich in the garbage.

I trudged up to my room, flicked on my fan, and lay down on my bed. The sun was almost gone, and my paintings of the sideways place—plum-purple and ruddy orange—looked bloody in the sunset. My head ached as if someone had taken a brick and pounded the top of my skull. I watched shadows creep across the ceiling. Tried not to think and couldn't *not* think.

No question: I'd done a number on Eisenmann's barn. So I had to be sleepwalking—and sleep-*biking*, come to think of it. That was the only explanation for my wet Chucks. The ache in my shoulders and arms was because I'd had to dangle from a rope tied off in the hayloft and needed one hand to keep from falling, the other to paint. The crescents of red paint beneath my nails just confirmed everything.

Then I thought back to the nightmare of the evening before: horses and blood and men screaming. A pitchfork.

For some reason, my eyes crawled to my desk. My drawing pad was squared there, a pencil worn almost down to nothing lying on top—and *that* was wrong. That pencil had been sharp the night before. As if in a dream, I opened my pad and started flipping pages . . .

I didn't start shaking until the next-to-last drawing. Because there was the barn I knew I'd never seen until today.

And on the very last page: a view of the town from a great distance and high up, from the hay door on the east side of the barn. Had to be. The fields and hills were right, and there was a smudge of lake, the foundry's smokestacks, and the big square clock tower opposite the town hall—

And one more building I didn't recognize at all that had an onion dome, like buildings in Russia. I stared. There was nothing like that in Winter. Not in this life—or world—anyway. And then I thought: *The sideways place?*

My whole body went clammy cold. *That* had never occurred to me before, that it might work like osmosis, you know? Maybe my mother and father could slip in and not get back out. But maybe that meant if something in *there* got out *here*, it couldn't get back either because a balance had to be kept.

I remembered that weird muttering, gone now. What if the muttering really wasn't *me*? What if something was sitting *behind* my eyes, *in* my head?

"Stop it." My voice was shaky and sounded really small. "Stop freaking yourself out."

But once I'd thought all this, it was impossible not to keep thinking. Uncorking the bottle and letting out the genie: That's what Aunt Jean used to call it, when you'd get a notion in

26

your head you just couldn't shake. You can't unthink a possibility once it's occurred to you.

So.

So what if the thing out at the barn was something that *I* really hadn't done? What if my *body* had been there, but not *me?*

I lay there, thinking about that, wondering what if. Then I cried again, pillow over my face in case Uncle Hank came home. While I lay there, my face all damp, I wondered what would happen if I fell asleep with the pillow still on my face. How long would it take for a grown man to suffocate a stupid teenager and would it hurt much . . . ?

Dumb things like that.

I don't remember falling asleep so much as my head got swimmy and my thoughts slipped sideways and *hot so hot july bright sun that hurts my eyes and dust, the smell of scorched metal because the wind is blowing the wrong way today.*

i run down main street because it is the day the train is coming and everyone is scared and excited all at the same time because THEY'RE coming . . .

Papa's in the foundry back in the ceramics workshop, the special clean room that keeps out soot and dust and he's painting something with lots of swirls and flowers and i'm not allowed there but i squirt through like a wet watermelon seed and burst in.

what's this, he scowls, what are you doing?

—come on, Papa i tug his hand —come on, come on . . .

he comes because we are all curious . . . there's a big crowd along the tracks and Marta is there in gauzy white and broad straw hat with a red red ribbon to match her hair band and i can tell Papa doesn't like that, but she is seventeen and going to college to be an interpreter and she is as stubborn as Papa, so stubborn Mama says they should both be irish instead of polish.

the train is going very slowly so we can all get a very good look.

the prisoners are staring out at us through the open boxcars and there are other men with rifles.

the prisoners' faces are still like wax like clay and they don't smile and neither do we.

but

but they have eyes like wolves.

golden and strange and . . .

i look away.

—no good will come of this. sheriff Cage stands next to Papa and he has blue blue eyes like the sky at twilight. i'd be happier the crops rot in the fields than bring them here.

the union boys and Papa mill around but Mr. Eisenmann is happy. he's very rich and so he didn't have to go off to war because the plant is so important because of all the iron and his father gave him the plant to run and so for Mr. Eisenmann the prisoners are good because they can work the fields and the plant and anything else needs doing.

the union boys don't like it. Papa doesn't like it. Eisenmann's out to break us, that's what they say.

the mayor makes a speech. the prison commander makes a speech. it's so hot sweat trickles down my sides and glues my shirt to my back.

Mr. Eisenmann is all gold, the ring on his little finger, the links of his gold watch chain, the buttons of his linen suit, even his cravat and his hair. he talks the longest about how the prisoners will stay in the old dormitories on the foundry grounds and how they will be good for the town and he brings a prisoner with white teeth and blue eyes to stand next to him and they are both gold in the sun like when Mrs. Grunewald talks about the gemini twins in school and Mr. Eisenmann puts his arm around the prisoner and calls him my friend and my right arm and my brother and this is all good only i don't think so and the union boys are against it all and my Papa most of all.

then the prisoner talks Mr. Eisenmann's friend talks and he has white teeth and his eyes are bluer than the sky ... his skin is brown as a nut because of being in the sun all the time and this makes his teeth look even whiter and his words are perfect ... his accent is less than mine and that makes me ashamed.

the sheriff shakes his head. —my boy's still over there. war's over and my boy still doesn't know when he can come home. bringing in prisoners to work when our own boys could do the work ... this ain't right ... and I don't care how many relatives folks here got back there ain't none of these people my friend ...

they take pictures of Mr. Eisenmann and the sheriff and the men with rifles and the prisoner with no accent and the good teeth ...

but then something happens and only i see it.

the prisoner looks at Marta and she stares back and then she smiles. and then his face changes.

it melts like wax. his jaw gets long and his eyes are yellow and then gold and his teeth are sharp sharp sharp as the pitchfork ...

and his lips are black and peel back and he is a wolf ...

he is a wolf and only i see it and there is blood, so much blood, Papa no, no Papa, don't ... no not the pitchfork no ... blood on my clothes and on my hands and it's sticky and smells like a milk pail left out in the rain ... t he horses smell it and they are stamping and kicking the stalls and i want to run run run run far far away but i have to be quiet ssshh ssshh ssshh ...

then the ghosts cluster round and they stab, they sting, they take my mouth, don't take my mouth please don't take my mouth, i need to scream, i need to scream Papa Papa Papa don't ...

III

When I woke up after one in the morning, it was to the taste of dust in my mouth and the sour smell of my sweat and images that made no sense.

And, oh yeah—I was still alive.

It was Thursday, a cereal day, and so when I stumbled downstairs after nine, Uncle Hank was in the kitchen, with a mug of coffee cupped in his hands. He looked up as I dragged in. "Christian. How'd you sleep?"

"Not too good." There was a bowl of Cocoa Puffs at my place. I usually had Wheaties or corn flakes. Cocoa Puffs used to be my favorite, only Aunt Jean said I didn't need the sugar. I hadn't had Cocoa Puffs since I was ten, but Uncle Hank had gone out and bought me Cocoa Puffs. I stared at the cereal and felt this big lump push into the back of my throat, and tears itched the backs of my eyes.

"Not surprised." Uncle Hank pushed the milk toward me. "Sit down and have something to eat."

"Okay." I ate my Cocoa Puffs. I didn't think I would be able to choke them down, but I did it for Uncle Hank. They tasted terrible and made me queasy. But I ate every last one. I even drank the milk just like when I was a kid.

Uncle Hank cleared his throat. "You're supposed to appear in juvenile court on Friday."

"Tomorrow? Isn't that kind of fast?" I licked off a chocolate milk moustache. Maybe they didn't need a lot of time when they had your sorry ass.

"A little." He'd missed a patch shaving, and there was dried blood on his neck. His eyes looked raw. "But it's probably best. Sooner you get this out of the way, sooner you get back to your life. Now, there are a couple of things going to happen today. . . ." He went over them: lawyer, social worker, psychological tests.

When he was done, I said, "What do you want to have happen?"

"How do you mean?"

"Do you want me to go away?"

He looked genuinely shocked. "No. Of course not, Christian. How could you think such a thing?"

My lips started trembling again. "But I've screwed everything up. Everyone hates me and no college will ever take me and—"

"Quiet." Uncle Hank's voice was all clogged, like he had a cold. He put his hand out to touch my arm. "That's enough of that. You haven't done anything gonna jeopardize college, I promise."

"You can't know that. Mr. Eisenmann . . ."

"Is pissed off and used to getting his own way, but it's not like you burned the factory down. We're talking about a barn, and a derelict at that. Anyway, you're going to juvenile court. Records are sealed. No college need ever know. In a couple years you can leave this and Winter behind—and that's okay, Christian. This is my life, but it doesn't have to be yours."

That made me feel a little better. Then I thought of something. "What did you mean yesterday when you talked about the barn seeing trouble?"

"Oh." Uncle Hank looked uncomfortable. "Well, there was a bad business happened there back before I was born. This was 1945, sometime in September, October. This would've been when your great-grandfather Jasper was sheriff. A man was murdered, that's all. Farmhand. Never did catch his killer, though everyone knew who'd done it because he ran off. Worker at the foundry, some immigrant. Abandoned his wife and two children."

"And they never caught him?"

"There was too much going on. That fire I told you about, the one that killed your great-grandfather and all those union boys and half the nonunion workers at the foundry, that happened maybe a week later. After that, well . . . I guess folks figured there were more important things to worry about. Anyway, technically, it's still an open case, but . . . " He shrugged. "No one really looks into it anymore. Killer's probably dead anyway."

"Why would Mr. Eisenmann want the barn?"

"Because he's Eisenmann and he wants everything. After the murder, wasn't any way the owner—I think his name was

Anderson—could work the fields. Things were bad enough during the war, trying to get enough labor to pick the crops and work the factory. Given the murder, people said the place was hexed. Haunted. Heck, someone back then even set fire to the farmhouse."

"Really? Why burn the farmhouse and not the barn?"

"Before my time, I don't know. Anyway, when I was a boy, we used to go out there on Halloween and try to scare ourselves silly. Of course, nothing ever happened."

My mouth was gluey, so I got up and filled a glass with water from the tap. "But I've never done that. I've never been there before. I still don't remember going there. Why would I go somewhere I haven't been and take spray paints I don't remember buying..." I drank my water, rinsed my glass, set it on the drain board, and then turned back to Uncle Hank. "Do you believe me?"

"It doesn't matter what I believe."

"That's not what I asked."

"I believe in *you*," he said, but his eyes slewed sideways, and a few minutes later, he said he had business down at the department and left.

I got the court-appointed lawyer for juveniles. She was okay, but she kept checking her watch, and I wanted to scream that she should just go see all those way more important kids than me already. But I kept my mouth shut. That's what I'm best at.

A social worker came. She spent a long time with Uncle Hank, and then she talked to me. She had this way of talking like she knew exactly how you were feeling and that made me kind of mad. (That's the one thing about people who say they want to help kids. I never come away with that feeling. I always think about how they're trained to talk to kids so kids will want to believe them, only they're adults and they have jobs and they must do this a hundred times a month, and they can't *all* be your friend.)

I also had to take a bunch of tests to see if I was crazy. One test was stupid and pretty long and asked a lot of questions over and over again, so I started psyching myself out, worrying that maybe they were trying to trick me by asking the same questions, then seeing if maybe I answered them differently than before. I thought about going back and checking to see what I'd answered but then I figured that this was what they *wanted* me to do and that it was a trick. . . . Then I decided I was screwed anyway, so what was the point?

Uncle Hank and I didn't talk much—which, come to think of it, wasn't really much different than normal. I'd said everything I could think of, anyway. There was this big hole in my chest, like I knew I was different and he'd done the best he could to protect me and here I was bringing him nothing but grief. Maybe it would be better if I just went away.

Court happened by Friday noon. There wasn't much I had to do except stand up when the judge called my name and say, "Guilty" and then keep on standing so the judge could tell me what a sorry piece of work I was, how vandalism wouldn't be tolerated, blah, blah, blah. Actually, it was good I didn't have to do much other than be present and accounted for. By then, I wasn't just creeped out by my dreams and what I'd drawn. I wasn't only scared. I was freaking out. I mean, if you just looked at the thing, yeah, I was quiet and kind of dreamy and geeky-weird and talking was hard, but I hadn't set fire to anything or robbed a bank or sold drugs. I wasn't a bit like some guys I'd known at school. Like this one junior last year named Karl Dekker, who'd gotten kicked out for vandalizing the school and drinking and a bunch of other stuff. So considering a guy like *him*, it would be harder to justify sending me away to, like, a boy's home or something. Man, if that happened, I would've left. I would have gotten out of town as fast as I could because they'd kill me in a place like that. The Dekker kind of kids? They're scary.

Besides, this was my *life*. I had plans, things I was supposed to be doing. I had my eye on art school; I mean, when I did *art*-art, it was pretty good, and something about the idea of painting like Rembrandt and Velazquez and Caravaggio excited me. The way they used chiaroscuro, all those inky shadows and sudden light and drawing in the dark, was a language I understood. And Dali or Picasso: I wanted to understand how they *drew* out what they painted as a person or watch. For me, when the painting was going well, it's like I said: There was this click in my head, like someone had thrown a switch somewhere and all of a sudden, I was on this different plane of existence. I know that sounds crazy, but I've read books about artists and writers and composers, and they all say the same thing: how when you're creative, your brain works differently. My science teacher called it an altered state of consciousness, right-brain thinking. Something like that.

Anyway, when all was said and done at court, my punishment came down to community service and reparations. Which was a legal way of saying I had to repair the damage I'd done—repaint that side of the barn. My community service wasn't bad, just working in the old-age home twice a week. Except the judge slapped me for eight hundred hours total, or some ridiculous number that would take me until past New Year's to finish. But still, it could've been worse. I didn't mind being around old people. The ones who remembered things were pretty interesting, actually, and I'd never had grandparents, so it was okay.

And I had to see a shrink too. Twice a week. So I guess maybe the test results weren't too good.

I figured that between the work on the barn, the community service, the shrink, and school, they were out to make sure I didn't have too much downtime.

The thing was, I'd done Eisenmann's barn in my *sleep*. Considering how my dreams had been going lately, I wasn't too sure they could put the genie back into that particular bottle.

IV

Saturday. Another dog day scorcher. I started on the barn. Sometime between Wednesday and then, Eisenmann had gotten a bunch of scaffolding put up.

"That's pretty high." Uncle Hank had sent Deputy Brandt with me because, technically, I was supposed to do this under the supervision of the court. Being a deputy, Justin Brandt filled the bill, and he'd volunteered. He was another one of the adults in town who didn't hold with the way everyone else felt about me, but that might've been because he wasn't all that much older than me. Aunt Jean had kind of adopted him when his father got disabled in a foundry accident.

Wrapping his fist around one of the scaffold supports, Justin gave it a good shake, grunted when nothing came crashing down. "Seems sturdy enough. You should be okay."

"Oh sure. Heights don't bother me." I lied.

Justin hooked his thumbs in his utility belt. "Why Eisenmann doesn't just tear down this old place, I don't know. The idea of making you scrape off red paint so you can paint the barn over in another color red . . . that's just plain mean."

That was an understatement. Before I could scrape anything off, I had to brush on an acid-based softener. Otherwise, I'd be chipping out wood. The softener didn't stink, but it would burn something fierce, so I also had to gear up in these coveralls and wear gloves and goggles, like those hazmat guys. Let the softener get to work, and then scrape off the paint without taking half the wood with me. I'd be lucky not to end up a puddle of grease on account of the heat.

Justin said, "Man, I'd like to help you, but if your uncle comes by and catches me, he'll have my hide. Still, I feel kind of stupid just sitting here with my thumb up my ass."

I laughed like he wanted me to, and that did feel kind of good. "I'll be okay."

"Uh-huh. You got enough of that Gatorade? Last thing I need is you getting heatstroke."

I told Justin I would be okay and got to work. A line of crows marched along the barn's roofline but rose in a chorus of harsh caws as I began to climb. Hauling that can of solvent, wondering if everything was going to hold, was the hardest part. The vibrations of my footfalls shuddered into the palms of my hands as I climbed the ladder. Those crows swarmed overhead, and I kept thinking: *This is when the whole thing crashes down and I break my neck.*

Once I was up there, I plugged into my iPod, fitted on the goggles, and got down to it. After a few nervous minutes, I settled into a rhythm brushing on softener, but I was sweating like nobody's business, the perspiration pooling around my waistband. Justin had brought along a book, and he pretended to read in a wedge of shade along the north edge of the barn. Maybe twenty minutes after I got started, I glanced over and Justin's deputy's hat was down over his eyes, his arms crossed over his chest. If my earbuds hadn't been in, I'd have probably heard him snoring.

The sun beat down on my back and head and arms; I was baking and basting at the same time. In maybe thirty minutes, I'd sweated through my clothes. Even the backs of my knees were wet, and my hands were clammy in their latex gloves. I chugged from a couple quart jugs of Gatorade Rain, but that made me have to pee. I might've just done the point and shoot—that high, the arc might've been kind of cool—but I was in enough trouble. So I was up and down.

I paced myself. I'm not a real athlete or anything, but my arms are pretty good. I brushed on softener working a left-to-right swath. By the time I reached the end, it had been about an hour, and then I could go back and start scraping. A couple hours of this, though, and my shoulders started to really ache and my arms were sore. I started to wonder if maybe I could get my hands on a cordless sander or power washer. I had to have *something* because doing this all by hand was going to take until sometime next summer.

My fourth time down, Justin woke up, yawned, stretched, smacked his lips a couple times, squinted up at me, and said, "Hey, you're doing okay."

"Mmmm." The right swastika was maybe half gone, a mess of red and gray flakes snowing the grass below. A big irregular splotch of weathered gray board flowered along the barn like a fungus. I shrugged and worked my right shoulder. The muscles between my shoulder blades felt tight. "But I'm never going to get done this way. I'll be here for years. Way more than eight hundred hours of community service."

Justin grinned. "Yeah, Eisenmann's one cruel SOB. But I got a cousin who does a lot of carpentry. You want, I'll see if maybe he's got some kind of machine for next time. I don't know a lot about painting, but there's got to be a better way than doing this by hand."

"Yeah." I armed away sweat. I reeked of greasy sunscreen I didn't need because of the coveralls. "That would be great."

"Come on, it's lunchtime. My treat."

But I shook my head. "If it's all the same to you, I think that I should keep going. I'm kind of worried that getting started again would be a hundred times worse."

Justin said I was probably right about that. He said he'd go into town, grab some sandwiches and drinks, and be right back. "You'll be okay, right?"

"Sure. Just me and the barn swallows."

The muttering started up as soon as the red dust ball of Justin's cruiser was out of sight.

I was on the scaffold again when that happened. Suddenly, my arm froze, the edge of the paint scraper pressed against old wood, and I started trembling. Cold beads of sweat popped over my forehead, and my teeth actually chattered the way they hadn't since I was a little kid with the flu. I thought about heatstroke, but I remembered that you weren't supposed to sweat. Then, just as quickly, the icy wave passed to be replaced by the muttering.

I wasn't too scared, which was really weird. Did this mean I was getting used to being crazy? Did crazy people even worry about things like that? But I was more ... apprehensive. The empty eye of that window the next level up seemed to yawn wider and wider and then this arrow of thought: the muttering—the voices—wanted me inside. Well, why not? It was hotter than heck, and the ground was so far away. ...

The crows had come back too, their claws digging into the roof, and I felt their glittery eyes drilling my back as I pulled myself over the lip of the window and into the barn. Inside, the first thing that hit was the smell, which is weird for me because I usually notice how things look first. But this time, it was the smell: the memory of sun-scorched timothy hay, a faint overlay of manure, and the fresher stink of bird poop. Heart thumping, I eased my way down a rickety old ladder from a kind of catwalk that went around the mow. The ladder groaned and squealed, and I kept waiting for a rung to crumble under my feet and drop me to the loft floor, but I made it down and I stood a sec, waiting for my legs to stop wobbling. I turned a slow circle, letting my eyes sweep over the barn and broken windows, unsure what I was supposed to see but drinking—*drawing*—it all in. The loft was cut by thick shadow, alternating with bolts of sunlight shooting through gaps in the roof. A flight of stairs led from the cupola and ducked through a square cut into the wooden floor. The mow was wide and above it ran bare wooden beams. I spotted an old rat's tail of rope curled around one beam, but it was frayed and would probably crumble to dust if you touched it.

The muttering in my head was ... well, it was there but holding its breath, waiting for me to notice—*what*? Then I saw it through the jagged gap in an east-facing window, and all at once, my vision narrowed and sharpened, like I was looking through a telescope, and the muttering surged to life.

I was looking at Winter, and it was the town almost exactly as I'd drawn it on the last page of my pad on the day I'd awakened from that first awful nightmare. There were the stacks of Eisenmann's plant chuffing ash gray smoke. There were fields alternating with tracks of oak and birch; and beyond, the cerulean lake seeping into a light turquoise sky. My gaze involuntarily clicked to the place in the landscape where I knew the onion-domed building ought to be . . . but, of course, it wasn't there. To the left was a copse of aspens on the southern tip of a small pond. From this height, I could see that someone had decided that was a great place to dump a load of old bricks, barely visible through weedy snarls.

I didn't know why I needed to see this. I didn't know why I was doing any of this. I decided I really needed to take a break. I was tired, sweaty, hungry, my head swimmy from the heat and, yeah, a little freaked out again. Best to rest and then Justin would come back and I'd have lunch and feel better.

The hinges of the second-story hay door protested when I tugged, but I got the door open, and a gust of cool air lifting from the lake pillowed against my cheeks. I leaned out a few seconds, letting the air wash over my face and then I felt calmer, ready for a nap. I sprawled with my back up against the boards and stretched out my legs . . . and the muttering dropped to a whisper, my thoughts got jagged and smells became sounds became colors and then I was falling—

V

I'll try to describe exactly what happened next.

I still smelled manure and hay, but the smell was stronger now, and horses nickered in their stalls below. My head filled with a swirly sensation like being on a roller coaster, and I swooped up and down the way you do when you're on the edge of a dream: not quite asleep but not really awake either. I knew I was in the haymow; the hard edge of splintering wood from the frame dug into my back, and I felt grit beneath my thighs.

I cranked open my eyes.

Everything had changed.

For one, it was high summer. I could tell from the gold and green of the fields stretching away toward the horizon. There were men in the fields to my right, bent over rows of bush beans, trailing lumpy burlap bags, which they filled. Two men on horseback kept watch. Each cradled a rifle. They were uniformed, but I couldn't make out if they were police or prison guards. To the left, I spotted two horses munching clumps of orchard grass, and still farther on, two jet-black horses ambled toward the mirror-still pond. The aspens were still there but not as tall.

I don't know what I felt, exactly. Part of me was confused, convinced I was dreaming. The other part was just . . . scared.

"Be happy you're not a prisoner," said someone behind me. "Otherwise, Anderson would be working you into the ground too."

I was so startled I almost fell out of the loft. My heart seized up and I gasped audibly. I turned.

On the floor of the loft was a mountain of loose, fresh-mown alfalfa. A thick rope, big around as my forearm and strong and new—and not at all that frayed curl I'd spotted before—was knotted around one of the wooden beams, and a sturdy ladder leaned against a post leading to some kind of ledge.

And there was a boy. He was much younger than me— maybe seven or eight—and thin, with a flop of brown hair and large brown eyes.

My tongue came unglued from the roof of my mouth. "What? Who . . . ?" But I already knew. His name was on the tip of my tongue: "Pavel."

"Yeah? What are you waiting for, David, let's go!"

"Go? Go where?" Then: "What did you call me?"

Pavel made a horsey sound. "Stop fooling around. I know you get to do this all the time, but some of us don't get the chance, so come on!" The boy whirled on his heel and scampered over to the ladder, ascending the rickety ladder like a small monkey. The soles of his bare feet were black, and he wore grimy corduroy trousers.

My eyes jerked to my own legs. My paint-flecked cover-alls were gone, replaced by a dusty denim overall and a white button-up shirt with short sleeves. What? *What*? I plucked at the fabric, and that's when I noticed that my hands weren't right; they were smaller, the wrists bony. A scar curved along the back of my left hand.

I wasn't me. I was—

"David!" High above, Pavel was reaching for the rope that dangled from the highest point of the loft. "Come on, you sissy!"

"I . . ." I staggered to my feet. They, too, were bare. "Wait, I . . ."

"WOOO!" Pavel pushed off. The rope carried him in a swooping arc like a trapeze artist, and then at the peak of his swing, above the thick mound of alfalfa, he let go. With a jungle yell, Pavel dropped like a rock and plowed into the hay. A second later, his head popped up like a jack-in-the-box. "Come on, David, you going to stand around all day?"

"N-no," and then I was walking, my body a little stiff, as if I were some kind of android getting used to his new skin, . . . which I guess was true. With every step, more of the body I was in took over and more of *me*, who *I* was, kind of took a backseat. Like an observer in a balcony. I felt my consciousness—me, Christian—pull back into the shadows. By the time I put my— the boy's—hands on the rope, I wasn't really me so much as—

"David!" From my vantage point looking down, Pavel was as tiny as a bug. His head was tipped back, his arms akimbo. "Come on, it's easy!"

Heart in mouth, I pushed off. I felt the rush of air through my hair—long, shaggy, fluttering around my ears—and the mow blurred. I wondered, too late, when I should let go, and then the boy's body took over. At the precisely right instant, my/his hands loosened, and we/he rocketed for the floor. The hay rushed for my/his face and

then the sweet scent of alfalfa envelops me, and I'm floundering for the surface, laughing and sputtering out stalks of hay.

Pavel's beaming. "Wow, that was great! Come on, let's do it again!"

Pavel's right and now I'm glad I invited Pavel, even though Mama's not happy because while the war's over, we've still got rationing and there's only so much laundry soap. I glance at the farmhouse and spy the two chimneys, and there is my own sweet mother shaking a rug from the upstairs window, and I'm happy because it's summer and school's out and the Germans don't matter.

But then I look east. There, straight ahead, is the town: the familiar smokestacks, the clock tower, the high spire of the old Lutheran *Kirke*, and that stark gold cross winking in the sun. I can see the onion dome too, a deep lapis surmounted by tinier echoes of the main dome. As always, it reminds me of Mama's nesting matryoshka dolls. You know the ones I mean? You open one and inside there's a smaller one and on and on until the last doll is no bigger than the nail of your little finger. That's what the White Lady's dome reminds me of.

(Who?)

My body flinches. That last thought . . . it isn't mine. That's not me. There's someone else in my mind and

I—me, Christian—I feel the boy tense as if he's suddenly aware that I am there, staring through his eyes, and he must look awful because his friend, Pavel, suddenly frowns. "David, you okay? What is it? You look sick."

"I . . ." I'm dizzy and I reel, my hand shooting out to clutch at a beam before I can topple to the floor so far below.

"Whoa!" Pavel's hauling back on my arm, and we're both stumbling away from the edge. "Whoa, you're gonna get us killed."

"Sorry." I sense the boy twisting around in his mind, as if he's trying to see into a dark corner. I turn to Pavel. "Don't you see him?"

"See who?" Pavel frowns, looks over his shoulder, and then back. He looks more frightened now than simply concerned; his dark eyes have gotten very big. "David, you better lie down. You don't look so good."

"No, no, he's here," I say, stupidly, "don't you see him?" Only I'm staring at a dark place where there's

(ME)

somebody staring, and then Pavel says something, but I don't hear him and neither does David because there's a sudden roar; the muttering swells and then

VI

Another growl of engine roar, a burst of crow chatter, and I jerked awake, my arms and legs spazzing so much I almost rolled right out of the open door. Gasping, I crabbed back, the heels of my hands snagging on splinters. The air was filled with a guttural rumbling like thunder only much louder. Confused, I inched back, glanced out, and got my second bad shock of the day.

"Hey, Killer!" Straddling his bike, Karl Dekker lounged in black leather and matching Docs. A cigarette was glued to his lower lip, and a red and black do-rag hugged his scalp. He didn't look any different than he did when he'd dropped out a year ago: mean and wiry, a sandrat with big knots of muscle from working the foundry.

If there was a person born mean, that was Karl Dekker. He'd singled me out ever since Uncle Hank busted up Dekker's dad's chop shop. The first time Uncle Hank did that was when we were in the third grade. Dekker's dad went to prison for nine months. I remember how bad I felt, how I tried to make it up to Dekker on the playground one afternoon. I woke up in an emergency room with stitches in my scalp and Aunt Jean trying not to cry.

Eventually, Dekker's dad made one too many mistakes, not only the chop shop (like three times), but he was a drunk and beat Karl. So that's when the social workers sent Dekker to live in boys' town for a while. Karl thought that was my fault too.

Not that I was the only one Karl hated. Two years ago, while his dad was getting back on his feet, Dekker went to live with the Schoenbergs. It had been Reverend Schoenberg's idea, and Dekker and Sarah had maybe hooked up, I don't know. All I *did* know was Karl made some kind of trouble and they turned him out too.

Of course, Dekker wasn't alone. He was never alone. He always traveled with two other guys—also sandrats, straddling their bikes and squinting up through curls of cigarette smoke. I didn't know them, mainly because they were so . . . the *same*. Dekker was Dekker. You couldn't mistake him for anyone else. These other guys, they could've been Curly and Larry or Athos and Porthos or Crabbe and Goyle. See what I'm saying? The only guy who really mattered, the only constant, was Dekker.

"Came by to see the handiwork." Dekker swung off his bike. "You did a pretty good job there, Killer. Not bad at all. You could be one of the real *bad* boys."

Curly and Larry spluttered, their mouths hanging open like dogs. Dekker said, "Come on down, Cage. You're not scared, are you?"

Yes. I swallowed, suddenly aware not only of how far out of town I was but that I was half dressed and totally defenseless.

I said, "I was just taking a rest." Like that answered anything. Dekker was poking around the can of softener, and I said, stupidly, "Hey, you got to be careful with that. There's acid in it."

"Ooooh." Dekker gave a mock shudder. "What do you think I'm gonna do, stick my dick in it? Unless . . ." He dangled the can from his fingers. "What a shame if this slipped or, you know, something happened to that scaffolding there or . . ."

"What do you want?"

He showed his teeth. "We got something to discuss, Killer."

"Stop calling me that."

"Stop calling me that," he mimicked and then said, "You coming down, or you gonna make me come up?"

What choice did I have? I fished up my sloppy tee and tugged it on. It reeked and the clammy fabric made me shiver. I hated turning my back, but I had no choice if I wanted to get down. I half-expected the scaffolding to collapse at any second. When I made it down, I turned, folded my arms over my chest and said, "What?"

"Want to talk to you about your uncle." Streaks of black foundry grime sketched the creases in Dekker's face, and his nails were ragged.

"What about him?"

"Know what he did?" Dekker leaned in. His breath stank of cigarettes. "He come by my old man's place. Said that anything like *that*," he hooked a thumb over his shoulder, "had to be the work of someone like me, that I musta imitated you just to get back at him."

To my surprise, I felt bad—and sad at the same time. Dekker was a jerk, and he was no one I wanted to be around, and he probably deserved much of what he got . . . but then, maybe, you could say that about me too.

"I'm sorry." I didn't see how I could make up for anything Uncle Hank had done, though. "That wasn't fair."

Dekker jabbed a finger in my chest. "Look who's talking fair. There's any trouble in town, your uncle comes out and sees my dad."

I didn't know what to say, so I kept my mouth shut.

"But here's what pisses me off." Another finger jab. "You're the one needs watching. Ms. Stefancyzk stuck her head through that noose her own self, but who helped? Who was the kid shooting death rays into her eyes?"

I knew where this was going: where it always went. What everyone thought in this crummy little town and talked about behind my back—

"And when your aunt bought it, you know who came tearing down to the shop? Your uncle. Said any drunk in these parts *had* to be my dad or one of my dad's guys. This is right before my dad got sent away, and there wasn't nothing to those charges, they were all bogus . . ."

"I was just a kid." Actually, I sounded like I still *was* and that made me mad. "I didn't have anything to do with it."

"Little kid, my ass." Dekker's face twisted. "Well, I was a kid too, but which kid got the short end? Who got sent away? Wasn't you . . . even though we know all about you, right? I wouldn't be surprised if you killed your aunt your own self. Ten to one, she took a look at something you drew and she couldn't stand what she saw and—"

That's when I punched Dekker in the mouth.

VII

So, okay, that wasn't bright. Actually, it was suicidal. Or maybe I had to stop Dekker from talking because every word . . . I didn't need to hear from Dekker what I'd already thought of myself.

My fist connected with his nose, and it felt like a bomb went off in my hand. The edge of his teeth cut across my knuckles, and fire streaked up my hand. Hitting Dekker hurt worse than I could've imagined, and I felt the blow shiver all the way up my arm and into my shoulder.

Dekker staggered. He lost his grip on the can of softener. The can flew in a short heavy arc before bursting open against his bike. A gurgling gush of yellowish goo drooled over the black body and chrome exhaust pipes like thick snot.

The other sandrats had gone dead quiet. Then they slid off their bikes.

"You *fuck*!" Blood trickled from one of Dekker's nostrils. His face flushed an angry purple. "You fucking ruined my bike!"

His guys moved in, and then they were crowding me back against the barn, probably so Dekker would have a nice solid surface while he whaled on me for as long as he liked. I saw him coming, and it was like this awful slow motion of a nightmare where the monster's coming and you know you've got to run, but the monster's gaining. . . .

"I'm going to cut off your fucking nuts," said Dekker. There was a glint of steel, an audible snick, and then I saw the knife.

"N-no," I said. I had nowhere to go but back, and in another second, I felt wood dig into my back. The knife in Dekker's fist looked like a scimitar. "Please, I'll pay for it. I'll do anything you want. . . ."

"Yeah, you will." Dekker's teeth were a smeary orange. His fist flashed out and back, and then a second later, a line of fire sizzled along my right forearm. "You're gonna pay *and* you're gonna do whatever I say."

Bright red blood welled from the slice—a long one—in my flesh. I clapped a hand over the cut. My teeth were chattering, and my face was wet with cold sweat. "I . . ."

"Shut up." The knife flickered again, and this time, I screamed as a seam of blood striped my left bicep.

"Hey!" One of Dekker's guys—Curly—was looking over his shoulder, and now I heard it too: engine grumble and the pop of gravel. Curly said, "Cool it. There's a car . . . shit, it's a cruiser."

"Everyone stay cool," ordered Dekker, and then he crowded in. I cringed back, but his knife had disappeared. He thrust his face toward mine until we were inches apart. His hot breath slashed my face. "Open your mouth about the knife, and you better hope I don't ever find you."

"Hey!" Justin was out of his cruiser, striding toward us. "Hey, you! Dekker! Back off!"

"We're cool, it's cool, Brandt." Dekker stepped away and turned, hands up, palms out. He looked back at me. "We're cool, right?"

Yeah. We were cool.

After Dekker and Curly and Larry growled off on their motorcycles—after I agreed with some version that had me nearly falling off the scaffolding, knocking over the softener all over Dekker's bike, and snagging my arms on nails—Justin said, "I'm gonna have to tell your uncle about this. I mean, I gotta turn in a report, and if Dekker presses charges . . ."

"He won't press charges." I was so dizzy the world tilted. "You heard him. All I got to do is fix his bike. What's another paint job?" I tried a grin, but the world spun and I swayed.

"Hey." Justin moved in, wrapped a hand around my left forearm below a band of blood from Dekker's knife. "Let's get these cuts taken care of."

I might have said something like, sure, but then the smell of blood filled my nose, and then my brain scrambled in a weird jumble.

ghosts

I recognized the feeling: the same splits along the seams of someone else's consciousness I'd experienced before

and teeth like knives and my mouth

when I landed in that other boy's body

don't take my mouth please

and then Justin was saying something, but I didn't get any of it

don't take my mouth

because gray ate at the margins of my vision, and then everything went *black . . . don't . . . please*

help me

help me

VIII

"Hank, you can't let him do it." Reverend Schoenberg forked pot roast and applesauce into his mouth, chewed, swallowed, and said, "He goes alone, and Dekker will kill him."

"I'll be okay." I sat beside Uncle Hank. As usual, Mrs. Schoenberg had made a fantastic dinner—pot roast with carrots and potato pancakes with homemade applesauce—only my stomach was too tied in knots, and the food tasted like sawdust.

Not that I wasn't grateful. A ton of eyes had lasered my back that morning in church, and conversations dried up as we slid into our pew, but no one had to be talking for me to know what everyone was thinking. I was sure everyone had heard about me fainting out at the barn the day before too. Now I had Steri-Strips on my arms, and a train track stitched on my forehead. So, I knew the Schoenbergs had invited us to Sunday dinner as a way of taking some kind of stand.

From across the table, Sarah said to me, "You should be careful. Karl Dekker's just the type of person who'd arrange for you to have an accident."

"She's right, and we know whereof we speak." The Reverend was a moon-faced man and a theology professor at the Ashburg extension of the University of Wisconsin. He liked books, gossip, and red wine. "You're lucky Justin was there when you fainted."

"If you ask me, he was lucky, period," said Mrs. Schoenberg. She and Aunt Jean had been best friends, and she'd made it her mission to make sure we ate a decent meal twice a month. "But luck doesn't last forever, Hank."

"I know that, Miriam." Uncle Hank accepted more wine from the Rev. "I've already talked to Justin Brandt, and he'll stick close while Christian's there."

"I'll be all right," I said. "I can take care of myself."

Of course, no one paid attention to anything I said. Probably didn't believe me, given everything so far.

I wasn't so sure I believed me much either.

The adults talked that to death some more, and then the Rev said, "So what's this about a body at the old Ziegler place?"

Sarah perked right up. "Body?"

Her dad waggled his eyebrows. "A *baby* is what I heard."

"Baby?" Sarah looked at her father and then Uncle Hank. "You mean, like a baby-baby, or a little kid?"

"I don't know how old and—" Uncle Hank shook his head at the Reverend. "You know I can't talk about this, Steve. It's an ongoing investigation."

The Rev made a horsey sound. "From a million years ago."

"Maybe not that long. I still can't talk about it."

"All right, decades. Anyway, I heard some folks from Madison are on their way up," said the Rev, like Uncle Hank hadn't said a word. (He and my uncle had done this before. The Rev wanted gossip, my uncle would say he couldn't, and then the Rev would just keep going until he got what he wanted.) The Rev splashed more wine into his glass. "Crime scene people is what I heard."

Uncle Hank shrugged. "Just the forensic anthropologist and her crew. They won't be here for weeks yet, no real rush on this end. Coroner says the body's been there for a real long time."

"No rush?" Mrs. Schoenberg's eyebrows went up. "If it were my house, I'd want a body out as soon as possible. For that matter, I might just move. The owner isn't a little, well, upset?"

"No. She's . . ." Uncle Hank thought a second. "She's an interesting woman."

"Oh?" I could practically feel Mrs. Schoenberg's ears prick up at that. "I don't think I've ever heard you find any woman interesting, Hank."

Uncle Hank gave a little laugh, like he was embarrassed, and said, "No, it's just I think she's more . . . fascinated. Real keen about learning all she can about the house."

"Well, if there was ever a haunted house . . . how long has that place been vacant? Twenty years?"

"Longer than that. Near as I can figure, the original owner, Mort Ziegler, lost his shirt when the Apostle brownstone business dried up in the 1890s."

"There aren't records?" asked Reverend Schoenberg.

"If there are, no one knows where. Place has been vacant all that time. Kind of strange, you come right down to it. Nice location, beautiful house. Didn't know it was on the market until the new owner moved in."

"Cost you an arm and a leg to heat. Think of the electrical you'd have to update. Is that how they found the body?"

"Yup, doing repairs. The crew was upstairs yanking out old insulation and getting ready to redo a lot of the stonework. They found the body when they dismantled the hearth. The Madison people said they'd bring up GPR—ground-penetrating radar—to go around the grounds and the rest of the house, make sure there are no more surprises."

"Any idea whose child it is?"

Uncle Hank shook his head. "But I'll bet it was one of the servants from way back, maybe even turn of the century. The house has been here that long, so it stands to reason. Nobody would care much about a servant or even notice that they'd stopped showing their face around town. You'd think there'd be rumors, though."

Sarah piped up. "I did this project in world history last year on superstitions. You remember, Dad? I used your account through the university to do the search? Anyway, there was this really weird superstition from Germany way back, when they used to put a live kid in the doorway or wall of castles or something for good luck and to keep away evil spirits."

Her mother scoffed. "Oh, that can't be."

"It is," said Sarah, looking annoyed. "There was this old castle named Vestenberg, where the mason built a special seat for this little boy in one of the walls. The legend was that the boy was given an apple to keep him from crying. Then they walled him up. They did the same thing in a church in another village. I did a report on it. I even got an A."

"That's disgusting," said her mother.

The Rev shook his head. "No, that's called a custom we wouldn't want to emulate. Religion's full of superstitions that make no sense to us but perfect sense to those who lived in the times. Actually, now that I think of it, it's really a commentary on Christ, isn't it?"

"How you figure that?" asked Uncle Hank.

"Think about it. A child is sacrificed, and he carries the apple of Eve's sin to his grave. Now, there's *got* to be a sermon in that." The Rev crammed a hunk of dinner roll in his mouth, gave a meditative chew, then inhaled more wine. "So, what do you think, Hank? Most everyone in Winter's got some German. Maybe they brought over a couple interesting customs from the old country."

"I suspect it'll depend on how old the forensic people think the body is."

"Can I come watch?" asked Sarah.

"Absolutely not," said Mrs. Schoenberg.

"Why not?"

"Because it's ghoulish, that's why not."

"Mom, it's *science*. What do you think archaeologists or paleontologists do? What if I want to become a forensic scientist?"

"She's got a point," said her father. "Miriam, it can't do any harm."

"Hank." Mrs. Schoenberg looked at my uncle for help. "Tell her she really can't do this."

"Well," Uncle Hank drawled. "Actually, Miriam, I can't see why not. Might be interesting for her, and I've known the forensics people to bring up grad students, so they're used to having younger people around. I'll have to ask the forensic anthropologist. If she says it's okay . . . sure."

Sarah beamed. "Great."

"Thanks a lot, Hank." Mrs. Schoenberg pushed back from the table. "Who wants pie?"

After we helped with the dishes, Sarah said, "Let's go outside."

We went around back. The swing set was weathered cedar, with black belt swings on chains and an eight-foot, dinged-up green slide. There were big divots scuffed out of the dirt from years of kids pushing off and digging in their toes. The seats looked too small and were a little tight, and I sat with my feet practically out straight in front of me. Still, it felt kind of good to be out there. Familiar. It occurred to me that this was the first time Sarah had made any time to actually talk to me in I didn't know how long.

She dropped into the swing beside me. The old chains creaked. "You think your uncle will keep his promise?"

"Yeah. But it's kind of . . . creepy."

"Hunh. You should talk. Anyway, if it's real, I might do this as my project for history . . . you know, investigate something local? It'd be kind of neat. You going to come out too?"

"Maybe."

"Good." She looked me square in the eye. "Why'd you do it?"

I knew she was talking about the barn. "I honestly don't know. I don't *remember* doing anything." I don't know why, but I told her the truth. Well, some of it: I left out the stuff about drawing the picture with the weird onion dome and dropping into another boy's body and most of the dream stuff. But it felt good to talk to somebody about what was going on, even if it was only half. I knew I was expected to talk to my shrink about this kind of thing, but I didn't know the psychiatrist except as an abstraction, and Sarah was right here, and we had some history. When we were kids—before Miss Stefancyzk—we used to play together and hang out. Then Miss Stefancyzk happened, then Sarah got popular, and then I started drawing the sideways place.

She listened seriously, twirling back and forth on her toes, her arms locked around the chains. "I don't see how they can get on your case for sleepwalking. In psychology, we read that sleepwalking might be a symptom of a brain problem like, you know, seizures. They going to test you?"

"Dunno." I started scuffing out a dirt sketch with the toe of my Chucks. "I took a bunch of other tests."

"Really?" She listened as I described what I'd done, then nodded. "The one with all the questions was the MMPI. It's a personality test where they can tell if you're lying or psychotic or something. That's why there were so many of the same questions. They want to see if you get paranoid."

"Yeah? Well, it worked."

"The inkblots—the Rorschach—test for psychosis too. So do they think you're psychotic? Because you know psychotic people, like schizophrenics and manic depressives and stuff, can be like totally out of touch, hearing voices and stuff."

That felt way too close to the truth. "Yeah ... well, everyone thinks I'm weird anyway."

"Well, you are. You know, always drawing stuff, eyes ... you're obsessive," she said. "But a lot of creative people are borderline crazy."

"They are?"

"Uh-huh. There was a whole chapter in the book about creativity and insanity. Proust was a manic-depressive. Virginia Woolf killed herself, and so did Sylvia Plath, Anne Sexton. Edward Munch painted his most famous stuff after he got sick. Van Gogh was just plain loony."

"Gee, I feel so much better."

She gave me a withering look. "My point is that maybe the people who create the greatest art aren't all that normal. I mean, Picasso had to be seeing and thinking with a part of the brain someone like me just can't."

I was amazed. I didn't know *anyone* was interested in the stuff I was. I had no idea that Sarah even knew about these artists, much less thought this way. None of the people she hung with knew anything beyond nail art.

She said, "So, you're an artist and you're weird. I can accept that, but you could try harder to fit in too."

"I don't think people here are interested in that. They've already decided what they think."

She was quiet a moment. Then, almost to herself, she said, "If people took the time to get to know you or if maybe you weren't always drawing, you know, weird stuff . . ."

"But I do, and they don't. It's okay."

"But it's not. You're not a bad guy. I mean, yeah, there was that stuff with Miss Stefancyzk, but that was just a coincidence, her singling you out in that note. And okay, you're strange. . . ."

"Thanks a lot. I guess it must be hard being so popular and having a soft spot for the weirdo everyone's freaked out about." I didn't mean it as sarcastically as it came out. Or maybe I did.

She looked startled, as if I'd slapped her, and then she flushed. "I'm trying to help."

All of a sudden, I got angry. I'd been effectively on my own for years—years. I was on everyone's shit list, and now she wanted to be my nurse or sister or therapist or something. "I don't need help. I'm doing fine."

"That's bull—" Her cell chirped. She glanced at the number, flipped open her phone, and then, with a fierce look at me, said, defiantly, "Hi, Stacy. No, I'm not busy. I wasn't doing anything, in fact." She hopped off the swing and walked off without a backward glance, cell phone to her ear.

I looked down at the sketch I'd made in the dirt. It was crude, but there was the curve of Sarah's face and chin. Her eyes, of course. Duh.

I scuffed the dirt bare and walked back inside.

On the way home, Uncle Hank said, "I got a call from that psychiatrist you're supposed to see. Name's Helen Rainier." He paused as if waiting for me to ask a question, and when I didn't, he said, "She wants you in her office after school on Tuesdays and maybe Thursdays or Fridays. She says she has to meet you to decide."

I thought about that. Between the work at the barn, the old-age home starting tomorrow, Dekker's motorcycle, and now the shrink on top of all my regular work, I wouldn't have any free time. Maybe that was the idea. But SATs and ACTs were coming up, and I needed to study.

For the first time since this all started, I got mad. Yeah, okay, I was a spooky kid; I was a geek and weird, but even *I* had a life. I knew it wouldn't do any good to talk about it, though.

Uncle Hank would just say what was done was done and I'd made the bed I had to lie in. Stuff like that.

So, instead, I asked, "Are you coming? To the psychiatrist's?"

"Not unless she asks. You want me there? I'll come if you want."

Yes, I thought. No, I thought. Heck, I didn't know. "No. What's she going to say that everyone else doesn't already think?"

Uncle Hank didn't have anything to say to that.

That night I didn't dream and I didn't end up in a little boy's body, looking out through his eyes. In the morning when I woke up, there weren't any new drawings on my pad either. That was fine with me.

IX

Monday.

My first day back at school. Not much had changed, though I got some more strange looks because of the stitches and my arms. At lunch, I spotted Sarah at a table with her friends. They checked me out and then started with the peek-giggle-whisper routine. Sarah threw me a worried look and half raised her hand, but she stopped in midair, like she suddenly realized what she was doing, and let her hand fall into her lap.

I got out of there and headed to the art studio. I never ate in the school cafeteria anymore anyway. We're allowed to eat lunch in a classroom, if we're doing work, so I'd been eating in the studio since freshman year.

Once in the studio, I unwrapped my sandwich and kind of stared at it. I didn't have much of an appetite. In fact, when I thought about it, I hadn't really eaten anything since that bowl of Cocoa Puffs the Thursday before. Every time I thought about what was happening to me—wondering if maybe I really was crazy—my chest got this suffocating feeling, like someone cinching down a rubber band around my ribs. I hadn't felt this bad since Aunt Jean died. And I was completely freaked out about the mental illness thing, all that stuff Sarah said. All I knew about mental illness was that people were unhappy and tried killing themselves or other people and took a lot of medicine that didn't really do them any good and made them fat or shake. The ones who didn't take medicine talked to themselves and had bugs in their hair and shuffled around in big cities with shopping carts loaded with crap and slept on park benches.

So if I were nuts . . . better to go to the sideways place. If I never found my mom and dad, it would be better to get eaten by something *there* than spend my life squatting on a dirty street corner and begging for handouts with a Starbucks coffee cup. Jeez, did homeless people even wipe their butts after taking a crap? I mean, if they didn't have a place to go, how would they do that, exactly? With scrap paper or their hands or what? I didn't even want to think about it.

With all *that* on my mind, I couldn't even work on my mom's portrait. Just . . . couldn't.

Aspen Lake was the old-age place, eight miles northwest of town. I'd been biking out that way a bunch of times. There's a very cool grove of white pines that goes on for what seems forever. Everyone in town says the trees were planted way back when Winter was big into shipbuilding. White pines grow straight, and the trunks were used for masts.

For me, there was something very peaceful about that grove. I guess you could say it called to me and drew me in.

Sometimes I'd hike in and lie down on a bed of soft needles and stare into the cool green darkness overhead. I liked the smell—the sharp tang of resin—and the fallen needles muffled all sound. The branches were high and thick, and the shadows dense, the temperature always five degrees cooler. That grove was always a place I associated with quiet, like things slept there. If that makes any sense.

Aspen Lake was west of that, and although I'd passed the entrance, I'd never turned down the quarter-mile drive to the home until that Monday. I'm a good biker, but that Monday my legs moved as if churning through molasses. I was not looking forward to this.

The place was X-shaped and looked like an airport, with a chalet-style entrance lobby. The lobby was a cross between a dentist's waiting room and a hotel: vinyl couches, overstuffed Leatherette armchairs, and low coffee tables strewn with ragged magazines. A huge plasma screen TV was mounted along the left wall.

The receptionist passed me on to the personnel manager, a sour-looking older woman with a beehive of silver hair named Mrs. Krauss, who seemed put out that I'd arrived at all. She peered at me over black plastic cat's-eye glasses. "You're ten minutes late." When I tried to explain about school and having to bicycle out, she shushed me with a wave of her hand and then pulled out a manila folder. She asked a bunch of questions and was even more pissed off when she discovered I didn't know CPR. She did the clucking routine with her tongue and made a phone call and scheduled me for a class at the Y the next town over. (The next class met on Saturday afternoons for two weeks. Terrific.)

Then she folded her hands on top of my folder and looked sternly through her glasses. Her eyes were the color of buckshot. "Let me be frank, Mr. Cage. I do not approve of the way in which you've come to us. At Aspen Lake, we pride ourselves on our mission. Serving seniors in need—providing them with a nurturing community and the closeness that comes with family—is also service to the Lord. I have only consented to take you on because you are the sheriff's nephew. As far as I am concerned, you will follow instructions to the letter. Your supervisor is responsible for assigning you to your duties, and you will report directly to her. Any deviations from your specified duties are to be approved by me, is that clear? In addition, you are to refrain from interacting with our guests in any way other than what is required of you. Many of our residents have memory problems and dementia; they are easily upset and agitated, and you are not to upset them more."

When she stopped to inhale, I said, "I won't upset anybody."

She gave me a narrow look. "You'll excuse me, Mr. Cage, but I've lived in Winter all my life. I know about you."

I felt my cheeks get hot. "You don't have to worry about me."

"I hope not." She held up a bony finger. "One slipup, one deviation, and I shall ask the court to remove you from this facility. Am I perfectly clear?"

"Crystal," I said.

"Do you have any experience with seniors?" Peggy McClellan was Wisconsin-lean, a big-boned woman with chipmunk cheeks and too-blonde curls. Mrs. Krauss had marched me through the lobby and out a set of double doors. We'd taken a connected breezeway to a separate building she called the

71

Lakeview House, and there she'd passed me on to Peggy—with relief, I thought. Another tick off the old to-do list.

"No."

"Well, what about grandparents?" When I shook my head, she sighed. "Okay, well, dinner's always kind of a busy time, but you might as well jump right in."

"Dinner? It's only five."

"The seniors eat early here, and believe me, it'll be six thirty or seven before we're finally done. After dinner, there's one last activity. . . . I think it's art today, and you'll help with that too, but let's get going, and I'll explain things as we go along."

She set off down a hall lined with open doors left and right. There were slots for name tags to the side of each door. None seemed to be vacant. Big wall clocks and date tags were set at either end of the hall. The air smelled like disinfectant, scrambled eggs, and boiled rice.

"This is our assisted-living wing," said Peggy. "We have about sixty guests, most of whom either have early- or mid-stage Alzheimer's or dementia. That means they can still pretty much take care of themselves, but the building's secured and our courtyard is fenced so they can't wander off. The oldest is ninety-one, and I'll eat my hat if he's not in skilled nursing by Thanksgiving. Trust me, when someone's looking over a fork like he's never seen one in his life, he's pretty close to the end."

"Where do they go then?"

She inclined her head. "Next door. Skilled nursing facility. That's for the ones who check in but don't check out, if you catch my drift. We'll get you a key card so you can get back and forth without having to come find me."

"Great," I said. At least Peggy was willing to cut me some slack.

"One thing, though. Some of the people here, when they start losing it? They can be . . . changeable. Some get downright mean, and I don't know if that's because of the dementia, or they were always that way. There was this one gentleman who liked to pinch me, not like he was being fresh. He *wanted* to hurt me because he was angry at his family, the world. He'd had a stroke and needed help feeding himself, getting dressed, going to the bathroom. . . . So he lashed out. He eventually wound up next door in skilled nursing. When he passed? I didn't shed a tear. But I always treated him with respect. That's the most important thing: respect. No matter what happens, you keep your cool."

"Okay." I thought back to my abortive brawl with Dekker: *We're all cool, right?* "So these are all bedrooms?"

"Uh-huh." She hooked a thumb over her shoulder. "Down the hall's the public dining room, living room, and common kitchen for those seniors who can still microwave popcorn and bake cookies without setting fire to the place."

"Wow."

"Yeah. That's happened once or twice. Off the living room are some of our activity rooms where we do things like art, yoga, dance, games, or watch movies. Sundays, one of the pastors from town rotates through, and a priest does Catholic Mass. Anyway . . ." She squared her shoulders like we were heading off to battle or something. "Right now, we go make sure everyone gets to the dining room, either on their own or we get them there. There are other caregivers who man the dining room so we can go next door to the skilled nursing unit and help out with meals."

"You mean, like feed people?"

"Mmm-hmm." Peggy eyed me. "You got a problem with that?"

"No. It's just . . . I've never done anything like that."

"First time for everything. You're going to do a lot of things here you've never done before. Get used to it."

By now, a few people were making their way to the dining rooms. They were the oldest people I'd ever seen, and the way they filed out of their rooms sort of freaked me out. It was like vampires coming out of their coffins at night. Or maybe zombies. It was really kind of scary. A lot of them thunked along with walkers or canes. Others shuffled or minced carefully, watching their feet. No one talked much because they were too busy concentrating on where they were going. I noticed a couple ladies in flowery dresses and old guys in trousers and sports coats, like going to eat dinner was the nearest thing they had to going out on the town. That made me feel . . . well, sad.

After Peggy gave me a crash course on wheelchairs, how to put on the brakes and flip down the footrests, we rapped on doors, poked our heads into rooms, and otherwise herded people into this big common dining room. The tables were for two and four. Everyone went through a buffet line where these people in hairnets doled out spoonfuls of mashed potatoes and slabs of meat loaf from warming trays, just like at school. Other workers brought plates of food to those residents who couldn't stand in line.

As I settled one old woman named Lucy at a table for four, she said, "Oh dear, I'm afraid I've left my purse in my room." Her face was wrinkled as a raisin, and she had vague, watery blue eyes. "Is it all right if I tip you tomorrow, young man?"

"Uh," I said.

To her right, another old lady with orange hair said, "Don't listen to her. She says that to anyone new. Give her a couple of days and she'll stop. But don't tell Peggy, all right? They'll move Lucy to skilled nursing, and she'll just wither and die there. Besides, as long as she can keep track of the tricks, we need her for bridge." To Lucy: "I've taken care of him, dear."

"A nice tip?" Lucy quavered. "A dollar?"

"Yes, dear." The lady with the orange hair patted her hand as a worker plunked down a plate before Lucy. "It's mashed potatoes, green beans, and meat loaf today."

"Oh, my favorite." Lucy gave me a sweet smile. "The secret to the tomato sauce is sugar and a pinch of saffron. Cuts the acid."

"Yes, ma'am," I said.

"Do you like meat loaf, young man?"

"Yes, ma'am."

"Would you like to join us?"

"He can't, dear." The lady with the orange hair took a dinner roll from a basket in the center of the table, thought about it, took another, and said, "He has to help the other guests."

"Oh, what a shame," said Lucy.

"Christian." Peggy was in the doorway, motioning me over.

I said at Lucy, "I'm sorry, ma'am, I've got to go. Some other time?"

As I hurried away, I heard Lucy say, "Such a nice young man. Next time, Regina, give him two dollars."

After the relative hubbub of Lakeview—and you really could see the lake, although it was man-made and about the size of a dinky wading pool—the skilled nursing unit next door was like walking onto a real hospital ward. Nurses in uniforms worked behind a big horseshoe of a desk with computer workstations and monitors and glassed-in cabinets with bottles of medications. Behind the desk, there was also a pretty woman with chestnut hair down to her shoulders and dark almond-shaped eyes, and I thought: *Caravaggio*. She had a handset pressed to one ear and was jotting notes on a pad, but she looked up and smiled as we passed.

"Who's that?" I asked Peggy.

"The doc on call. She switches off with two other docs in town. She usually makes her rounds at the end of the day when she's done at her office or first thing in the morning. We call her at night if we need to."

"Do you need to a lot?"

"More than we'd like to sometimes. We can run a code and take care of someone in an emergency situation, get them stabilized, but if they get really, really complicated—like they need surgery or something—we transport them to Ashburg Memorial. Sometimes they come back, sometimes they don't. Most times, they do. We're set up as a hospice too."

"You mean, people die here?"

The look Peggy threw me practically screamed *DUH*. "Where else? Believe it or not, it's better to die here than a hospital. When I go, I want to go at home in my own bed. If I can't do that, then I'd want a place where I can look outside and see water and trees, have my things in my room. There are worse ways to go."

The unit was large, arranged in a big square around the nurses' station, and held about a hundred guests in need of more intensive care, Peggy said. It was also much quieter, a place where you instinctively lowered your voice, though I could hear the occasional beep-beep-beep of machines coming from some of the rooms. A lot of the residents were in hospital gowns and lay in aluminum-railed hospital beds. The smell was really different: the antiseptic odor again, but now I caught the scent of age, the stink of diapers. The people here weren't necessarily older than the seniors next door, but they really were frailer, all spindly arms with wattles of sagging skin. A lot of the seniors were tied up in their wheelchairs or bedside chairs with a kind of sling Peggy called a posey. A few sat in the common area where a TV chattered to itself in one corner. As we passed through on our way to the kitchen, some of the old people looked over. Their faces were blank and nearly featureless, like when I molded something out of clay that hadn't worked and so I'd taken a loop tool and skimmed off all the detail in large curls until the clay was smooth again.

Peggy retrieved a big metal, cafeteria-style gurney loaded with covered trays. "Okay, so here's the drill. Some people we have to feed. Other folks can feed themselves, but you have to check every couple of minutes or else you'll be cleaning peas off their laps or the floor. Also, you've got to be sure to match the tray with the right person, you got that? Let's take care of the people who don't need to be fed first; then I'll coach you through feeding a few of them. Oh, and be sure to say everyone's name, and then tell them what's on the tray to orient them."

A half hour went by in a blur of covered trays, napkins tucked under chins, cut-up meat loaf, bowls of quivering Jell-O and mushy peas, and other bowls of colored glop that were probably pureed vegetables and looked like baby food. Still, I was getting into it a little, not so freaked, because the work wasn't hard. You just had to get over being creeped out, and then it was easy. Well, easier.

So everything was going okay. Yeah, Mrs. Krauss was a jerk, but Peggy was okay. Lucy had been kind of sweet. I was feeling kind of good, actually—so that alone should've tipped me off that things were about to go really, really bad.

I was on the last set of trays when I saw the doctor at the end of the hall. She was busy reading a chart, and then she peeled off into one of the rooms . . . and I felt this little, tiny mental tug, like a fishhook in my brain. I stopped dead. *Something* was pulling at me, stroking my brain with sticky fingers, and it was coming from *that* room, where the doctor was. Something was drawing me. . . .

So I eased down to the door. To the left was a name tag, written with black Magic Marker, slotted into a metal holder: **WITEK**. To the right, I saw a strange brass tube, inlaid with colored glass and crystal, stuck at a weird angle to the right doorjamb.

Inside was a single hospital bed and there was this brittle-looking old guy propped up on pillows. His arms were sticks, and his face was so sunken his cheeks looked like axe blades about to cut through his skin. There was something wrong with his face. The whole right side drooped, like molten candle wax, like he was Mr. Eisenmann's mirror image only not scarred and definitely not a gargoyle.

The doctor was talking to the old man. I couldn't hear what she said, but her voice was kind, like what I imagine a mom might be like with her kid. She was leaning over the old guy, flicking a penlight back and forth across his eyes. Her back was to the door, so she didn't see me.

But I sure saw those paintings.

There were five: all in frames and most were oils, I thought. The canvases were relatively small, maybe twenty-four- and thirty-inch squares. I was too far away to make out any of the details, but it didn't matter—because I felt this queer little *thrum* in my head. Not quite a sound but definitely physical and

(?)

then that weird floaty feeling caught hold and then I was falling, the way I had right before those nightmares and in the barn and

I'm sweating and my tongue is glued to the roof of my mouth, and I wish I had a penny to spend for an ice that Mr. Grinstein is selling at the corner from his white handcart, like it's May Day or the Fourth, but I don't have any money and besides the prisoners will be here soon, and I don't want to miss that.

So instead, I squirt to the front of the crowd of people lining Main Street to the foundry's gates. It is still blindingly hot, so bright that everything looks bleached and bone white. Even though the prisoners have been here for a few weeks, people are still curious. Papa's forbidden me to come. He says that these men are our enemies and we have better things to do than gawk, but I don't understand that because Papa spends a lot of time with them. In fact, Papa told us at supper that Mr. Eisenmann has taken him out of the ceramics workshop for the time being. Papa's only job now is to make drawings of the prisoners because that's what Mr. Eisenmann wants. Mr. Eisenmann says that this is history in the making, and he wants Papa to record everything—and Mr. Eisenmann himself, of course, because he's the town's history too.

I spy Marta across the street, close to the gates. Of course, she's there, making eyes at the prisoners, who make eyes back. She's with some of her girlfriends, and all of them are wearing nicer clothes than normal. Marta stands out, of course, with her gypsy looks and brown skin and red hair band. Papa doesn't want her here either, but she comes every day so she can watch when the prisoners get back from the fields. Mama and Marta have quarreled, their hands flashing, because Mama and Papa believe that Marta should be modest, but she only shouts with her hands that there are no other men in town because everyone is either away at the war or too young or too old. Besides, all her friends are there and where's the harm?

I know where there's harm: in making eyes with wolves. If Papa knew what she was doing, he would beat her and not allow her to work at Big Brown because the wolves are there too. Miss Catherine wants a new house, but Mr. Eisenmann says that Big Brown should do very well, only it will need a lot of work and the wolves can do that. Mr. Eisenmann and Miss Catherine have quarreled about this in public because my mother says that Miss Catherine is headstrong and willful. We're not supposed to notice the quarrels, but everyone does. The rich are not like the rest of us; that is what Papa says.

There is a grumbling from down the street, and now the trucks are coming back in boiling spumes of red dust. The truck beds are open, and the prisoners are there, along with some guards, who cradle their rifles like babies, and laugh and joke with the prisoners. There are seven trucks and only one guard per truck, and that doesn't seem like very much to me. A prisoner drives each truck. With no guard. I think: *All they would have to do is push the guards out of the truck or kill them, and then they could escape.* Only these men won't do that. They're fed and have a place to sleep and money too. Here, Papa says, they have it good and know it.

The trucks squeal to a stop at the foundry gates. I taste grit in my mouth and spit red, and my eyes sting. Pavel's scrubbing his eyes with his fists, and muddy tears streak his face, but he is jabbing me with his elbow too: "They don't look so tough. I heard most of these are Wolfsangels, only they're the wolves that got caught now, aren't they?"

I see that he is right, because all their eyes are yellow, and when they smile, they grin like wolves, showing all their teeth.

Across the street, Marta and her friends are smiling and waving and holding out little wrapped parcels of sweets. A few of the prisoners reach down to snatch at them, and that reminds me of what I've read from the books Mama's brought from Poland, about knights and how a lady might hand one a ribbon or a glove or a kerchief to show that he was *hers*. That is what Marta is doing, and it makes me uneasy because there is the gemini, the golden prisoner who is Mr. Eisenmann's right arm, and he's taken a parcel from Marta and said something slowly so she understands and they're smiling into each other's eyes, and I'm thinking: *Doesn't she see that he's . . . ?*

There is a scream, very high, like an iron spike piercing the air, and then a woman shouts: *Fritz-Fritz-Fritz Hueber!*

All the men in the trucks turn and then, in the second truck, one prisoner leaps over the wooden slats and sprints toward the crowd. People start screaming, and Marta looks confused, not understanding at first, and I'm jostled as everyone lurches away, the crowd parting like the Red Sea. Around the trucks, the guards are bewildered. Then someone in the crowd screams, and that seems to throw a switch in the guards because a few bound after the prisoner, their rifles held high so they don't shoot anyone by accident: *HALT-HALT-HALT!*

The woman screams again: *FRITZ!* She pushes past, and it's Mrs. Grunewald from our school, and then she and the prisoner are hugging and crying and she is screaming: *Oh we thought you were dead, we thought you were dead....* Everyone else is gawping, and the guards pound over now and shout: *Get back everyone get back, Hueber, let her go and come back here, back away, don't make us shoot you, Fritz....*

Then another prisoner shoves through, the one with no accent and good teeth and yellow eyes—slit eyes, eyes like a wolf. It is Marta's gemini, and he's shouting in his flaw-less English: *Get back everyone be calm he means no harm.* He goes to Hueber, who is crying with Mrs. Grunewald, and he puts his arms around the other prisoner, and they're talking together.

Mrs. Grunewald's face is blotchy, and there are white stripes on her cheeks from where her tears have cleaned away the dust, and she says: *He's my cousin. We thought Fritz was dead, but he isn't, here he is and ... oh oh, we thought he was dead....*

Then someone in the crowd—the minister at St. Luke's Lutheran—shouts: *It's a miracle. It's a sign from God! These are our brothers!* And then other people start nodding, and some begin to weep.

Mr. Eisenmann comes running through the foundry gates into the street, and even though he is in his shirtsleeves and they're rolled to his elbows, he is as he always is because he's like a king: all gold, and his gold ring flashes, and his gold chain with its twinkly fobs is very bright. He talks to a few of the guards and then walks with the prison commander to speak with the prisoner with the yellow wolf eyes. They talk together, heads bent, their hair spun gold in the sun.

Eventually, everyone calms down. Mr. Eisenmann makes a speech about family and brothers and how war divides, and he talks about the Civil War, which I know nothing about, but everyone else who is not new here does. All around, people are weeping; I hear whispers, muttered talk about how there might be others—brothers and cousins and uncles. Across the street, I see Marta smearing away tears from her cheeks because it is all so touching. Even the wolf is crying.

But looking at Mrs. Grunewald and Fritz Hueber, I also wonder if maybe what the rabbi says is true: that we are all brothers under the skin—even if some are wolves.

A hand falls on my shoulder. Startled, I twist my head around and there is Papa. His face is black as a storm cloud, his eyes are thunderous, and I expect a beating. I cringe back, and my feet tangle. . . .

And then he's on me: *What are you*

". . . doing here, Christian? That tray belongs to Mr. Griffith."

I blinked and nearly dropped the food tray at Peggy's feet.

Before I could say anything, a monitor in the old man's room gave a little *eep* of alarm. The doctor's head whipped toward some machine and then back at the man on the bed and then she took his hand. "Mr. Witek, can you hear me? Blink if you hear me."

More bleeps from the machine, and now my fingers began to itch, and I thought: *Give me a pen, give me a pencil, anything. . . .*

"Well?" Peggy was semi-pissed. "Mr. Griffith's room is two doors down."

"Ah . . ." Confused, I looked from the tray to Peggy, then to the old man on the bed. "Sorry. I wasn't . . . I got mixed up."

"Uh-huh." Peggy's eyes clicked over my face, and then she nodded. "That's okay. Let's just keep moving. . . . Sorry about that, Doc."

"No problem." The doctor was studying me with a curious expression I couldn't read. "Are you all right?"

Well, I just dropped into another kid's body, only this time it was like a hand slipping into a glove, like time travel, and I was awake. . . .

"I'm fine."

"We got it covered, Doc." Peggy was steering me away. "No problems, right, Christian?"

Later, after the dinner rush, Peggy didn't ask what I'd been doing or why. That was good. Because I didn't have any answers.

X

After that, my entire body went creepy-crawly-twitchy, like ants on my skin. I couldn't get that old guy with the paintings out of my head or the whole dream thing. I'd been *awake* this time. Maybe Sarah was right; maybe I was having seizures or something. There was a scritchy-screechy feeling in my head like nails raking my brain. I told myself to calm down, take it easy, but I also knew that I had *not* imagined being drawn, and I wasn't daydreaming. It was time travel all over again, just like the barn, and it started at the threshold to the old guy's room. . . .

No, correction: it really got going when I got a look at those *paintings*.

After an hour of clearing dinner trays and settling people into rooms, Peggy said, "Would you help Mr. Nelson down to the activities room for the art class? I'm going to take a smoke break."

The activities room was set up with about twenty easels. The teacher looked up as I wheeled in Mr. Nelson and pointed me to an empty spot. A rectangle of drawing paper was clipped to the easel: a shaky, half-finished Japanese-style wash of bamboo and some kind of attempt at a bird. I spotted his brushes, and it was all I could do not to grab them.

"Hey," I said, as I slotted Mr. Nelson before the easel and kicked on his brakes, "that's pretty good."

Mr. Nelson's lips parted to reveal irregular yellow pegs ground down almost to the roots. "Thank you. I used to draw a bit, but then life caught up with me, and I had to go to work to support my family." He fumbled up a brush, and I half reached to steady his hand but quick jammed my fists into my pockets as he said, "Now they're supporting me, and I've got all the time I need to draw."

I muttered something about that being nice. Then the teacher moved in, and I backed away. The urge to draw was so overwhelming, though I had no idea what was begging to flow out of my hands and onto paper. I turned, thinking: *Get out, get out, just get out . . .*

"Young man," a familiar voice quavered, "young man."

Lucy. I hadn't seen her. She lifted a hand like she was a student in class. "Young man, I need your help."

"Be right there, Lucy," the teacher called, and then he jerked his head at me. "Go keep her company a second, would you?"

So I was trapped. Lucy's picture was a mess. She'd been trying to do a copy of a portrait of her done maybe ten years back by someone else. The older portrait was actually pretty good—and a little disturbing, if you knew how to look. In that picture, your gaze snapped to her eyes: blue, sharp, a little angry, the irises stark against the whites—like a surrealist's vision of what a doll's eyes might look like. But the rest of her face was deliberately blurred, like another Lucy was trying to step outside her body, or maybe it was just that the perspective had been flattened and smudged, her image like something scissored out of a magazine and slapped onto paper. But I could've sworn another person was there, stepping out of Lucy's body: not quite a shadow, not a ghost, but as if Lucy were giving birth to another version of herself. Imperceptible but there nonetheless. There was virtually no color other than Lucy's accusing blue eyes and a bloodred sweater. Everything else—her skin and features—was gray with smudges of a sick, putrid yellow, like something oozing out through her pores. The background was a frenetic, spastic wash of various shades of cool gray mixed with 6 percent blue into slate and pewter and a little green. Maybe the artist had sensed that Lucy was losing it.

Lucy's attempts at a copy had produced only an amorphous muddy blob floating in the center of the paper: A vaguely egg-shaped head with tiny pellet eyes, an off-kilter nose glued to one cheek. A slash for a mouth. A Cubist's nightmare, actually.

"I just can't seem to get it right." The hollows beneath Lucy's faded denim eyes were wet. A tear trickled over the cracks and crevices of one pruned cheek. Her fingers were black from charcoal, and when she smeared away tears, she left a watery smudge. "Could you help me? I can't seem to find myself. I used to . . . but I can't now."

That made me feel really sad, and I kind of choked up. "Sure," I said. I found a clean piece of paper and clipped it to her easel and took down the artist's portrait because I thought, well, maybe it upset her. Then, without thinking, I reached out and took her right hand in mine.

The moment of contact was a snap, a charge, like a little electric shock. I stiffened and Lucy gasped, and her fingers twitched. My mouth was dry, and I said, "We'll . . . let's draw it out together, okay?"

"All right," she said, her voice faint as if from far away, or maybe that was just my head starting to balloon. She/I pressed the charcoal against the paper and made the first hesitant swoop of a cheek and jaw—and then I thought: *Don't look. Just let it come out. Just draw. . . .* So I closed my eyes.

And then I felt it happen, the magic, and I was floating, my head expanding.

Disjointed images and sensations flickered bright as flashbulbs: a hot summer's day that was so brilliant the sidewalk was bone and it hurt to look; the high screech of a train whistle in the distance; grit in my eyes; a flutter of white dress; a fan of lush black hair. Everything faded away, the itch in my hands, the voice of the teacher, the murmurs of the other seniors. I was only dimly aware that Lucy's movements were more fluid, no longer hesitant, no longer *old* but swift and sure and graceful, like we'd found an island of calm in the center of a hurricane. The only sounds in my ears were the soft scratch of charcoal on paper and the steady thump of my heart.

In time—I don't really know how long, but I do know that I didn't want it to end—Lucy went still and then I heard her say, "Oh my."

I opened my eyes.

There is an oil by Whistler called *Symphony No. 1, The White Girl*. The auburn-haired girl is tall and regal, dressed completely in a floor-length white dress with lace around the collar and cuffs buttoned tight around her wrists. She's standing on a fox-skinned rug, but the fox's face is playful, almost like a teddy bear. The portrait is soft and gentle, almost a dream.

Lucy wasn't quite Whistler's girl but close. The girl in *her* picture wore her hair in an old-fashioned kind of bun that revealed the graceful swan's curve of her neck; her dress was square-necked with loose, gauzy sleeves. The bodice gave way to a cinched waist and then a flow of skirt that just brushed the tips of her black shoes. She was turned slightly away, looking back at the viewer over her left shoulder, a parasol balanced over her right. In the background, there were tracks and a station platform and a blocky locomotive just moving in, the words **RIO GRANDE** clear and unmistakable. But the girl was Lucy, no question. All you had to do was look at the eyes.

"Oh my God." The teacher, over my right shoulder, and then I saw that Peggy and the doctor were there too. I realized then that I was still holding Lucy's hand. I dropped it like I'd been scorched. "I . . . uh . . . I . . . I was just help . . . *helping* . . . "

"I'll say," said Peggy.

But Lucy only stared at the drawing. Tears dripped down her cheeks, but she—oh, *she* was beaming. "Oh," she breathed. "*There* I am."

XI

So Mrs. Krauss was pissed. Her mouth was screwed so tight it almost disappeared. "You were not to do anything other than what Peggy assigned and *I* approved."

Sitting in the chair next to mine, the doctor said, "I don't get what you're so upset about. You're always talking about how much help you *don't* have. I've talked to the teacher, and he thinks Christian's fine, a natural." To me, she said: "You did good."

I nodded. My mouth was very dry, and I could hear the click in my ears as I swallowed. Even now, the whole episode felt unreal, like it had happened to someone else.

The doctor was saying, "Lucy used to be an elementary art teacher a long, long time ago. But she's got Alzheimer's, and well, you can see what's happened to her work."

I slicked my lips and the roof of my mouth. "You mean, that picture of her, the one with her in a red sweater . . . *she* did that?"

"Uh-huh. Her illness was just starting. The thing about Alzheimer's is that while it affects the entire brain, it really whacks the right parietal lobe." She touched the right side of her head. "That's where people visualize things in their head and then translate that onto paper or canvas. Over time, her ability to visualize herself has diminished."

"Is that why she can't even draw her own face anymore? Even when she's looking at it?"

"Yes. She's gotten so bad we've thought about not allowing her to go to art anymore because it upsets her so much. Today, I'm glad we did because what you did for her was . . . amazing. It's like you calmed her down enough to tap into her visual memories. I've no doubt that her drawing was all muscle memory, a picture of herself from long ago. That's why there's the parasol, the dress, the train." She shook her head again. "Truly amazing. You've got a real gift."

Yeah. Lucky for me, this time my gift didn't get anyone killed. "Is that the same thing as what's going on with that old guy? The one with all the paintings?"

"We do not gossip about our guests," Mrs. Krauss put in.

The doctor either didn't hear or decided to ignore her. "Mr. Witek? No. He's had another left-hemispheric stroke."

Mrs. Krauss leaned forward. "Doctor, this is privileged medical information."

The doctor threw Mrs. Krauss a cool, sideways glance. "No, this is information that any caregiver needs in order to serve our residents better. Or would you prefer that Christian just muddle along?"

Mrs. Krauss's eyes slitted, and her face hardened. But she flicked a hand, giving permission.

The doctor said to me, "Mr. Witek's latest stroke occurred about three weeks ago. The way your brain works, a stroke on the left affects the right side of your body. He's got right-sided paralysis now because of the stroke; that's why his face droops. Of course, he had profound memory problems before, but I can't begin to assess them now. I can only imagine that everything is much worse. Anyway, he was just transferred back to our facility a few days ago. There's not much more a hospital can do for him."

"Why?"

"Because Mr. Witek is going to die," the doctor said, "and soon. Even if he hadn't suffered a stroke, his Alzheimer's is in its terminal phase. Most patients live ten to fifteen years, max. He's been ill for ten, so . . . at this point, he's a DNR: Do Not Resuscitate. He can't eat or drink, so we're keeping him hydrated and comfortable."

"How long can he live like that?"

"Not long. He wasn't eating before the stroke, and his body's eating itself. It's a normal part of dying. So, a few weeks, maybe a month."

"Why can't you feed him through a tube?"

"Because that's not what's in his living will. Someone has power of attorney. Perhaps a relative, but I don't believe anyone visits." She looked at Mrs. Krauss. "Are there any relatives?"

Mrs. Krauss said, "None of which I'm aware."

"So we're his family," said the doctor. "The biggest problem now is that if he's in pain, he can't tell us. I have to infer. I've reduced his sedation, gradually, to see how much he wakes up. I'd rather not snow him with meds, but he's bound to be confused no matter what. Actually, he had this very peculiar delusion: intermetamorphosis, the delusional belief that people are body-hopping, switching identities."

Whoa, that sounded a lot like what I'd felt in the hayloft and just today. "Wow. Really? I mean, can people do that?"

"Body-hop? Oh no. It's a delusional misidentification syndrome caused by profound brain dysfunction. Anyway, I don't know what he's thinking now because we can't communicate. Although . . . there are reservoirs of brain function we can't fathom, or perhaps reliably measure. You'd be amazed how some people have these startling moments of clarity at the very end. No one knows why, but we observe it quite often."

"So he can't paint anymore."

"I'm not sure he's ever painted. The way I understand it, those pictures were done by—"

"We're getting a little far afield now, aren't we?" Mrs. Krauss interrupted. "I don't see how this is relevant. I understand that you're fairly new in town, Doctor, and so you may not appreciate the reluctance we feel here in discussing one another's lives. In a small town, everyone knows everything about everyone else. We strive to maintain some distance."

Hunh. Like anyone had ever done that for me. The doctor either didn't understand or wasn't cowed. Maybe both. "All I have to do is examine his medical records for the relevant history and . . ."

"And you may do so at your leisure. Now, *you*." Mrs. Krauss threw me a look. "You are excused. I need a moment with the doctor."

I got up to go. "I'm really sorry, ma'am," I said to Mrs. Krauss. "I just . . . Lucy needed help. I didn't mean any harm." Thinking of the judge: "I really don't want to lose this job."

The doctor said, "You didn't do a thing wrong, and I'll note that in the medical record. In fact," she grinned, "you were awesome."

"Yeah?"

"Yeah. I don't think I can write that in the record—it would sound a little weird coming out in court—but if anything *does* end up with the judge in any capacity, the medical record will be part of that. Might even be made public, I don't know. But I'll be sure to document what happened today—and my assessment of your behavior and contributions."

I had a feeling she'd meant that more for Mrs. Krauss than me because Mrs. Krauss's face suddenly pinked. If that look had been daggers, the doctor would've been skewered.

"Okay. Thanks," I said.

"My pleasure," said the doctor. "See you around, Christian."

It was dark and there was no moon, so I followed the headlight on my bike all the way home. There were no cars on the road, and as the blackness closed around, I let my mind go.

Okay. To say that I was freaked out would've been an understatement. I really thought I was losing it, big time. The first time, I'd had the awareness that something was happening to *me*, Christian Cage. Yes, I'd been that kid, David, but the sense that there was something wrong in my/his head had been there from the start.

This time, that hadn't happened with Mr. Witek. It was literally a case of here one instant, there the next—and it happened when I saw *them*, the paintings. There'd been the draw, the same kind I felt when I'd painted all over my walls, like a door waiting for me to have the courage to step through into the sideways place. . . .

The thing was, I wasn't being honest with myself. Forget being honest with the doctor or anyone else; they already thought I was crazy, even if the doctor had been okay. But the thing with Lucy? Oh yeah, I knew that feeling. That little click in my head happened when I painted, at the moment I separated the thinking, critical part of my mind from what I was actually *doing*. When the click happened, it was like another set of eyes opened up in my mind, and I painted what *they* saw. I drew *from* them. And I knew that because I'd done it before: with Miss Stefancyzk. And Aunt Jean. Now . . . Lucy.

Shit, I'd have to be careful.

That night, after Uncle Hank thought I was asleep, I painted over the door on my wall. There was no way, there was just no way I was going through there—or letting them out.

Then I went to bed, expecting to dream or time travel or body swap or whatever. But nothing happened. Thank God.

XII

I got to my first shrink's appointment about five minutes early. The waiting room was empty. A closed door opposite the entrance obviously led to the shrink's office. I'd seen in movies how shrinks usually had a little light or bell or something that told them when a patient had come in and then the shrink always opened the door like maybe three seconds later. So I didn't sit. Figured, heck, I'd just have to get right back up. Only the door didn't open and didn't open—and then just when I started to feel stupid, the door opened.

"Hello, Christian." Today, she was wearing a white, buttoned shirt open at the throat, blue jeans, and brown cowboy boots. But it was her. "I'm Dr. Helen Rainier. Come on in."

I didn't move. "*You're* Dr. Rainier? But . . . they call you Doc, like you're a real doctor."

"Because I am? All psychiatrists are, and I've had additional training in neurology and geriatrics. So I'm boarded in both. Actually, triple-boarded."

"Why didn't you say anything?"

"What did you want me to say, exactly? And would you have wanted me to do that in front of Mrs. Krauss?"

That was a good point. "Well, that's a good point."

"Yeah, I thought so too. Everyone at Aspen just calls me *Doc*, so . . . I didn't see any graceful way to bring it up, and I didn't want to embarrass you. Winter's a small town. Most people are pretty sensitive when it comes to seeing me, and we hadn't set any ground rules yet."

"So, uh, what do we do?"

She stepped away from the door. "Coming in would be a start."

And here I'd been all prepared to hate her.

There were three rooms: a playroom with toys and an easel off to my left, the room where Dr. Rainier saw her adult patients to our right, and another door directly ahead. I pointed to that. "What's behind there?"

"Nothing important." She tilted her head to the right. "Want to come have a seat?"

I hung back. "Who goes in that room? With all the toys?" *And the easel . . .*

"Kids, mainly, ones who are too young to want to just talk. Do you want to go in there instead?"

I eyed a box of crayons and colored pencils, watercolors. A blackboard. "Ah . . . maybe another time."

Her main office was big, with floor-to-ceiling bookshelves along one entire wall, a bank of windows opposite that over-looked the lake, a desk with a computer workstation, a couple of sling-back chairs. She gestured me to one and then dropped into the one opposite. She said, "Let's talk about here versus Aspen Lake first, okay? At Aspen, we work together, so it's nothing heavy. Just whatever comes up, and we may not run into each other that much. Here, we work together too, but . . ."

"You get to call the shots."

Her lips moved in a small smile. "You could put it that way, but not really. Anything we talk about will have to be a two-way street. The thing is, we might also run into each other around town. I usually leave it up to patients to approach me. So if you spot me, I won't say anything unless you say something first. That way, you control things, not me."

I liked that. "What do I call you?"

"What do you want to call me?"

I thought about that. "Dr. Rainier, if that's okay."

"That's fine." She fingered up a sheaf of papers. "I've got the court's report, the sheriff's report, and the results of the psych testing. There's other stuff here from the time when your mother left: the report your uncle filed and an assessment by a court-appointed social worker."

"I don't remember any of that." It also hit me that I hadn't thought about my mother in days. It felt like years. "My mom didn't leave."

"Oh?"

But I was already sorry I'd said anything. I just shrugged and then folded my arms and looked at the wall of books. "You read all those?"

"Uh-huh."

"So you're smart."

"I'm not sure that reading a lot translates to smarts. You can read Swahili too, and not understand anything. I once picked up a book on quantum physics, and I could read all the words, but I didn't understand a thing."

"That's different. You read Swahili?"

"No. French and German. What about you?"

"I take Spanish. I wanted to take Japanese, but the school's too small to afford a teacher."

"Why Japanese?" Then her face cleared. "Ah, you must like anime."

I blinked. "Manga. Yeah. I like *Hellsing*. Alucard is awesome."

She was nodding. "I know that one. What do you like about Alucard?"

"Well, you know it's Dracula backwards, right? He's just . . . awesome. He's got this great red coat, he's kind of creepy, and he goes after ghouls and bad vampires and . . ." I stopped.

"What is it?"

"This tells you about me, doesn't it? I mean, that I like this kind of stuff."

"Well, you also like art, and that says just as much about you."

"You don't want to know all about me."

"Why not? We all have our dark places, Christian."

"Right. Like what bad things have you lived through?"

She cocked her head, studied me for a long moment that stretched into three and then four—enough to get a little uncomfortable. She said, finally, "Here's what I'll tell you. I don't have to have a heart attack to know how to treat one. In a way, it's the same thing here. I don't have to be an axe murderer to understand how to deal with one. But—" A smile flitted across her lips. "There is the old saying about shrinks: either you have to be incredibly normal to know what crazy looks like or it takes one to know one. Let's just say that I'm comfortably in-between."

"So . . . not too crazy?"

"I have my moments, but . . . no, not too crazy."

I liked her for that. "So how come you're not scared of me?"

"You mean, beyond the fact that you're not holding a gun to my head? What's to be scared of?"

"I dunno," I said, feeling stupid. "A lot of other people are."

"You mean because of what happened with your teacher? Betty Stefancyzk?" She shrugged. "I wasn't here then. I don't know anything more about it than she had a nervous break-down. How that's related to you, I don't know. But if the reports I read are right, she'd been diagnosed with manic-depressive illness. Ten to one, she simply didn't take her meds."

"She said it was me in her note."

"So what?"

"Well, I . . ." I thought of the power flowing out of my fingers with Lucy. And Aunt Jean. "I don't want to talk about this anymore."

"Okay. So then let's talk about the barn. How come that happened?"

"I . . . I don't remember doing it."

"So you were sleepwalking. What do you think you were painting? A nightmare?"

Yeah, but someone else's. I remembered what Uncle Hank had said about a murder, and for the first time, it occurred to me that maybe *that* was what I was seeing. Like what they talked about when you heard about haunted houses, a psychic residue. Except why *now*? I'd lived in Winter my whole life, and I'd never gone out to that barn or ever *heard* about a murder. I said nothing.

She said, "I guess it's easier to talk about how everyone hates you and is scared of you, right? I mean, that's a part of you, like your name."

"If you say so."

"Is that what you want me to put in my notes?"

"Look, I had a bad dream. I sleepwalked. That's all."

"But why there? And why swastikas?"

"I don't know."

"You think it has something to do with *Hellsing*?" At my frown, she said, "The Nazis. They're all over *Hellsing*, right? And you like manga, so . . . maybe that's where the swastikas came from."

I didn't think so. "I don't think so."

"So what's your theory?"

"I don't have one." I pulled on my lip, then blurted, "Did you know that someone was murdered there?"

Her eyebrows arched. "Really? No, I didn't. Tell me."

I told what little I did know and then said, "I keep meaning to look it up, but I've been kind of busy."

"Okay. And you think this means . . . what?"

"*I* don't know. I'm not the doctor."

She chuckled. "Touché. Well, I think that maybe you heard about this at one point in your life and it surfaced now."

I was shaking my head before she finished. "You heard Mrs. Krauss. This is a little, tiny town, and there are things people don't talk about. This is one of them. I've never heard about this, never."

"You had to have known, Christian."

"I don't see how. It's not something Uncle Hank would talk about. Heck, he barely knows anything himself, it's been so long, and other than the fact that it happened in 1945, that doesn't explain the swastikas. I mean, Nazis? In Winter?" I shook my head. "Never happen."

After that, the hour—well, fifty minutes—was up. Leaving, I asked, "How do you know my uncle?"

"Ah. Well, you know that case your uncle's working? The baby in the hearth?"

"That's *your* house?"

"The very one." She held the door open. "See you Friday."

"Why didn't you tell me?"

Uncle Hank chewed a mouthful of stew very carefully. He swallowed and said, "Well, it really wasn't any of my business now, was it?"

"What are you talking about? You're investigating a body in *her* house, and she's my shrink!"

"Would it have changed anything?... No? Then," he spooned up another mouthful of beef and carrots, "no harm done."

I frowned. Stirred my stew a few times. My appetite was still terrible. "What do you think of her?"

"Dr. Rainier?" He gave this careful thought. "She's an interesting woman. A lot of other people, men and women, they'd have been long gone out of that house, completely spooked. She's very... analytical about it. To her, they're just bones. She's an interesting person."

"Yeah, you said that." Was there color in his cheeks? "How often are you going out there?"

Uncle Hank was, suddenly, very busy salting his stew. "As often as I need to."

"Uh-huh. So how often is that?"

"Depends. There are logistical matters. Updates." Then he eyed me in a way that said no more questions. "Eat your stew before it gets cold."

I did what he said. But I thought: *Hunh.*

XIII

So things kind of settled down for about two weeks, which, all things considered, was weird. Now, in hindsight, I realize that it was because it was the beginning of the end.

At school, the other kids stopped poking each other every time I went by and settled back into treating me like a bad smell. Dekker was waiting for me one day after school but then got all buddy when Jason rolled past in his cruiser. After that, Dekker just told me I could do the paint job on his bike in another week and then we'd be cool. Uh-huh.

I saw Dr. Rainier every Tuesday and Friday. She was okay. Mainly, we were kind of feeling each other out. I didn't tell her anything, really. I mean, shrinks aren't mind readers. Thank God.

I did the home on Mondays and Thursdays, with the possibility of the occasional Sunday. Things at the home got routine pretty fast, though Peggy kept me away from Lakeview

House most of the time. The few times we *did* go on the unit together, she kept checking to make sure I stayed right with her. On the other hand, she loosened up enough that she said I could come extra days if I wanted to speed things up and get all my community service hours in. So I said, sure, I'd try to come by on Wednesdays. . . . I mean, might as well fill up the afternoons, right?

So yeah—the week was full. I did homework and took tests and stuff. And I kind of calmed down enough inside so that I could actually feel hungry again, and Uncle Hank said he thought it was because of all the extra work I was doing at the home. I let him think that.

The muttering just kind of . . . died. I tried not to think about it because I didn't want to jinx anything.

My dreams didn't change, though, and that was bad. They came in snatches, always the same thing: a dark space, the smell of hay and blood, the horses screaming and men shouting, but everything was garbled. I always had the weird feeling that I watched through eyes that weren't mine, though I didn't know whose. That boy's? David? Had to be.

It rained the next weekend, so I wasn't able to go to the barn, which didn't exactly slay me. Staying away helped too, a little. Sometimes I'd snap awake like a rubber band, and I almost felt as if the answer, whatever that was, was on the tip of my tongue. I'd try drawing what I dreamt, but they weren't, well, *right*. Just . . . images and sometimes not even that. More like hints of sensations: Something bright, that rust smell. The screams of horses and men.

Definitely the barn, I thought. No way in hell I wanted to find out more. I was good with that.

105

Oh, and one other thing: the door on my wall didn't reappear. I was good with that too.

On Wednesday the following week, in history, big groans all around the room. One kid said, "A paper on local history? Nothing ever happens here."

"Oh no," said Sarah. "People find bodies in their walls all the time."

"Except that," said the kid. "And you've already got dibs, so what does that leave?"

"Listen, not every paper has to be on something as sensational as what Sarah's doing," said the teacher. "You've got the history of the foundry, for one, and the Eisenmanns after World War I. There's the union unrest of the '30s and '40s, the big fire of '45, the town's contributions to the war effort, and so on. There are plenty of areas that tie us into the state and national level, and world events after World War I. I'll get a list of general topics together, and then I'd encourage you to use your imagination."

After class, Sarah paused by my desk. "So . . . I've interviewed Dr. Rainier."

"Yeah?"

"Uh-huh. She's pretty nice." Sarah was studying me.

I gathered up my books. "That's good."

"You going to come out when the anthropologist gets here?"

"Maybe . . . look, I got class."

"So what are you going to work on?" she asked as we moved into the hall. I saw people look at us and then each other and do the elbow-nudging routine. Sarah either was ignoring them or didn't care—and I had to wonder about that.

"Well, I was kind of thinking about a murder myself."

She looked interested. "Yeah? Which one?"

"Hey, Sarah!" It was one of her girlfriends, and I saw Sarah frown and then nibble on her lower lip.

Sarah turned back. "Look, I—"

"Yeah. See ya," I said and walked away.

So, yeah, I was thinking about the barn when I got to Aspen Lake that Wednesday afternoon. As I pedaled past the grove of white pines, it seemed to me that they exhaled air that was much colder than usual. Farther back, the shadows seemed almost solid. I got this urge to veer off, plunge into that darkness—but I pedaled on past. No more ghosts.

Then, on the approach road to the home, I saw a quartet of crows lift from the remains of a squashed rabbit, and I had this funny, really weird feeling like: *What are you guys doing out here?* Like they were the same crows from the barn, right? Dumb. But I twisted around in my saddle as they swarmed back down over that roadkill. One crow tugged a rope of intestine, and I looked away.

Peggy was off. The woman in her place—Stephanie—was tiny and brown, like a house wren. She had eyes like a bird too: quick and bright, darting all over the place, always sliding off my face until I finally figured out that she was freaked out to be working with me. She kept shooing me away from the trays: "Oh now, I can do that" or "No, no, you go help out in the dining room, why don't you?"

But they didn't need me in the dining room. So after I'd settled Lucy and some other people in wheelchairs at their spots, I wandered out. . . .

And thought: *I got a key card. Why the heck not?*

The nurses in Lakeview didn't pay me much mind. If Dr. Rainier was around, I didn't see her. So I walked straight to Mr. Witek's room. Stood in the doorway. Listened to the monitors go *bip-bip-bip*. Propped up on his bed, Mr. Witek looked pretty much the same as the week or two before, only this time his eyes were closed and his mouth sagged open and I could hear his breath every time he inhaled. He looked asleep or in a coma.

My heart was banging against my ribs, and I was breathing kind of fast. *Calm down.* I smoothed moist palms over my jeans. I don't know what I was expecting—well, that's a lie. I *did*. I was hoping for that little *thrum* again but nothing happened. I knocked softly on the doorjamb. "Mr. Witek?" Then again and a little louder: "Mr. Witek, it's me, Christian."

Of course, he didn't answer. Duh.

But something changed. I felt it in the air, a subtle plucking at my brain, like fingers at the strings of a harp.

My eyes crept to the decorated brass tube on the doorjamb. Now that I was close enough, I saw that there was also some kind of symbol, also fashioned out of brass, near the top. It kind of looked like some kind of letter, like a *W*—and for a brief second, that tip-of-my-tongue feeling, the one that grabbed me every time I woke up from one of those weird dreams, surged through me: *I know what this is. . . .*

Pulling the door shut behind me, I stepped across the threshold.

For a second, I just stood there. My knees trembled, and my hands were still wet. Besides the monitor, I caught the faint ticking of the IV pump. The room smelled sour, like the old man needed a bath or to have his sheets changed.

The paintings stared out from the walls: a few landscapes and what looked like a family portrait of mother, father, daughter, and son. The closest, to my right, was a woman reclining on a couch. Her skin was like alabaster, and her arms were thrown back over her head and sank into the lush tangle of her hair that cascaded like molten gold over the deep forest green pillows. She wore only a shimmering cream-colored silk robe with black trim and bloodred chrysanthemums, and the robe sagged around her neck, and the faintest crescent of pink nipple was visible along her left breast. She looked directly out of the frame, completely unself-conscious, more than a hint of invitation in her dark eyes. Her lips, full and blush red, were parted to reveal small, even, white teeth.

The woman was posed against a long picture window with a stained-glass transom. The stained glass reminded me of Tiffany, a style called French Nouveau: stylized tulips, water lilies, and pond grasses. The picture window looked out on a garden. To the right, I saw a brass fountain: a woman in Grecian costume pouring water from an urn. To the left were an enormous willow and those kinds of wrought-iron benches that completely encircle the trunk.

I looked for the artist's signature and found nothing but an odd symbol: a six-sided star and two letters in the center, *MW*. Two numbers above and below the star at twelve and six o'clock: 4 and 5.

That thought, again: *I know this. . . .*

Then my eyes clicked to the oil to the right of the portrait—and a forest of hackles prickled along my neck.

There was no mistake. There were the same rolling hills, the tracts of deep green woods, and the thin ribbon of lake along the eastern horizon. The square brick clock tower and the foundry alongside. Even the curls of smoke rising above the buildings were the same—and there was the azure blue of that onion dome: the White Lady.

It was the oil of the sketch I'd drawn the night of my first nightmare. And then I'd seen it again, in the barn, as David.

"Oh my God." My whisper was like a shout in my head. Goose bumps rose along my arms, and I felt a cramp in my groin, like I had to pee. I thought I heard something coming from the old guy, and my head whipped around, my mouth open, ready to scream. . . .

He was lying there just as he'd been: the bellows of his chest moving with every breath, his jaw unhinged and his mouth all caved in on account of his having no teeth. Beneath his half-closed lids, I saw the slivers of white and his eyes jerked from side to side. Dreaming . . .

My hands came alive at once, with a ferocious sting of electricity. The fingers actually spazzed and twitched, and I thought: *a pencil, a pen, anything . . .*

Then I saw a slim packet on the bed stand to Mr. Witek's right. Had it been there before? I didn't recall. The packet was a khaki canvas roll and lay atop an artist's sketchbook. Before I knew what I was doing, I'd picked up the roll. Instantly, the pain in my hands eased. Not all the way but a bit. I tugged at the ribbon and unrolled the packet and caught just the faintest whisper of turpentine.

They were brushes, each slotted into a separate canvas holder. They were the kind you used for oil painting. Some were stiff hog hair for thick paints, but there were also softer, sable-hair brushes, and all types—flats, rounds, a few filberts, daggers, and scripts—for very fine work. The brushes were in excellent condition. Their toes were absolutely perfect, the lacquered dark wood of the handles unblemished with the size of each brush in tiny gold numbers, and a name done in an ornate script: **Dynasty**.

I knew these belonged to the artist who'd done all these paintings—to *MW*. Obviously, the *W* must mean "Witek."

I looked at the old man, licked my lips, and then said: "Mr. Witek, sir, do you want me to have these? Is that why they're here?"

Of course, he didn't answer. His breathing didn't even change. It was like having a conversation with a corpse. Still ... I looked at the packet of brushes in my hands and then at the old man. Then I tucked the canvas roll into my hip pocket and pulled my shirt out so no one could see. I felt like a complete thief—but that didn't stop me from scooping up that sketchbook either.

The sketchbook was old, the pages yellowed and spotted with age. There was no information on the first page, only a date, written in black ink: 07-08-45.

The second page was a pencil sketch, a head-and-shoulders portrait of a young man in three-quarters profile, his left side toward the viewer. The man looked to be in his early twenties; his face was lean, a little hungry-looking, with a fringe of bangs over a high forehead. The man's lips were very thin and uneven, with a scar bisecting his upper lip just below his nose, and there was another half-moon scar puckering his left cheekbone. The eyes were a little too close together over the bridge of a narrow nose, and there was something off about them, a look that reminded me of a flounder. A lazy eye? Maybe. I could just see the curved frame of spectacles jutting from the man's left breast pocket. His shirt was open at the throat, and there was something in white—a letter?—just visible below the hump of the left shoulder. There was a name penciled below, followed by some kind of code: *Daecher, L.K. 31G-5293.*

A hum of recognition when I saw the name. Daecher? No one in town with that name, but . . . I quickly leafed through a few more pages and saw that they were all pencil portraits, all men, all with codes next to their names.

Puzzled, I looked down at the old man again. "Sir . . . Mr. Witek . . . I don't know what this is all about or if you can hear me, but maybe you can. . . . I mean, can you blink or some—"

"*What* are you doing?"

I nearly let loose with a yell. As it was, I jumped back from Mr. Witek's bed, turning so fast that I almost smacked Stephanie in the face. She glared, her beady bird's eyes narrowing as she saw the sketchbook. "I said, what are you *doing* in here?"

"I . . ." I swallowed and then did the absolutely wrong thing by hastily replacing the sketchbook on the nightstand, just like a guilty guy caught with his hand in the register. "Nothing . . . I was just talking to Mr. Witek. . . . "

"Talking?" Stephanie bustled toward the bed. "How could you be talking to—" She broke off and a hand flew to her lips. "Oh my God."

Mr. Witek's eyes were open.

And the very next second, my head exploded.

The sensation was huge and immediate and physical, like being clobbered from behind, this huge KEBANG, a blinding flash that was also physical, a ripping open of some fissure and the muttering—gone for so long—jostled in and *you*

you

YOU

YOUYOUYOUYOU

XIV

Mr. Witek's eyes didn't waver—he didn't blink—but he was seeing me, *really* seeing me for the first time, and the words in my mind were screams, and then there were so many voices

he's crazy I hate peas little bitch's not wearing panties I'm three weeks late little bitch she thinks that because I'm old I can't get it up better call security if I could just find myself that's right come closer let's see those little titties oh I'm so lost

all overlapping in a blurry cacophony, like water gushing out a burst dam. I screamed, my hands clapping to my temples as I stumbled back from the bed. My legs got tangled, and I flailed, knocking over an IV pump with a huge *crash*.

"What is it, what's the matter?" Stephanie was shouting. She actually took a step back. "What's wrong with you?"

Her frantic thoughts bulleted out: *Call security better call security hell if I'll take the blame . . .*

"My . . . *head* . . ." I gritted my teeth, doubling over with the pain. My vision sheeted red and then white, like a lightning bolt had jagged across my eyes. All of a sudden, something hot and wet spurted over my lips, and I backhanded bright red blood as more gushed from my nose. The pain was so intense, I thought my eyes were bleeding. "It . . . *hurts*. . . ."

"Let's get you out of here," said Stephanie and plucked at my arm. "Come on, you need to go sit down."

"N-no," I said. Another burst of pain in my head, blistering and fiery as napalm

oh I've lost myself hurts my eyes . . .

and all of a sudden, I thought: *This is what it's like to die . . .*

Another jumble of images flickered: a train, white gauze, a lace parasol. . . .

"Oh God, it's *Lucy*." I took one lurching step for the door, swayed, and grappled for a handhold. I hung onto the wall, my bloody hands smearing rust over cream paint. *Not me, it's her, it's . . .* "Quick, you have to get help! Something's happening . . . something's happening to Lucy."

But Stephanie was already moving fast.

lock him in he's nuts he's crazy

trying to get out and lock me in.

"N-n-no." I grabbed for her, but she shied away. A sickly gray fog was steaming over my vision, and the fluorescents had dimmed, and the objects in the room, Stephanie's face, they were becoming fuzzy and indistinct, grainy the way the world seems to dissolve at twilight.

Then I saw something new: the potato-shape of a head, but not with pellet black eyes this time. This time, the eyes were wide and startled, the face twisted in a grimace, the slash of mouth bleeding black because the hand holding the charcoal was failing, falling, the world spinning away. . . .

That got me moving.

"No! Stop! You don't understand!" I stumbled for the door, grabbed the edge before Stephanie could slam it in my face and yanked. Stephanie fell back with a sharp cry; the door bammed against the wall hard enough that the painting of the woman in silk crashed to the floor.

"Get out of the way, get out of my way!" Then I was pushing past, into the hall, still shouting, *roaring*: "Call Dr. Rainier, call the doctor, it's Lucy, it's *Lucy*!"

I took off for the exit at a dead run.

no, don't, help me, help me, help me, don't leave, don't

XV

At the commotion, a few of the nurses had come into the hall, but they moved aside fast, breaking up like startled ducks as I tore out of Mr. Witek's room. I must've looked like a maniac: blood slicking my chin, staining my shirt, my hands rust-colored, my eyes

all that blood must have killed Stephanie got to get out of here

wild, but then I was blasting past, screaming something about Lucy again and calling Dr. Rainier, and I saw one nurse grab a handset and start punching numbers into her phone

security

and then I hit the exit doors at a dead run, banging through. A second later, an alarm shrieked from the intercom, spiking my ears and then words, but not the ones I'd expected: *Code blue, Lakeview Common Room; code blue, Lakeview . . .*

Oh God, I was too late! I galloped down the breezeway, swiped the key card, and banged into Lakeview in seconds.

Images slammed against my mind, breaking like waves. The halls were crowded with old people, all talking and thinking excitedly, and I bullied my way past, squirting through, people moving aside once they got a good look at me. There was another crowd outside the common room—the one where they held the art class—and now I could hear a gabble of voices.

"Excuse me. . . . I have to get through," I gasped, shoving my way to the front. "I have to get through, let me through, let me . . . !"

I stopped, dead.

Lucy's friend, the woman with the orange hair, was huddled to one side, an aide hugging her as she wept. There were upended easels and paper and brushes on the floor, multicolored footprints from where people had stepped in spilled paint as they scattered.

Lucy's easel had overturned when she toppled out of her wheelchair, but I could see the charcoal portrait—that lump of a head—very clearly, and it was exactly as I'd seen it in my mind. There were backs huddled around, but I could see Lucy, spread-eagled, her dress speckled with tiny blue flowers bunched up around her hips, her thighs fish-belly white. Lucy's eyes were jammed wide, her mouth open, a look of surprise and agony on her twisted, withered features—and that's when I realized: she'd drawn the moment of her death.

No. *No.* She'd *drawn* herself to death.

Oh God. It felt like my brain was leaking out of my ears. *Oh God, it's like Miss Stefancyzk . . . it's like what I did to Aunt Jean. . . .*

Dr. Rainier was doing CPR: "Get me a tube, get me an ET tube right now, and I want some access . . ." Then she saw me. "Christian? Christian, what—?"

But I couldn't stay there a minute longer, not one more second. Instead, I turned and ran.

XVI

No one tried to stop me. I slammed out of the home, jumped on my bike, and took off as fast as I could pedal. It was near dark, the light going fast, and the sky a brilliant wash of orange and peach to the west but cobalt blue directly overhead. Maybe three minutes out from the home, an ambulance screamed in the opposite direction, light bar and headlights flashing.

For one brief second, as the headlights tacked me against the graying twilight, I thought: *Hit me. Please hit me, just hit me, hit me, and this will all be over.* . . . Maybe I thought about swerving into the ambulance's path, maybe not. It's such a jumble now, I don't know. Of course, the ambulance didn't hit me but blew past in a blast of exhaust and a swirl of grit.

I kept on. I guess you'd say I was losing it. I was beyond freaked out. My thoughts tumbled. The wrong person had died. What good had I ever done anyone? First, my dad and then my mom and then Aunt Jean and . . . Everything I touched turned bad. I thought about not going home. I wasn't sure where I could run or what I might do for money or anything. Maybe go north to Canada, sneak across the border, live off the land or get a job in some tiny, little town and hunker down and never touch another piece of chalk or charcoal or pencil or brush. . . .

Brushes. The *brushes*. They were still in my pocket. Why had I taken them? Because they'd been on Mr. Witek's nightstand like some kind of sign? Great, that was something a crazy person did. And touching them, taking them had touched off something, started a ball rolling, and now it was picking up speed, and it was all, *all* my fault. . . .

My face was wet with a mix of blood and my tears, my mouth full of the taste of salt and rust. My heart felt like it was going to burst wide open, and I was crying and pedaling and weaving all over the stupid road. My headlight gave out two miles from home, and even though I kept hoping for it, no one hit me either.

I don't know when I realized that the muttering in my head was gone. Had it faded even before? Maybe my brain had automatically kicked in some kind of override switch, like in a movie when the engines are going critical and the whole ship's gonna blow if the override doesn't get its act together. I don't know.

I half-expected Uncle Hank's truck to be in the driveway, but it wasn't. Probably no one had told him what his crazy nephew had done now—not yet anyway. But I knew that he'd be home soon, and by then, I had to think about what I was going to do because Krauss would kick me out for sure, and then the court would . . .

I just couldn't think about it anymore. I dumped my bike, banged in through the kitchen, and pounded upstairs. The blood on my face was tacky, my shirt stiff with it. I peeled out of my clothes and underwear, and then I cranked on the shower and ducked under the water while it was still icy. Stupid, maybe, but I remembered reading about some old monk or saint or something and how he'd stand in an ice-cold pool for hours to get rid of all the bad feelings he had pent up inside. For him, I think it was sex. For me, it was . . . I don't know. Murder? Knowing that I'd touched death? Knowing I'd killed someone *again*?

The shock of the water stole my breath, and I grunted, my mouth tightening into a grimace as I turned my face into water that was so cold the spray felt like needles. Good, good, pain was good because I was bad, I was no good, I deserved whatever I got. . . .

The blood on my face swirled, pale red, down the drain. By then, I was panting, my heart booming in my chest, my skin getting numb. I started to shake and couldn't stop, just the way they say when you go into shock. My teeth clacked together, and I bit my tongue, tasted fresh brackish blood—and I wasn't dead; I was still alive and I thought: *Okay, you want to die? You do it like Miss Stefancyzk, or you ride your bike off a bridge, or you find a car and wrap it around a tree; you do it with a gun or a rope or fire or . . .*

And then I was weeping again, all of a sudden, and so wobbly my knees buckled and I curled up on the stall floor, letting the icy water rain on my back. I was so cold; I was in agony. I kept waiting for my heart to seize up, but it didn't—and then I remembered that Uncle Hank would be here soon, and if I wanted to die, it would have to be somewhere else because I couldn't bear the thought of him finding me. There'd be no way he wouldn't blame himself, and that was wrong; that *was* evil.

Swaying up on my knees, I reached up, groped, turned the water to hot—felt it turn from icy to tepid to steaming to boiling. It took a while for the steely cold in my gut to loosen, and then my skin got so hot, it felt like it was going to peel off, so I dialed the temperature to something I could stand. Gritting my teeth, I soaped up; I lathered every inch, and still I didn't feel clean. At the end, I started crying again, sagging against the tile as water pounded my neck and shoulders. But I wouldn't let myself fall.

I didn't hear Uncle Hank over the rush of water until he pounded on the bathroom door. "Christian! Christian, you all right?"

I thought about pretending that I couldn't hear but considering that Uncle Hank had broken down locked doors to get at people, I figured that would only delay the inevitable.

"I'm okay." I twisted off the water. "I'll be out in a couple minutes."

Silence on the other side of the door. Then: "Dr. Rainier called just as soon as she could. She's on her way over. She was pretty worried about you." A pause. "Me, too."

"I'm okay. She doesn't need to come."

Uncle Hank chose not to get into it. "I'll be waiting downstairs. There's a fresh change of clothes just outside the door."

I was so stunned, I forgot to thank him, and by the time I remembered, he was already gone.

They were waiting for me in the kitchen, mugs of fresh coffee steaming on the table. Uncle Hank looked tired and sad and worried. Dr. Rainier just looked concerned, and they both kept throwing looks at each other in that way adults have when they're trying to figure out the best way to talk to the crazy kid. They waited while I poured coffee, sloshed in milk, and dumped in a couple tablespoons of sugar before Dr. Rainier said, "It wasn't your fault."

I concentrated on stirring. I didn't turn around. "You wouldn't understand."

"Try us," said Uncle Hank. "Help me understand why you ran out of there. You scared Dr. Rainier half to death. She said there was blood all over your face."

I turned around then. "I had a nosebleed." I sipped my coffee. It was too hot, and I burned the roof of my mouth.

"Stephanie said you were acting"—Dr. Rainier chose her words carefully—"very erratically."

I actually gave a bleak laugh. "I'll bet those weren't the words she used."

Uncle Hank said, not too heatedly, "Watch that."

"It's okay." Dr. Rainier actually smiled. "She said you were acting, and I quote, *nuts*. Is that accurate?"

Yeah, that pretty much covered it; hadn't she even thought those exact words? "From her point of view, I guess." Heck, even from my point of view.

Dr. Rainier pulled out a chair at the table and nodded me toward it. She waited until I dragged over and then said, "What happened, exactly?"

I debated. What could I really tell them? Lemme see, well, I went into a room I shouldn't have been in the first place; there's a painting on the old guy's wall that's exactly the same as the one I drew in my sleep the same night I spray-painted swastikas and eyes on Eisenmann's barn. Oh, and I stole the old guy's brushes; then I got a flash of Lucy as I'd drawn her—or maybe as she'd drawn herself, only it was like this cosmic Ouija board and so she couldn't have done it if there wasn't some kind of power I was tapping into. Then I saw/felt her *draw* out her death, and I freaked out; I got this headache, I smeared blood all over the place, bolted from the room and tore into the next building—and I could read people's thoughts, if only briefly.

Oh, and that poor little baby someone walled up in your hearth, Doc? I think that's tied in somehow too.

Right. There was no way I could tell the whole truth and no lie I could figure out that would cover everything that had happened. So I said, "Do you believe in ESP?"

Uncle Hank frowned. To her credit, Dr. Rainier didn't even blink. "Well, I could be psychiatric about it and answer a question with a question, like what do you believe, but . . . I don't know. Sometimes I wish I could read my patients' minds. The most gifted therapists I know have cultivated empathy to a fine art. And it's a fact that couples with solid, long-term marriages pretty much know what the other person is thinking. Identical twins report finishing each other's sentences." She paused for a second to look at me. "I think that can look like ESP, but it's more likely that they—and those gifted therapists—are picking up on subtle nonverbal cues. It's how experts in kinesics—body language—do what looks like mind reading but is really close scrutiny of clusters of behaviors."

"So . . . you don't believe in it."

"Reading minds? Throwing thoughts around? No, I don't. I'd like to. I studied the stuff in college, even did a research paper on it. But that probably says more about me than anything else." She cocked her head. "Are you saying that you think you can read other people's thoughts?"

"All I know is that I felt like I had to go into Mr. Witek's room, like it was . . ."

drawing

". . . *calling* me," I said. "Maybe it's all those pictures, I don't know."

"You mean, the fact that you enjoy painting and drawing."

I nodded. "But when I got in there and saw them, I . . ." I snuck a glance at Uncle Hank and then said to Dr. Rainier, "I realized that I had drawn a picture almost exactly the same as one of Mr. Witek's paintings."

Uncle Hank sat up a little straighter. Dr. Rainier didn't notice. "Then you must've seen the painting before," she said, reasonably.

"No. I hadn't even met Mr. Witek then. I drew this picture the same night that I . . . that I guess I spray-painted Mr. Eisenmann's barn. I can show you." I slid off my chair. "Just a second."

I don't know what they talked about while I was gone, but I heard the low growl of Uncle Hank's voice—"It's the first I've heard of it"—and then they both stopped talking as I came into the room. I opened my pad and then turned the drawing around so they could both see.

"That's what I drew," I said. "If you go look at Mr. Witek's painting, everything's the same, even the direction of the smoke from the foundry."

Dr. Rainier and Uncle Hank stared at the drawing for a good minute; then Dr. Rainier tapped the onion dome. "What is this? Do you have a building like that in town?"

Uncle Hank shook his head. "Haven't got a clue."

"It looks Russian or Eastern European."

"It's called the White Lady." When they looked at me, I continued, "Well, at least, that's the name I've heard."

"From whom?" asked Dr. Rainier.

"I'm not all the way sure, but I think I got it from Mr. Witek the same way I got that drawing of Lucy with that parasol."

Uncle Hank said, "What? What drawing?"

Dr. Rainier said slowly, "Lucy drew the picture, Christian. You calmed her enough so she could reach down and pull out the image she wanted."

I shook my head. "No, that's what you think. It felt more like . . . When I took her hand, it was like a Ouija board."

Her eyebrows tented. "What?"

"Ouija board?" Uncle Hank demanded. "*What* drawing?"

Dr. Rainier explained and then said, "But there was nothing magical about it, and it certainly has nothing to do with what hap—" Her voice cut out abruptly, and her eyes slitted. "What is it, Hank?"

Uncle Hank passed his hand in front of his mouth, like maybe if he could stop himself from saying it, whatever came out of his mouth wouldn't be real. His eyes clicked to me and then back to Dr. Rainier. "You've read Christian's files, right? So you know about Betty Stefancyzk."

"Of course, I know, but . . ." Now Dr. Rainier was looking at both of us the way you do some kind of weird bugs. "You can't be serious. You believe what she said? Hank, she was mentally ill. She'd stopped taking her medications. She was delusionally fixated on Christian."

"Maybe," said Uncle Hank, slowly, "but don't you find it kind of weird that she and this Lucy at the home . . . that both, ah, incidents involved Christian's drawing something? With Stefancyzk, it was a picture of a house Christian drew in class, only her note said Christian drew it out of her, as in *stole* it. With this Lucy, it was *her*."

Dr. Rainier opened her mouth and then closed it. She and Uncle Hank just looked at each other, and then Uncle Hank's head moved in a tiny nod. "Got to be more than just coincidence," he said, so low I could barely hear him. Then his gaze crawled to me. "Christian, why did you ask about ESP?"

I said, as calmly as I could, "Because I saw Lucy draw her death. I saw it in my mind." I pointed at the picture. "I *drew* that. I . . . I *took it out* of something—and I'd never seen Mr. Witek's painting before that. But it's an exact match."

Uncle Hank didn't laugh. He didn't say I was crazy. He said, "And?"

"And I think it means that . . . he . . . he *told* me."

"But Mr. Witek can't speak," Dr. Rainier said.

"No, ma'am," I agreed. "Not in words."

XVII

We pretty much left it at that. I mean, what else was there to say? No way I was going to spill everything. I was in enough trouble as it was.

Before she left, Dr. Rainier said, "Christian, I think it's best if you skip the home for the rest of the week and come on Monday. Give things a chance to settle down."

"You think they'll let him come back?" asked Uncle Hank.

"Technically, he hasn't done anything wrong." To me: "The way I understand it, you were interested in Mr. Witek's paintings, you tried talking to him a little bit, and then you had a nosebleed. Is that about right?"

"Uh . . ." Not *exactly*. "Yeah. What about Lucy and Stephanie?"

"You let me handle all that. I need a chance to think about what you've said, but I don't think you can be fired for a premonition. You had a *hunch*." She fastened her eyes on mine. "Isn't that right?"

I saw where this was going. I nodded, and her face smoothed.

"That's what I thought, and that's what I'm going to write into the official record," she said. "Losing it with Stephanie will be harder to explain, but you were having a nosebleed and you were upset. So far as I can tell, there was no harm done except, perhaps, to Stephanie's dignity. You might actually have done some good for Mr. Witek. He responded to you by opening his eyes. He hasn't done that for anyone. I checked him before I came over, and while I wouldn't say he's ready for a round of golf, he's not worse either. One more thing. I'd like to see you tomorrow instead of Friday, okay? Let's just touch base."

That was all right with me. Friday was a teacher workday and no school, so having the whole day off would be kind of nice. "Sure."

"Good." She smiled at me, but when she turned to go, she touched Uncle Hank on the arm. Just a brush of her fingers. "I think we'll be fine," she said—mainly to Uncle Hank, I thought.

Uncle Hank's voice was husky. "God, Helen, I hope you're right."

Helen?

I wasn't hungry; my brain was churning and my stomach too, but Uncle Hank scrambled up eggs and hash browns and made me eat. We didn't talk—no shocker there. After the dishes, I said, "I'm going to bed."

"All right." He was sitting at the table with the last of the coffee. "You sleep well now."

I walked to the hall but lingered in the doorway a moment. "Why is Dr. Rainier helping us so much?"

His face was cop-blank. I'd seen that look a hundred times before, so I knew he was hiding something. "Any doctor worth her salt's gonna do what's best for a patient."

"But she's . . ." I didn't want to say *lying.* "I mean, she's pretty much told me what to say. Is that allowed?"

"She's giving you the best shot you've got to stay out of as much trouble as possible."

"Okay." I debated before asking, "So how much do you like her?"

For a moment, I didn't think he was going to answer the question. To be honest, I was pretty surprised I'd ask. We're not exactly talkative, my uncle and me. His eyes shifted to his coffee and then back to me, and he said, "I loved your Aunt Jean very much. But I've been lonely, and Dr. Rainier . . . she's smart, tough. Got guts, get right down to it."

And beautiful. But I didn't say that.

"I like her, Christian. I like her very much. But I'm also not going to do a thing about it."

I couldn't believe my ears. Looking back, Uncle Hank must've been exhausted or else he'd have never revealed so much. You have to understand how private he is, not just because he's sheriff but to protect me, I think. I'm willing to bet that there's a lot of talk and gossip and heat I don't know about, even now, because he made sure I didn't hear it and wouldn't suffer more than he felt I already had.

People had tried to fix up Uncle Hank before. He's only forty-one. Sometimes he feels older to me, but that's because he carries around the weight of so many lives. He once said that you didn't understand mortality or real grief until you stood over the body of a high school kid on prom night.

The way he talked about Dr. Rainier, like it was a done deal, made me feel sad. "Why not? If you like her . . . Aunt Jean would understand."

"It's not that. I know your aunt would. We talked about it a lot, actually. Even though Winter's pretty quiet and we haven't had a murder in I don't know how long, things happen. Your great-grandfather died in a fire, after all. Drunks'll run you off the road and roll outta their cars, not a scratch on them and leave you as a smear on the road. There's black ice and tornadoes and fools driving their trucks out onto the lake when the ice is too thin. This life will kill you a million different ways to Sunday. So your aunt and I, we'd already had that talk about what to do and how to go on if something happened. Of course, we figured it would be me, not her." His blue eyes bored into mine. "You don't know how many nights I wish it *had* been me instead."

My chest got tight, and my eyes burned. Uncle Hank's face blurred and broke apart the way light does through a prism, and then I was crying again. Yes, he would surely hate me if he knew. . . .

You know what really got me? Uncle Hank thought my tears were because I felt bad for him, . . . which I did. But he got mad at himself for making *me* upset. He wrapped me up in a bear hug, patted my back, rubbed my hair the way he had when I was about ten or so, and kept telling me everything would be okay.

When he pulled back, his eyes were moist. "You all right?" I'm about four inches shorter, and he ducked down a little to grab my eyes. "It'll be okay. We're going to get through this the way we always have."

I said something like yeah and sure and thanks, and then I got out of there. Only when I was in my room did I realize that Uncle Hank never had answered the question.

So, of course, I couldn't sleep.

I was ashamed. Here, I'd been ready to, you know, *die* or run away, but Uncle Hank was hanging tough. He didn't think I was a bad person.

I felt like a little kid inside, like there was this other me who was about five and wanted to be told everything would be okay. Maybe everybody feels that way. In history, we were talking about the Iraq war—there are a lot of local guys who're army or National Guard—and someone said wounded guys call for their mothers. People kind of giggled, and the teacher snapped at us. But I didn't laugh. I *understood* that feeling. Maybe only kids who've had parents hang around until they're all sick to death of each other don't get it. I did.

So that's when I decided that I had to help myself. I'm seventeen, for heaven's sake. Yeah, I was worrying about colleges and stuff, but it hit me that kids in college had it easy. Things are still done *for* them: their meals, their schedule, all that stuff. All a college kid has to do is get to classes, do the work, and figure out how to do laundry.

But take someone like Uncle Hank. No matter how much horror he saw, he dealt with it—because nobody else would or could. The same for Dr. Rainier, I'd bet. Somebody had to be responsible. So I had to do that too.

I pushed out of bed, went to my desk drawer, pulled it open, and unrolled the canvas brush roll. The brushes felt as right and natural in my hand now as they did back at the home. I'd *drawn* and been drawn to Mr. Witek's room, and the moment I'd picked up the pouch, Mr. Witek opened his eyes. There was a message in all that.

So, enough self-pity already. I could be scared. I could be freaked out. But things were happening; there were messages being sent my way and tasks that, perhaps, only I could do. I just had to figure out what and why.

So that's what I did: fired up the computer and made a list of the things I knew and could remember from my dreams and what I'd heard. It was a short list: the White Lady, Mr. Witek, a murder back in 1945, a fire in September or October of that same year. After a few seconds of staring at the list, I added *Marta. Anderson farm. Foundry dormitories. Prisoners at Eisenmann Foundry.*

Then I Googled.

I realized that without a last name, I wouldn't get far with Marta. Ditto on the farm. All I could find on the foundry involved the company's website, which gave an abbreviated timeline and history of the Eisenmanns. The reading was fairly skimpy. The company's founder, Sigismund Friedrich Eisenmann, immigrated to the States from Germany in 1856, along with his second wife and nine children. The son of a cattle farmer, Sigismund had dreams of being a businessman and settled first in Chicago, working as a shoe salesman by day and attending college at night, earning his degree in metallurgy seven years later. Shortly thereafter, he came to Wisconsin to visit cousins and met a local businessman named Kramner, also a German, who wanted to take over a local foundry that was apparently going under. The two struck up a partnership, purchased the foundry, and operated it jointly as Kramner-Eisenmann Manufacturing Company for ten years churning out farm implements and residential items like cast-iron tubs, plumbing fixtures, and kitchenware. When Kramner died, Eisenmann took over sole ownership, and the company has stayed in the family to the present. The Eisenmann *I* knew, Charles, was Sigismund's great-grandson. Charles's son, Jonathan, currently managed the bulk of the company's day-to-day operations, but Charles Eisenmann still had the final word.

One thing that I did find pretty interesting, though: Sigismund faced a serious shortage of skilled workers as his company grew larger. There were—still are—large German, Swiss, and Austrian populations in Wisconsin, many of whom came over in waves beginning in the 1840s. By the time Sigismund arrived, these first immigrants had established communities that welcomed new workers, and Sigismund realized that he could lure skilled craftsmen and ironworkers to his company if he provided them not only with a community but a means of integrating into American society. So he built dormitories: comfortable living quarters in which workers lived rent-free. Their meals were provided. Classes in American history, English, and business were offered twice a day to accommodate the shift workers; workers were put on a path to citizenship. The idea was to get the workers to view the company as family and stay put once they'd arrived.

Hunh. I clicked back to my list and checked off *dormitories* as the real deal. Which freaked me out a little, because that

meant at least part of my visions or dreams or whatever . . .
were real.

Searching for prisoners or a prison in connection with
Eisenmann's company was a big zero. So was the White Lady.

Plugging in *Winter, Wisconsin, murder,* and *1945* got me
a single useful hit, the first paragraph of an archived item on
"National News" from the *New York Times*:

> Milwaukee, WI, October 23: Residents of the tiny rural
> hamlet of Winter continue to grapple with the aftermath
> of what appears to have been a particularly vicious and
> senseless murder. Walter Brotz, 45, was found slain in
> a horse barn on October 20. He had been stabbed re-
> peatedly with a pitchfork, which was found at the scene,
> smeared with the victim's blood. Mr. Brotz, an employee in
> the brass plant at the Eisenmann Manufacturing Company,
> was reported missing by his wife, Gertrude, on the evening
> of October 19, when he was last seen leaving work with
> several companions.

When I read that word—*pitchfork*—my stomach clenched.
There'd been a pitchfork in my very first nightmare.

Unfortunately, that was all I got. If I wanted to read the
rest of the article, I would have to pay and since a) I didn't have
a credit card and b) I didn't have any *money*—that was kind of
a nonstarter.

I searched for *Walter Brotz* but came up empty. Still, I put
his name on my list. At least now I had the name of the murder
victim. Maybe there was more at the town library or at the Historical Society. Sarah would know. I checked the time: almost

eleven, too late to call, though I had her e-mail address from way back. Hopefully it was still good. So I wrote:

To: preacherskid@magna.com
From: ccage@magna.com
Subject: research

Hey, Sarah:

Sorry to bug you, but I'm getting started on my history project, and I'm drawing a big zero. I think what I need might be at the Historical Society, or maybe the library, but I'm not sure. Since you know who to talk to there, would you mind if I came with you? When are you going next? I have to work on Saturday, but I could go on Friday after school.
Thanks.
Christian

I hit Send, hoping she might check her e-mail tomorrow morning, and then maybe we could talk at school. Then I sat back and studied my list. Without more details, it seemed to me that searching for a 1945 fire was a waste of time. Here there'd been a murder in the same year, and I'd only found one news story about it. Maybe the Historical Society people would have more.

That left only one item: Mr. Witek. It hit me then that I didn't know his first name, which made me feel stupid. But I plugged in *Witek*, *Winter* and *Wisconsin*. I paused, thought about it, and added *painter* then hit Enter.

The next second, my mouth dropped open. I clicked on the first result, and a short entry from Wikipedia opened on my screen:

Mordecai Mendel Witek (b. April 3, 1905–?) was a self-educated realist painter. Dubbed the "Andrew Wyeth" of Wisconsin regional art, Witek immigrated to the United States from the tiny Polish town of Oswiecem (later renamed Auschwitz) 1935. Initially settling in Milwaukee, he found employment as a painter of fine ceramics and porcelains at the Eisenmann Manufacturing Company in the small northern town of Winter and moved there in 1940. He continued to paint watercolors and oils, predominantly landscapes, but garnered both praise and censure after his painting, *Katarina at Sunset*, won Grand Prize at the Milwaukee Lakeside Arts Festival in 1943. A critic at the time described the painter's style as "subversively sexual." The painting caused a minor scandal when it was revealed that the young woman in question was the fiancée of a local businessman. Witek continued to reside in Winter, where he divided his time between his factory work and various commissions, and he was active in Winter's small but vibrant Jewish community.

Later events would cast a cloud over his short-lived artistic success. Today, Witek is remembered chiefly as the prime suspect in a gruesome murder of a fellow factory worker that occurred in October 1945. Local residents believed the murder was motivated by a love triangle, a claim substantiated by the factory's owner, Charles Randall Eisenmann, who was also injured and horribly disfigured in the same incident. The murder remains unsolved, however, as

Witek disappeared. The artist's subsequent whereabouts and presumptive date of death are unknown, though reporters of the time believed that Witek fled the country, possibly to Canada or Israel.

⁓

Wow.

I must've read that entry six times. An artist? And *Jewish*? As far as I knew, there were no Jews in Winter. But that last name was too unusual. This had to be *my* Witek's father.

I did a quick calculation. Sixty-five years had passed since the murder. Mordecai Witek had been forty *then*, so he was dead for sure. Mr. Witek was, what? In his seventies? So, in 1945, he'd have been a boy. . . .

"Papa," I whispered. Yes, Mordecai Witek's *son*. David.

And another mystery was solved: Mordecai Witek was the man who'd scarred up Mr. Eisenmann all those years ago.

Holy crap. No wonder Mrs. Krauss hadn't wanted to talk about it.

I clicked on the hypertext link for *Katarina at Sunset*.

The painting that flashed onto my screen was breathtakingly beautiful, and I could see why Witek might be compared to Wyeth right away. The woman, Katarina, sprawled on a slope of forest green meadow, and I even recognized the spot because of the barn perched on a rise in the far distance to the right. To the left was a two-story farmhouse: white, with black shutters and a weather vane and two brick chimneys. The painting had been done at Eisenmann's barn, at a point in time when the house still stood.

As with Wyeth's *Christine's World*, Witek's Katarina faced away from the viewer, but that's where the similarities ended.

141

Instead of gazing at a house, Katarina looked up the hill toward an absent sun, its memory sketched in a sky dyed in vivid swaths of iridescent blue and a bright pink that seemed almost alien. The colors roiled across the sky in luminous bolts and splashed over the meadow and the woman lying there like unearthly water.

Katarina was also completely naked.

It's hard to describe, even now, what the picture really looked like. You couldn't see Katarina's face, but maybe it was the languid line of her back and the way her golden hair whipped around her head that made me think: *Bernini.* There's his famous statue of St. Theresa in St. Peter's, the one where the angel is stabbing her through the heart and Theresa's in ecstasy, and I remembered that several critics had suggested that Bernini had studied the faces of women in . . . well, *orgasm* to get just the right expression.

That's what popped into my head when I looked at that painting of Katarina. She was having sex—and she'd reached *that* moment—only we were supposed to imagine it. I could see why people at that time would've thought it was racy, especially with all that lurid color. It was a little like Rubens that way, only he splashed red against his women's thighs instead of pink.

My eyes fixed on a small detail at the bottom right of the picture. Zooming in, I was able to magnify that portion of the painting—and there it was, that same six-sided star with the letters *MW* in the center and two numbers, one above and one below: 3 and 9.

Now, I understood: a Star of David and Mordecai Witek's initials. For the artist, his Jewish identity had been something he'd taken pride in.

It was then that I realized something else.

I'd seen this woman before in another portrait, in Mr. Witek's room, hanging to the right of the door.

Katarina was the woman in the silk kimono with the red chrysanthemums.

XVIII

My e-mail chimed: Sarah. I checked my watch; it was a few
minutes before eleven.

To: ccage@magna.com
From: preacherskid@magna.com
Subject: re: research

Christian, you don't write or talk to me for over two
years and now already we're like pen pals or something?
LOL just pulling your chain.

Yeah, sure, you can come with me to the Historical
Society. I'm going tomorrow right after school because I
have to do something with the family on Friday <groan>.
I'll show you who to talk to and how to use the databases.
Hey, I heard about what happened at the old people's home
because Dad got called. What did you do?

Hey, do you have IM? If you have IM, we can do that
instead of e-mail because it's faster. I'm sarah13. IM me.
Sarah

I did have IM, only I hadn't used it for years. I'd never had
any buddies, so it seemed a waste. But I logged on and then typed:

ccage: Hey, Sarah, it's me. Christian.

I wasn't expecting a reply, thinking that maybe she'd already gone to bed, but she came right back:

sarah13: So what happened?
ccage: Nothing.
sarah13: That's not what I heard.
ccage: What did you hear?
sarah13: That you helped her make a drawing and now she's
dead. People are saying it's like Miss S.

I was about to type *No, it wasn't like Miss S at all*, but I didn't.
Not that this wasn't partially true. With Miss Stefancyzk, I had
been furious, as volcanically angry as a seven-year-old can be.
I remembered the feeling well: this deluge of emotions and
thoughts that were alien to me, ones that involved knives and
faces that morphed into monsters' masks, and then I *drew* that
house out of her, the one she kept locked away in a steel vault in
her mind, but I found it, oh yes, I did. . . .

But now I wondered: What if the images and emotions
I'd had then weren't mine? What if, like Stephanie and the
other people at the home, a door had cracked open in my mind

and Miss Stefancyzk's deepest, darkest thoughts had leaked in? Hadn't Dr. Rainier said that Miss Stefancyzk was manic-depressive and probably hadn't been taking her meds? So what if she was tipping over the edge all along and then . . . ?

And then I came along, with some kind of weird ESP-ish power to channel all that rage and have it come out my fingers, the same way I tapped into Lucy's images of herself as a younger woman and the awful instant when she had the heart attack that killed her. But I hadn't been angry with Lucy. I liked her. So what was I *drawing*? Nightmares? Destiny?

And the way I visualized my mother and saw the sideways place where I was too frightened to go—what was it, really? Heaven? Hell? Purgatory?

And then there was Aunt Jean. What had I seen there? I couldn't imagine my Aunt Jean—sunny, ready with a smile, always good to me—with such a pit of blackness in her soul. No, I'd killed her all right. She made me angry, and my mind had lashed out, and then I'd drawn that wretched picture. She'd taken one look, and it was like all the blood drained from her veins, and the horror in her eyes, like she'd confronted the thing that scared her most. . . .

I shied away from that particular memory. I typed:

ccage: I was in an old guy's room when it happened. I had a premonition and then my nose started to bleed, and I freaked out.
sarah13: Wow. Are you okay?
ccage: Yeah.

I couldn't think of anything else to say, so I waited. It hit me suddenly that I was having a conversation that you'd almost call friendly. Not entirely *truthful*—I wasn't *that* crazy—but comfortable enough. I thought back to the times when Sarah and I had played on swings and climbed trees and I wondered how it was that you went from playing games to actually talking.

Sarah typed:

sarah13: Hey, I'm having a Halloween party at my house. You want to come?

I was so stunned I just sat there and read the message again. Finally, I wrote:

ccage: Yeah?
sarah13: <eye roll> Duh. Of course, *yeah*. I was thinking that you're so good with painting and all, maybe you could make some kind of mural. You know, something creepy, like a graveyard or haunted house or something.

I should have known. This wasn't about me. I typed:

ccage: Maybe. I might be busy.

As soon as I hit Enter, I wished I hadn't. I wanted to type something about being an asshole, but I didn't.

A long pause. Then:

sarah13: I'm trying to be nice to you! Do you know how many people don't like you? Do you know how many people think you're flat-out weird?
ccage: Everybody. We've already had this conversation.

sarah13: God, you make it so hard for anyone to be nice to you.
ccage: Yeah? So where've you been for the last two years, Miss Popular?

Now I was being an asshole and I knew it. I wrote:

ccage: Sorry. I'm being an asshole.
sarah13: You're just now figuring that out? I'm done. It's almost midnight. I'm going to bed now.
ccage: Good night.

Sarah typed *SCREW YOU* and logged off.

I got in bed, but I didn't fall asleep right away. My thoughts pinballed around my skull, and my eyes kept snapping open. The moon was waning, perhaps three-quarters, and so my room wasn't completely dark. Silver light leaked in around the edges of my drawn shades, and the paintings on my walls seemed to glow.

To *move*.

Subtly. Stealthily. As if aware that anything more than the most minute of movements would make me run screaming from the room.

I held myself very still and thought: *Maybe this is it. Maybe this is the night the drawings come to life and just take over, draw me in. . . .*

Wasn't this what I'd been waiting for? A way of slipping into the sideways place and finding my parents? It had been days . . . no, a couple of *weeks* since I worked on that charcoal of my mother, and that made me freeze up inside. I couldn't do that, could I? If I stopped looking for her, wouldn't she stop looking for me? Her face would just evaporate like steam or something, and all that would be left would be pictures. . . . So I should go. I should let this happen.

Right. If I really wanted that, why had I freaked and whited out the door? Maybe because I really didn't have the guts at all. It was my bike ride home all over again when I'd thought about suicide. I was too scared to be in this world and too frightened to leave it.

I yawned. I would never fall asleep, never . . .

The ghosts still mutter, but there is another somebody, different from the rest. I see him, he sees me, my mouth is still gone, but my mind begins to burn, to itch and I think nothing, Papa's son is nothing; Papa's son did nothing but watch and now there are ghosts and wolves and my mouth is gone. . . .

Papa says that he and the other men will meet at the White Lady after shul to talk about the wolves. The wolves will break the union. Mr. Eisenmann wants to break the union. Papa says Mr. Eisenmann's using the wolves for Miss Catherine's house. . . .

Katarina at sunset, Katarina's white skin and her breasts, her body . . .

I have to be quiet, can't move, mustn't let them see that I am there. Papa has sent me away; he thinks that I've gone, and Miss Catherine has given all the servants the day off, told them to leave and not return until later. There is only the butler who stands guard at the front door, and he's easy to get around. I've often come by to visit Marta, and I'm nobody and small for my age, and so I creep down the back steps. I know all the ins and outs of this house because of Marta, and so long as I am quiet, which isn't hard when Marta and I talk . . .

The air smells green from ferns and huge potted plants. Water bubbles and splashes in a tumble of stones because there's a real brook that gurgles through the day room. Light spills through the long picture window, and jewels of color sparkle on the pale stone floor from the transom's stained glass. Miss Catherine lies on a satin divan, and she is so beautiful; it hurts to look, and the sun fires her fine kimono from behind so you can see the shadow of her breasts and the curve of her hips. I know Papa sees her because he's painting; his back is to me, and I'm crouched behind a trio of pots, peering through a fringe of palms. Papa tells her to move first this way and then another and his brushstrokes are so thin she glows like the alabaster lamps of the White Lady.

Neither sees me. My face burns with shame for spying. I know I shouldn't have disobeyed Papa, but there is something I don't like about what is happening here.

If I had only seen it sooner—if I had seen—I could've stopped the darkness and blood and the slash of the pitchfork.

Papa and Miss Catherine think they are alone. Miss Catherine has lips like ripe peaches, and there is color in her cheeks, and when Papa tells her to adjust her arms and to turn more to the right, she laughs and pouts and makes Papa come and move her arms for her. . . .

No, Papa. I am screaming this in my mind as he throws down his brush in disgust. I see that she's playing a game, like a queen, and what I can't understand is why Papa doesn't see it too—unless, maybe, he doesn't *want* to understand. Maybe he *wants* there to be something he can claim is an accident. But I scream, silently: *No, Papa, don't, stay away, don't!*

Her gown falls open, and she guides his hand. "I know what you want," she says, and now I know for certain that it is a game for the two of them. Papa's hand is on her breast, and Miss Catherine is pulling him down, and he's fallen on top of her, and her hands are in his hair, and now she is naked and her hands are under his shirt, and now they are both moaning. . . .

I am not aware that I have screamed—out loud and for real—until they both jerk their heads around and stare. Papa's hair is mussed, and his pants are sagging around his hips, and his eyes are shocked. Miss Catherine screams, and her hands fly to cover her breasts.

No! No, Papa, no! I turn and I am running out of the room, flying through the doors that open with a loud BANG! The butler's been dozing in his chair, and he startles at the sound; he is all elbows and knees, and he's struggling out of the chair, but I'm running down the long hall for the front of the house, and there are tears in my eyes. . . .

"David!" It is Papa. He is chasing after, but I keep running. I burst out of that grand house and into the blinding day, past all the wolves who are working on the grounds and turn to stare with their yellow slit eyes, but then I'm sprinting down the hill, away from the wolves climbing all over the house, away from all of them. Papa's cries are fainter and then they fall away, and the only sounds are my sobs and the seagulls wheeling in the blue sky over the lake, and they are screaming too, just as the horses scream and the men . . .

And now there's blood. There's blood on Papa's hands, there's blood everywhere, and the horses are screaming. . . . Catherine and Marta and the wolf . . . no Papa no, help me, somebody, please so scared, i want to stop seeing this, i'm so scared somebody please somebody help me help me help me

XIX

So, of course, I spazzed awake about three seconds before my alarm went off. My head was full of confused images and mutters, and I knew I'd been somewhere else—back in time, with the boy, *as* the boy—but there was nothing clear, just a jumble. I grabbed a pad and pencil from the nightstand the way Sarah said she had when they had to write down their dreams in psych—and just about fell out of bed when I saw what was already there.

Two scrawled words:

HELP ME

I didn't throw the paper away.

Maybe I should have.

Oh, the things you know in retrospect.

I got my second shock when I looked at my wall. Maybe the muttering in my head—oh yes, it was there again—should've tipped me off.

Because the door was back.

Cold sweat popped out all over my face and chest.

The door had no knob. But there it was, in precisely the same place, the edges crisp and clean, only this time I had used Mordecai Witek's brushes because the pouch was unrolled, a long-handled bright smelling of fresh turpentine. (Even in my sleep, I took care of my brushes. How strange was that?)

So my brain had decided to take over in my sleep and force my hand . . . so to speak. Whatever lived in the sideways place was just behind that door, pressed breathlessly against the skin separating it from this world. (Apparently, even my subconscious had limits, which was kind of hilarious when you got right down to it. Sure, make me bike a gazillion miles and dangle from a rope to spray-paint a barn, but whoa, watch that doorknob.)

Another thought occurred to me, though. What if that final step, *drawing* the knob and then turning it . . . what if that had to be my *choice*? Something I did *consciously*, understanding what might happen? I know. It sounded crazy to me too, and I was becoming an expert on crazy.

But you know what it reminded me of? *Revelation 3:20: Behold, I stand at the door and knock; if anyone hears My voice and opens the door, I will come in to him and will dine with him, and he with Me.*

Now, I'm not a whacked-out Christian-type. But everyone knows that quote from Revelation. Sarah's dad said in confirmation class that the reason God didn't barge in was that you had to bring your head to God along with your heart; the two couldn't be separate, and it had to be your choice. Another thing Reverend Schoenberg had said was that whenever you saw a reference to a door in the Bible, it also represented the way in which heaven and truth, angels and God, communicated with people.

So . . . was the sideways place really heaven? Some kind of truth?

Then I thought of something else: Mr. Witek's door, the weird tube on the jamb. How I'd stood there and knocked and felt the pull, like I was being invited in . . . only our roles were reversed then, weren't they? I hadn't brought any kind of truth with me. No, the truth had been in Mr. Witek's room; the truth lived in those pictures and whatever was locked in Mr. Witek's memory.

The truth flowed from my fingertips.

I closed my eyes. Thought about counting to ten and made it to four.

The door was still there.

"Go to school, you jerk," I said. "You've still got work to do."

But I left the door where it was. I wrote down what I could tease out of the tangle in my brain: a garden room, a stream, stained glass—and then I thought: *Idiot, you're just remembering the painting. You're incorporating the painting into your dreams, and you think it means something.*

Well, maybe it did. Damned if I knew what.

School crawled by. Sarah didn't look at me the whole day, and I figured I was on my own. At lunch, I didn't go to the cafeteria, but I also stayed away from the art studio. Instead, I went out to the playground and sat on a swing while the little kids ran around and played kickball. Watching them brought a lump to my throat, and I wanted to cry. Those kids were so lucky. They didn't have to worry about anything getting out of control; all they had to worry about was making it to the base before they got tagged. The little kids were laughing and horsing around, and there were so many of them, they were like ants boiling over the playground. But it was nice seeing how happy they were. Made me wish I was little again.

Although, of course, little kids are pretty vicious too. I should know. I've certainly been on the receiving end all my life. You try being the one a pack of kids will cut out from the group, make sure you're real far away from the school so no one will see, and then beat the crap out of you. That was one thing Marjorie was wrong about. You didn't need to live in a city to experience people being the animals they really were deep down inside.

I was scuffing out to the bike rack after school when I heard Sarah behind me: "Wait up!"

"I thought you were mad at me," I said as she trotted up.

"I *am* mad at you." She was wearing jean capris, and her hair was up in a ponytail, like Betty in those Archie comics. Not that I've ever read them. Since I was eight, anyway. Sarah looked kind of cute. She said, "What are you looking at?"

"Nothing." We pushed out to the breezeway and hung a left, heading for the bike rack at the side of the school. I saw her glance at a knot of other girls in the parking lot, all of them pretending not to stare, and then away. I asked, "You know, if you don't want to do this . . ."

"Can we talk about something else other than your insanity, please?"

"Uh . . . okay." I wracked my brain for something to say. "How's the research going?"

"Pretty good, thanks. I called the sheriff's office today, and Marjorie said the anthropologist was probably coming up tomorrow or Saturday."

"Hey, that's cool. Would you . . . uh . . ."

She stopped, planted her hands on her hips, and said, "No, I don't mind if you come. I said I didn't mind before. What do you need, Christian, an engraved invitation?"

"Uh . . . no, no, I don't need that. Thanks."

She rolled her eyes and started walking again. "You're welcome."

"So who does the baby belong to?"

She shrugged. "Could be anyone's, right? Until the anthropologist tells us how long the body's been there, we can't date anything or anybody. But get this . . . the house wasn't always the way it is now. There's the original house that dates way back to the 1720s when it was owned by a French trapper."

"You're kidding. I didn't know the French . . ." My voice died, and my throat seized up.

"What?" Confused, Sarah shot a look at me and then turned to stare in the direction of the bike rack. "Oh," she said, only it came out more like a moan.

Dekker was there, standing next to a red motorcycle— probably his dad's. When he saw that we'd spotted them, he elbowed his two guys—Curly? Larry? I didn't think they were the same two sandrats, so probably Athos and Porthos, but who knew. Their heads turned our way at the same time, and it was weird, like a pack of animals watching prey.

Without realizing what I was doing, I stepped in front of Sarah. "What do you want?"

"Now, is that any way to talk to someone who could press charges and get your ass off probation and into jail?" Dekker gave a silent dog's laugh, and then his eyes shifted. "Hey there, Sarah."

Sarah was silent. I felt her sidle up to my right elbow.

Dekker pulled a face. "What, you don't want to talk to me?"

"Leave her out of this," I said. (I know, I know: like a bad movie.)

"What you going to do, Killer? You going to hex me too? I hear you've been up to your old tricks again." To Sarah: "I'd watch my step around this boy, if I was you."

"Well, thank heavens, I'm not you, and no, I don't want to talk to you," said Sarah. "I've got nothing to say to you. But remember one thing, Dekker: I'm a witness. You do anything, I'm here to say what happened."

"Ooooh." Dekker mugged for Athos and Porthos, who cracked up, their cigarettes bobbing. "I'm so scared of the preacher's kid." His eyes slitted. "Come on, Sarah, you know we could have some fun together. Remember last summer? You were happy to see me then. . . ."

Poor Sarah was the shade of a plum. "Hey," I interrupted. "You want to talk to me, here I am. What is it?"

"What, you want her too? Well, good luck with that. These preachers' kids, they get all hot, but when it comes to putting out—"

"What do you want?" I asked again.

"Why, I do believe the boy's sweet on our little Sarah." Dekker twisted around to grin at Athos and Porthos. "Won't *he* get a surprise."

"Fine." Stomach jumping, I turned to Sarah. "They're just dicking around," I said, as casually as I could, although the words felt strange in my mouth. "Let's go."

"What did you . . . Hey, *hey*!" Dekker's voice was sharp and peremptory. "Don't you turn your back on me, you little prick!"

I turned back, expecting that the next thing I'd see would be his fist hurtling for my nose. But nothing happened. I waited a beat and then said, "What do you want?"

"What I *want*," he bit off the word, "is for you to get your ass out to my place this Saturday. My bike's gonna be ready, and you still got to make good on fixing it. You got that?"

"Yeah, I got it." That would also mean I couldn't work on Eisenmann's barn, but the barn wasn't going anywhere, and since Dekker would find some way to break my arms if I didn't show up, better I do his bike. "We got to go."

"Yeah? Where to?"

"Anywhere you're not."

Dekker feigned a blink. "Excuse me? Say what?"

This time, I kept my mouth shut.

"Naw, come on, Killer," Dekker said. Athos and Porthos were smirking the way coyotes grin. Dekker swaggered a few steps toward us; I eased back, bumping into Sarah. "Come on," said Dekker, "I want to hear it again."

I said nothing. Dekker was maybe a foot away, close enough to throw a fast jab or flick out his knife again. He must've read my face because his wolfish eyes shifted to my arms. The bandages were long gone as were the Steri-Strips, but when his gaze clicked back, he made a little feint and laughed when I flinched. "What's the matter? Scared I might cut you again?"

"Dekker." It was Sarah. When I looked, she had her cell out and she'd taken five steps back, out of Dekker's reach. Her thumb was poised over the Talk button. "You have ten seconds before I call 911."

Dekker's smile dribbled away, and his eyes sharpened. "You don't want to do that, Sarah. I was just playing." But he backed up a step, then two.

"Great. I'm not." Sarah sounded a lot older than seventeen. Her voice was flat, no-nonsense. "Now you've got *five* seconds."

Dekker's eyes narrowed. "You little holier than thou bi . . ."

Sarah jabbed Talk.

"Son of a . . . " Dekker's face was purple, and he was so angry that his lips trembled. He whirled on his heel as Sarah said, "Hello, yes, this is Sarah Schoenberg, and I'm at the school and—"

"Let's go!" Dekker stomped his bike to life and throttled up, gunning the engine. Athos and Porthos were already astride their bikes, and the three whipped their motorcycles out of the parking lot. "Saturday!" Dekker screamed back at me, and then the three growled away.

When I turned to Sarah, she was closing her phone. "What about the dispatcher?" I said.

"Oh, that." She eyed me calmly. "The battery's dead."

As we were getting on our bikes, I said to Sarah, "Maybe this is none of my business, but what was all that . . . did you and Dekker . . . ?"

My God, the things that were popping out of my mouth. What was I thinking? Sarah was the only person who would *talk* to me, and now I was digging into her life like some nosy brother.

159

"You're right." She pulled out her bike and swiped at the kickstand. "None of your business."

The Historical Society was housed in an old, wooden two-story mill house next to the river, and there was only one car in the parking lot when we got there. The main reception area was large and filled with a mish-mash of bric-a-brac from different periods in Winter's history. The room smelled musty, like it needed a good airing.

The lady behind the front desk looked up, smiled when she saw Sarah, and said, "Hello, dear." She only glanced at me before continuing, "How is the research coming?"

"Great," said Sarah. "Christian's doing a project and needed some help."

"Oh." The lady's gray eyes fastened on me. "What exactly are you researching?"

"Mordecai Witek," I said. "I'm especially interested in the murder."

"Yes, isn't everyone."

"There isn't much on the Internet."

She gave me a tight smile that showed no teeth. "Some things are best forgotten. You didn't live through the war, so you wouldn't know, but there are many of us who are just as happy to let sleeping dogs lie."

"Yes, ma'am," I said. "So how do I find out more?"

Her smile wilted. She pointed toward a side room. "In there. Newspapers, principally. Sarah knows how to use the microfiche and databases. There are two terminals, so feel free. I am, however, leaving promptly at five."

That gave us about an hour and a half. We thanked her and headed for the microfiche and computer terminals. Old photos hung on the walls: the foundry, the town hall, and groups of people in old-fashioned clothes waiting as a trolley trundled down the center of Main Street.

"Is she always like that?" I asked. When Sarah shook her head, I continued, "So why is she giving me a hard time?" Sarah just shrugged.

The microfiche reader squatted next to long gray file cabinets, and Sarah pointed to a label that read in spidery ink script: *Tribune* 1/1887–12/1923. "Each drawer has boxes with microfiche of the paper dating back to when it started in 1883." She pulled open one of the metal drawers, which was filled with square boxes, each representing a year's worth of newspapers. "Over there, next to the computers, is the *New York Times* and the *Milwaukee Journal Sentinel*. You can cross-reference once you've got a date." Tugging on a pair of white gloves lying in a box on top of the file cabinet, she pulled out a random box, thumbed on the microfiche reader, and showed me how to thread the film and which buttons to push to advance the film, go back, and zoom. "Once you get the hang of it, it's really not so bad," she said. "The layout of these old papers is pretty similar. National headlines at the top, local news about halfway down, obits in the back. You get a sense for what you're looking for; you should be able to find it pretty quickly."

"Mmmm." It sounded like a lot of work. The computer databases were straightforward enough. Typing in *Mordecai Mendel Witek* didn't do much more than bring up the same information I already knew, though.

"Who's that?" Sarah asked, reading over my shoulder.

"An artist who used to live here. He was pretty famous, for a while."

"You're kidding. In Winter?" She read the Wikipedia entry. "Wow. I didn't know any of that. No one ever mentions it."

"You heard the lady out front. Some things are best forgotten." I thought of Mrs. Krauss. "Some people probably want the past to remain just that. Dead and buried and forgotten."

"Yeah, but a murder's pretty sensational. At least *you've* got a date. I'm still backtracking through old deeds to figure out who lived in Dr. Rainier's house when."

At the mention of Dr. Rainier's name, I groaned. "Oh crap. I forgot my appointment."

"With whom?"

"Ah . . . Dr. Rainier. She's . . . uh . . . I'm supposed to see her."

"Oh." Sarah arched her eyebrows. "Well, call her."

"Your cell's dead."

"*Christian*. Miss Maynard has a phone."

I didn't want to use the phone in front of that woman, but I didn't have much of a choice. I dragged back to the front and explained that I needed to make a personal call. To my relief, Miss Maynard pointed me to a small office behind the front desk. "Use the phone in there. I like to keep this area free of traffic."

"Uh. Sure. Thanks." Like there were people breaking down the doors to get in. Once inside the office, I closed the door, dialed Dr. Rainier's number, and prayed that it would flip to voice mail.

Of course, it didn't. "Dr. Rainier."

"Uh, Dr. Rainier, it's Christian."

"Christian. Where are you? Your session started fifteen minutes ago."

I said, "I'm really sorry. It just slipped my mind. Could I make it up tomorrow?"

"Well . . ." I heard her flipping pages. "I don't have any hours, I'm sorry. Can you make it today? Say, later? Six fifteen? Otherwise, I can see you Monday, but . . . I think it would be better if you came in."

I calculated rapidly. The Historical Society would close at five. It would take me a half hour to bike to Dr. Rainier's office, which was on the other side of town. I'd have to wait, but I was the one who'd blown the appointment time, so . . . I could do homework in the waiting room. "Sure, that's okay. I don't mind waiting. Uhm . . . am I in trouble?"

"For missing an appointment? Of course not. I could be Freudian about it and suggest that maybe you *want* to miss, but you don't have to be an analyst to know that. Yesterday was pretty awful."

That was an understatement. "No, it's not that," I said and was surprised when I meant it. "I'm at the Historical Society." I gave her a thumbnail sketch of what I'd learned so far and added, "I wanted to find out more because I think . . . well, it might be important. Maybe it would explain some of my dreams."

She was quiet a moment. "I've done a little research of my own, and I'll be very interested in what you find, Christian."

"Research on what?"

"I'll tell you when I see you."

"Okay." I thought of something. "How is Mr. Witek?"

"Fine. None the worse for wear, although he's definitely waking up. He still can't talk, but he seems to be responding more purposefully."

That would go along with the way my nightmares seemed to have more . . . coherence. They were still fragmented and panicky, still just a collage of sensations and images, but this last one definitely felt as if there was some story there too.

I said, "That's what I thought."

"Oh?"

"I'll explain when I see you."

I could hear her smile. "Touché. Anything else?"

"Yes. What is Mr. Witek's first name?"

"Uhm . . . David."

Of course. "Okay. Thanks. Uhm, you wouldn't happen to know if he has any brothers or sisters, would you?"

"Sorry, can't help you there. All I know is that he's got no living relatives."

"Okay. Thanks again."

"You're welcome, Christian. See you in a couple hours."

⁓

"Well?" asked Sarah when I got back.

"She was cool." I slid into a chair before a computer monitor, typed *Marta Witek* into a couple of the databases. In my dreams or time travels or telepathic contacts—I really didn't know what they were—Marta seemed a lot older than the little boy, David. If I was remembering right, David's father had told both of them to stay away from the foundry. So maybe it was worth a shot.

There was nothing in the databases.

I decided to cut to the chase. I tugged a pair of gloves and found the microfiche film spool for the relevant year. I threaded the film onto the machine and then fast-forwarded through the newspaper pages, pausing occasionally as they flickered by to get my bearings. I slowed at October, and it was then that I realized that Winter's newspaper back then had been a weekly that appeared every Wednesday. So there would be nothing on the exact date in question—October 20, the day Walter Brotz's body had been found. The Milwaukee newspaper item had appeared the following Tuesday, so I would have to go to the October 24 edition of the Winter paper to find the story.

The story, not surprisingly, was front page news, a screaming headline:

LOCAL MAN STABBED; FOUNDRY OWNER INJURED
MANHUNT ENTERS FOURTH DAY

"Holy crap, I found it," I said to Sarah. She crowded in to read over my shoulder.

Local residents continue to express shock and disbelief over the brutal stabbing death of Walter Brotz, age 45, on the evening of October 19. Karl Anderson, of 2752 County Road AA, made the grisly discovery upon arriving at his barn on the morning of October 20. Mr. Anderson reported hearing groans issuing from the barn and discovered the murdered man in a lake of blood. The murder weapon, a hayfork, was still embedded in the victim's chest. Lying nearby, Anderson discovered foundry owner and town celebrity Charles Randall Eisenmann, who was also injured. Mr. Eisenmann is currently being treated at St. Agnes Hospital, where doctors report that the millionaire is weak from loss of blood but out of immediate danger.

Sheriff Jasper Cage issued a statement reporting that Mr. Eisenmann has named Mordecai Mendel Witek, age 40, as the attacker. No official motive has as yet been uncovered and law enforcement officials decline to speculate; however, rumors have begun circulating over

Mr. Witek's apparent infatuation with Milwaukee heiress Catherine Bleverton, age 25. Readers will recall that Mr. Eisenmann and Miss Bleverton recently announced their engagement and are scheduled to be married in the spring of next year. This reporter cannot confirm stories that Miss Bleverton's house staff have been taken in for questioning. Miss Bleverton could not be reached for comment, and it is not known if she has been questioned in conjunction with the investigation.

Sheriff Cage has enlisted the services of the Clarendon and Hunter counties sheriff's departments to coordinate the manhunt now under way, although as time passes, the prospects for Witek's apprehension dim. At the current time, Witek's immediate family—his wife, Chana, and their two children, Marta, age 17, and David, age 8—remain in protective custody.

"Protective custody," Sarah said. "Hunh. More like the sheriff was probably keeping them under lock and key so Witek couldn't hide out with them."

"No, I think it's more than that." I pointed at the heading of the next paragraph.

Jewish Community Stunned

Albert Saltzman, president of Congregation Beth Tikva, has expressed his profound shock and sorrow over the news. "None of us would ever have believed that Mordecai would be capable of this," Saltzman said. "The one thing we hope is that our Christian friends and neighbors realize that this is the act of one man and not reflective of Winter's

Jewish community, which has existed here for over fifty years. Winter is our home, and for those of us who've recently arrived from the horrors of Hitler's Reich, Winter has been our salvation. Our commitment to social reform has nothing to do with our deep and profound appreciation and love for our Christian brothers."

Despite this sentiment, tensions between Winter's Jews and local residents have been building for several months over Eisenmann Manufacturing Company's decision to utilize prison labor to make up for the current nationwide manpower shortage. The Jewish community has been particularly vocal in opposing both the importation and use of prison labor, and their sanctuary has been the scene of both union meetings and community protests against the same.

"I still don't like it," says one Jewish man, who asked not to be identified. "Bringing those men here? It's a slap in our face, that's what it is. I don't care how many beans rot in the fields or cast-iron tubs don't get made, these men should never have been brought into our midst."

Of note is the fact that Witek had recently been named as the union's representative in ongoing negotiations. As of ten days prior to the murder, however, talks had broken down and the foundry faced the near-certainty that Witek would recommend that the local call a general strike. News of the union's intentions sent Eisenmann Manufacturing stock tumbling and created a ripple effect throughout the region, angering many. There is the widespread belief that the Jewish-dominated union local, most of whose members hail from Eastern Europe, is taking advantage of the nationwide shortage of skilled laborers and might be behind the recent call to close Camp Winter.

"You have no idea how much we depend on that foundry," says Edith Werner, owner of Werner's Bakery on 13th and Main. "We serve the foundry people. Sure, there's the farmers, but there's no way I could stay in business if I had to rely on seasonal farm labor. Mr. Eisenmann's family has been the best thing to happen to Winter. Without them, we wouldn't even be on the map, and there are some of us thinking of circulating a petition that we rename the town after the Eisenmanns. It's really their town, and we're their people. If that foundry shuts down for more than a week or so, I'll go under. Those union people, those Jews, I've heard about the trouble they're making in Chicago and New York. They like the Socialists so much? Let them go back to Russia."

"That's ludicrous," says Saltzman, when informed of the prevailing attitude. "We're Americans. Our people have faced persecution after persecution. Our parents came to this country for the freedoms and opportunities for which this nation was founded, and those of us who came a decade ago were fleeing the very oppression for which our soldiers have fought and died. None of us wants to return to that. One of the beauties of America is the freedom to insist upon social justice, and that's what we're doing."

In line with Mr. Saltzman's assertion, it is of interest to this reporter that prevailing opinion has not stopped the synagogue's board of directors from continuing to show support for union officials. An emergency meeting of union members is planned for this coming Sunday, a move that has outraged certain members of the Christian community.

"Sunday is God's day," declares one pastor, who asked to remain anonymous. "For these people to hold their meeting on the Sabbath is an affront to every decent Christian in this town."

Several church groups have suggested that they would organize their own vigils.

Synagogue officials had no comment.

—

"Wow." Sarah dropped into a chair. "I didn't know anything about this, did you? The murder and the unions . . . there was a *synagogue* here?"

"That's what it says. Do you realize that there may not *be* any other Jews left in town except Mr. Witek?"

"I can believe it. I've never met any that I know of, and the mayor has a meeting every other month with all the pastors and stuff to talk . . . I dunno . . . religion or something. Dad's never mentioned any Jewish people." She ran her gaze over the story again. "And a prison? I didn't know that either."

"Me either." To say that I was stunned is putting it kind of mildly. Reading that newspaper article was like opening some forgotten closet and having all this junk spill out. Remembering my list, I read the article through again. At the article's mention of Marta, I wrote *Sister, age 17* and next to David, I penciled *age 8*.

"What are you doing?" Sarah peered at my list. "Hey, you already knew some of this."

"Not really. I'd just heard it around." I was busily penciling in new items now: unions, Chana Witek, Albert Saltzman, Beth

Tikva . . . and Camp Winter? What was that? The prison? I said, "Hey, isn't there a way to print out a copy of this?"

Just as Sarah showed me what to do, Miss Maynard stuck her head in the door. "I'm closing up in five minutes. You two need to wrap things up."

My eyes jerked to the wall clock: quarter to five. "But you close at five. We've still got a couple minutes. Ten, at least."

Her face hardened. "There are things that need doing that I always do in a certain order. Miss Schoenberg here has never complained. Now I'm sorry, but if you want to use our resources, you will abide by our rules."

She didn't sound sorry. Sarah jumped in: "No problem. We'll be out in a few minutes." Sarah waited until she was gone and then hissed, "Don't piss her off."

"Sorry." I wasn't, though. "There's just so much stuff. I mean, we got a bunch of things."

"Well, *you* did. Too bad we can't just get a key and do this on our own time. I didn't get anything done."

"I'm sorry." This time, I meant it. "I took up all your time."

She patted my shoulder. "That's okay. Really, I could be at this forever, figuring out who owned the house when— and that's not even counting if maybe there were boarders or which servants were here when and all the renters. Better for me to wait until the forensic anthropologist gives us an approximate date."

I was reaching forward to unlock the microfiche from its holder when my hand accidentally knocked the rewind button. Several pages blurred by before I shut the action down, and when I looked again, I was on August 22. My gaze snagged on a small headline in the bottom right corner: Camp Winter to Close.

And beneath, in much smaller type: Prisoners to Head West.

I glanced at the copy of the October article I'd just been reading. That had mentioned a Camp Winter too, and I wondered again if that had been the name of the prison. I reached forward to center the page, but then Maynard appeared right at my elbow, like a schoolteacher.

"We are closing now." She reached forward to unlock the film holder.

"Sorry," I said, beating her to it. "I'll get it. I just want to . . ." I quickly hit Print, the machine chugged, and three seconds later, a copy of the newspaper page slid into a holding tray. Without even glancing at the paper, I jammed it into my pocket and hit the rewind. In twenty more seconds, the spool of film was back in its box, and Sarah and I were heading out the door.

"Thank you," Sarah called over her shoulder. "See you maybe tomorrow?"

Maynard gave a wintry smile. "I don't work on Fridays," she said and locked the door behind us.

Walking to our bicycles, Sarah said, "Witch. What did you get?"

I told her and then said, "I'm not sure I really got it. I didn't have time to center the page in the viewer." I fished the crumpled paper from my hip pocket and smoothed it out on my bike seat. I saw at once that the print was horribly crooked, tilted on a left diagonal. But the story was there, the letters a little smeary but legible. I scanned the article—and that chill finger tripped up and down my spine once again.

"What's the matter?" Sarah touched my arm. "You look like you've seen a ghost."

"Not a ghost." I turned the paper around for her to see. "But just about as bad."

Sarah's eyes widened as she read. "Oh my God," she said.

Dr. Rainier scowled. "I don't believe it."

"It's true." I pulled out the copy of the news article.

She read straight through, her scowl deepening. When she reached the end of the story, she turned the paper over, saw that it was blank and then looked up at me. "Where's the rest?"

I was chewing the side of my thumb. "I didn't get a chance to read the rest. Heck, I barely got *that*; the lady was so hot to get us out of there. Ten more minutes, I'd have gotten the rest and maybe found even more. But . . . I mean . . . I didn't know *anything* about this. *No* one in town has *ever* talked about it. Uncle Hank's never said anything."

"Your uncle hadn't been born yet. He was born in . . . what? Late sixties, early seventies?" She tapped the paper with a fingernail. "This would've happened more than twenty years before, and from what I can gather, it sounds like something you might not want to publicize."

"You think?" I gave a disbelieving laugh. "So here's the thing: just when, exactly, did the Nazis come to town?"

⁓

Okay, "Nazis" was a bit extreme. Maybe.

See, I was right about one thing: Camp Winter was a prison, but not just any old prison. Camp Winter was for prisoners of war—and the PWs who came to live and work in Winter were Germans, captured overseas and shipped stateside.

Kind of explained the swastikas, though.

⁓

There was tons of information on Google. Dr. Rainier read.

"Well, it says here that between the years 1942 and 1945, there were about half a million prisoners of war in the United States. They weren't all Germans; there were Japanese and Italians too. Apparently, we started bringing prisoners over here in 1942 because there were rumors that Hitler was going to air-drop weapons to all the PWs in Britain—"

"Why do all the articles keep calling them PWs and not POWs?" I asked.

"If I had to guess, I think it's about propaganda. *Germans* kept POWs. *We* just held prisoners. It's all about semantics."

"Wow. I didn't know any of this. No one's ever talked about this kind of thing here."

"Yeah, I've noticed that's kind of a theme around here," said Dr. Rainier. She tapped her computer screen. "Anyway, it says here that since the Allies were planning an invasion of North Africa, the U.S. agreed to take custody of all PWs captured from November 1942 on. They shipped the prisoners back here on liberty ships and housed them at military installations."

"But there are no military bases here—at least, not in Winter. I mean, there's the National Guard, but . . ."

"Hang on, I'm getting there." Click-click. "Hmmm. The first camp selected was Camp McCoy down in Monroe County. McCoy served as a base camp but eventually housed most of the Japanese prisoners and . . . oh, this is interesting. The very first prisoner of war to arrive in the United States went straight to McCoy, a guy named Samaki Kazuo captured at Pearl Harbor.

"Anyway, the military established other base camps around the state, wherever there were manpower shortages. A bunch of PWs worked in canning factories; others worked in the fields. They would stay until the work was done—sometimes only a few months—and then move on."

I thought about my vision—when I'd been David Witek— of men bent over rows of beans—and then of the other two uniformed men with rifles on horseback: guards.

Dr. Rainier was still talking: "But there were also requests made to loan out prisoners to other industries. In fact, it says here that there were prisoners farmed out to every single state except Nevada at one point or another. The pay was minimal, about eighty cents a day, but the theory was that you kept people busy and gave them some money in their pockets so when they were released, they could go back and start their lives fresh. As near as I can make out, there were prisoners of war in the U.S. until late 1946 . . . so, more than a year after the war was finally over."

She made more interested-sounding noises. "Well, this might explain why no one knows. This paper—guy out of Madison—says that the whole thing was kept very low-key: virtually nothing in the national newspapers. Because of various shortages, small-town newspapers weren't published as regularly, a lot of news got diluted, and even on those rare occasions when prisoners escaped—"

"Escaped?" I was thinking of my time trip: one guard per truck, the prisoner driving. "Like got away?"

"That's what it says."

"Did they catch everyone?"

She studied the paper a few seconds and then shook her head. "Doesn't say. You know, I'm not sure you would report something like that back then. Can you imagine the response? Can you imagine it *now*? People in Wisconsin love their guns. They'd shoot each other on general principle."

"Yeah. Some lady might've blown her husband coming back from second shift."

"Exactly. Anyway, in a lot of cases, when prisoners escaped, the story was never really circulated because by the time the paper came out, it was old news and the guy had been caught. You know, I'm amazed these communities tolerated the prisoners at all."

"Are you kidding?" When she turned a surprised look in my direction, I went on: "You're not from here, so you don't know. Most everyone in town is German or just about, one way or another. That's one thing I *do* know about Winter history: the first Eisenmann went out of his way to make Germans and Austrians feel right at home, and most of them stayed."

"Well," said Dr. Rainier, thoughtfully, "I'll bet some of those German PWs would've felt right at home."

"You know, though," I said, "one thing I don't get. The article from August says that Camp Winter was supposed to close. But if you look at the article from October, it's still open. So what changed? Why would it still be open? If they're working the fields . . . well, that's all done. There's no work left to do in Winter except . . ." I stopped.

"Except in the foundry," said Dr. Rainier. "Except for Eisenmann."

We stared at each other a moment. "Would Eisenmann have done that?" I asked. "Used the Germans?"

"To break the union?" Dr. Rainier cocked her head. "He's a businessman. They're cheap labor. Why not?"

"Boy." Dr. Rainier huffed out a breath. "Imagine being Jewish and knowing what's gone on in Germany, and then the richest guy in town brings in German soldiers. No wonder the Jews here were upset."

"Yeah, but where did *they* all go? How come there aren't any left?"

"Well, there *is* one." She shook her head in disbelief. "I can't believe I'm so stupid. I've walked by that mezuzah on his door every day and never really looked at it." I'd never heard the term before, and Dr. Rainier explained and then said, "But, of course, that's what it is. Makes me wonder how many other people even know that he's Jewish."

"Or why he came back. Maybe he's always been here."

"I don't think so. Like you said, it's a small town. Granted, I haven't gone over his entire chart, but he's been at the home for the last ten years or so and fairly incompetent for the last four."

I said, "Once he's gone, then they're all gone. Forever. When Mr. Witek dies, it'll be like the Jews were never here."

"You know what they say: History's written by the winners." Dr. Rainier tapped the newspaper story about the murder. "Sounds like there was a fight brewing between the union local and Eisenmann. In this case, it sounds like the town pretty much identified the union with the Jewish community. That's understandable, considering that the union met in the synagogue. But I'll tell you what really bothers me—that little bit about some church groups being upset about the meeting on a Sunday. Maybe . . ."

"What?"

She chose her words carefully. "Maybe things got . . . out of hand."

I went cold all over when Dr. Rainier said that. "Like, maybe there was a fight. A big one. And the Jews lost."

"That's what I'm thinking," said Dr. Rainier.

XXI

We were nearly through the hour when Dr. Rainier said, "I don't know if this is the right time to bring this up, but I've been doing some digging myself and found some pretty interesting stuff—at least as it concerns Mr. Witek."

My mind was still grappling with the image of German prisoners

the prisoners are staring out through the open boxcars

marching down Main Street and so it took me a second to focus.

"Yeah?"

"Yeah." Dr. Rainier folded her hands over her knees. "You asked me if I believed in ESP, and I said no. But then I got to thinking about what you'd said about when you drew that picture, the one that's the same as in Mr. Witek's room, and so I did a little research of my own."

"On ESP?"

179

"Sort of. On brain injury and changes in function following such an injury. Mr. Witek's stroke happened about a month ago. About a week before you came to the home, he had another . . . event. I don't really know what you'd call it, but his brain showed a sustained and very intense burst of activity. If I'm not mistaken, it happened right around midnight, and I recall that when I looked at the record the next morning and went over it with the neurologist at the hospital, we both agreed: it looked like a variant of high-intensity REM activity but predominantly right-sided."

"REM sleep. I've heard of that. Isn't that when you dream?"

"That's right. There's so much about the brain we don't know, and when a patient's in terminal-stage Alzheimer's, you've got widespread dysfunction. Some regions of the brain may actually be disinhibited."

"Disinhibited . . . You mean, they wake up?"

"That's a good way of putting it. Newborns have a whole repertoire of reflexes we adults don't. That's because their brains are immature. As you grow, you develop more function that covers over these primitive reflexes."

"So, in Alzheimer's, it's like the brain goes into reverse."

"Somewhat. So, *maybe*, some brain capabilities we never fully appreciate come to the fore—not just the return of primitive reflexes but perhaps other functions and abilities. . . ." She paused for a beat, as if for emphasis, then continued, "Faculties we would never see otherwise."

Other abilities. Other faculties. I knew where she was going with this. Abilities like . . . telepathy? Like my brain as some kind of receiver?

She said, "Now, it's a fact that sleep architecture is greatly disturbed after you've had a stroke. Some patients barely sleep at all, and this, of course, leads to a lot of post-stroke confusion and disability. What happens to dream sleep after you've had a stroke is pretty interesting too. Depending upon which side of the brain you have your stroke, you can either dream more or less. Mr. Witek had a left-sided stroke. People like him dream more and for longer periods of time, and it doesn't take as long after they've fallen asleep for REM sleep to begin."

"So Mr. Witek has been dreaming a lot."

"Yes, but." She held up a finger. "He's been doing something else too. You know what a flashback is? And a seizure?"

"Not really. I mean, I've heard of them, but . . ."

"Okay, let me put it this way. Someone who's suffered a traumatic event frequently has flashbacks: periods when they actually relive the event in every detail. Sight, sound, smell, you name it. It's like suddenly being swallowed up in a virtual reality bubble. Many people who have what are called partial complex seizures will also experience powerful feelings of déjà vu. Patients with PTSD frequently show more right-sided brain activation during a flashback than people who are just remembering something and then telling you about it."

She was losing me, and I told her so. "How does this relate to me?"

"When you went sleepwalking and drew that picture? That was very close to the time when Mr. Witek's brain manifested this bizarre and unexpected activation."

"Why would his brain do that? I mean, was it because of the stroke?"

"Maybe. Or maybe his brain was always that way. But he had a normal and intact brain, relatively speaking. His stroke postdated his slide into dementia where people tend to dwell more in the past anyway. My point is that perhaps this peculiar brain activity was masked when more of his brain was healthy. Then he has his stroke; the left-side of his brain goes a little kaflooey, and then the right side is back with a vengeance." She paused and then asked, "Were you having headaches?"

"Yes. I still have them. Right here." I pointed to my left temple and then pressed the top of my head. "And here, like someone's bashing me with a brick."

"Is this the first time this has ever happened to you?"

"For the headaches? Yeah."

"What about the other stuff? The drawing you did of Lucy with the parasol and the . . . vision you saw before you got to the activities room? Where you got into someone's head? That ever happen before with anyone other than Miss Stefancyzk?"

I wanted to tell her about Aunt Jean. But I couldn't. So I shook my head. I'm not sure she believed me. But she said, "Remember what I said about empathy? I've known some exquisitely gifted therapists who really were able to immerse themselves into a patient's worldview. Their boundaries were very fluid. So that made me curious about intuition, telepathy, things like that."

I wasn't sure I'd heard right. "Do you really believe in telepaths?"

"Let's say I don't disbelieve. There's plenty of literature on people who've unlocked amazing talents after a head injury: artists, writers."

"Yeah, but a lot of them were crazy or just plain weird," I said, remembering my conversation with Sarah. "Well, that's me, I guess. So you're saying I'm a freak?"

"No," said Dr. Rainier. "I'm saying that you may not be the only one."

She handed me an open manila folder. "Here are some citations I pulled up last night."

The International Journal of Applied Parapsychology and Neurology
Research Trends in Parapsychology
Phenomenological Inquiry
Transcultural Trends in Paranormal Psychology

Voodoo. That's what Uncle Hank would've called it.

She said, "Christian, I think you've had some kind of ability for a long time and you know how to suppress it. Perhaps strong emotions cause this ability to express itself, the way certain stimuli can promote a seizure. But there's been a change—only not in you. The change has been in Mr. Witek. That drawing you did of the oil painting in his room would suggest that his mind has found *you*. The onset of your current problems happened very close to Mr. Witek's stroke—"

"My headaches. You mean, I felt his stroke?"

"Possibly. At least, part of it. I'll also bet there's more that you've experienced that you haven't told me. . . . That's okay." She held up a hand like a traffic cop. "A shrink isn't a mind policeman. You're entitled to keep certain things private—so long as they're the *right* things." She added after a second, "That was a joke."

"I . . . I'm not getting a lot of humor right now."

"I understand."

"Do you?" My voice ramped up a notch. I was gripped with this weird, shaky feeling, like I was going to scream or cry or explode. "Do you, really?"

"Yes." She reached out and circled her fingers around my wrist, very gently. "I think you and Mr. Witek may be working together, or your mind provides a conduit Mr. Witek's lacked. You're special, Christian, in ways that most of us can't really understand. As for Mr. Witek . . . well, I think his stroke disabled part of his brain but either freed or activated another. He's probably lost time sense he had before, because of his dementia. So what if the stroke has triggered flashbacks to something in his past? Or caught him in some loop where that's all his brain *can* do? And what if he's always had these flashbacks but kept them under wraps?"

She let go, swiveled in her chair, fingered up a piece of paper. "Right here, from the *International Proceedings of the Academy of Parapsychological Psychiatry* . . . there's a case study of a stroke victim who suffered from unremitting flashbacks to a car accident fifty years earlier that wiped out his whole family. He couldn't control the flashbacks, and they seemed much worse when he would enter REM sleep." She looked up from the paper and held my eyes. "You and Mr. Witek might be synergistic because I've been decreasing his sedation little by little, letting him wake up. Clearly, the scene you drew and the barn have significance for him—and now we know why."

"Because the barn's where the murder happened," I whispered. My lips wouldn't work quite right; I felt as if I'd been out in a blinding snowstorm for way too long, and I was stiff as a board. "Because that's where a man died."

"That's right," said Dr. Rainier softly. "For poor David Witek, history stopped right there, when he was just a little boy. No wonder his mind returns there, to that barn."

I nodded as if I agreed with her—but I knew something now that she couldn't possibly because I hadn't told her. I hadn't told anyone: not about the dreams or falling into that little boy's body.

Mr. Witek's memories didn't circle that barn like a drain because his father had killed someone there. Poor Mr. Witek thought about that barn all the time because when his father murdered Walter Brotz, Mr. Witek—David—was there.

XXII

"Don't be crazy," Dr. Rainier said when we were done. "I've kept you way over, it's nearly eight, and it's dark. I'd be nuts to let you bike home."

I didn't point out that a shrink being nuts was probably not a good thing. On the other hand, maybe it takes one to know one, like she said. "But I've got my bike."

"Which you're going to load onto my truck. I've already called your uncle and left a message."

"What? *When*?"

"When you rescheduled. You didn't call, did you?" When I shook my head, she tsked. "Christian, you need to learn that people care about you."

"Not everybody."

"Even if it's only one person, you owe your uncle the courtesy of letting him know where you are. He worries about you."

More like worries what I might do next. That's what I thought but didn't say. Anyway, Dr. Rainier wouldn't listen to any objections. She clicked off her office lights and shoved me out the door. "Let's go."

Whatever Uncle Hank was going to say pretty much died behind his teeth when he saw Dr. Rainier standing there. Before he could recover, she said, "It was my fault, Hank. We rescheduled and then I wouldn't let Christian bike home in the dark. You got my message, right?" When he nodded, she said, "So, here we are."

"Yes." Uncle Hank's lips twitched in the ghost of a smile. "Here you are. Well, at least he listens to *you*."

"She didn't give me a choice," I said.

"Uh-huh," he said, with mock dubiousness. "Well, come on in. You had your supper yet?"

"What are you offering?" She said it seriously enough, but I saw the laughter in her eyes—and it suddenly dawned on me that the two of them were *flirting. Flirting!*

"Penne in primavera sauce," said Uncle Hank. "Salad. Picked up a loaf of bread, did it up with garlic. And I might scrounge a bottle of wine somewhere."

I did a double take. This late, we usually do canned hash and eggs or something. But penne? Garlic bread?

Dr. Rainier only smiled—which kind of answered my questions.

It was a really nice dinner. Not that we don't eat well. Uncle Hank's taught me to cook, and he's actually pretty darned good at it himself. We're just rushed a lot, that's all. And we're two guys. So. You know.

But this was nice. The food was great, and the whole thing was comfortable, having all three of us at the table. Uncle Hank and Dr. Rainier acted like they'd known each other a long time. You could see that they fit, and I knew they liked each other. It made me think again about what Uncle Hank had said—how he wouldn't say or do anything with Dr. Rainier—and I wondered why not. Then I thought: *You idiot, it's because of you.* Of course. I was Dr. Rainier's *patient.* He wouldn't do anything to interfere with what was best for me.

As weird as it sounds, that made me start thinking about leaving again. About how Uncle Hank might be a lot better off if I wasn't around to keep spoiling things. . . .

"Christian?" Uncle Hank eyed me across the table. "You all right?"

"Fine." I screwed on a smile and tried not to look at Dr. Rainier. (Stupid; *she* couldn't read minds. Still.) Scraping back my chair, I gathered up my dishes. "I still have homework, though." That reminded me. "Uncle Hank, I need to do more research at the Historical Society, only they close early on Fridays. I'll be able to get in tomorrow because it's a teacher work-day, but if I need more time, is there any way you can get me in?"

"Well." Uncle Hank's eyebrows tented in a frown. "I don't know. I hate to inconvenience people. Have you ever thought of just asking? On your own?"

Yeah, right, like people were going to open their doors to the town curse. That must've shown on my face because he held up a hand. "You know, that was dumb. Of course, I'll help if I can. I can call first thing tomorrow, see if maybe there's some way you can use their resources after hours. After all, you are working on a legitimate project."

"And Sarah," I put in. I felt Dr. Rainier's eyes on me. "She's helped a lot . . . and . . . you know . . ."

"Fair enough," said Uncle Hank, and then he snapped his fingers. "I forgot. The anthropologist will be here tomorrow."

Dr. Rainier perked up. "Really? Oh, Hank, I wish I'd had more warning; I would've shuffled patients so I could be there. What time?"

"Marjorie said bright and early, around about eight or so."

Dr. Rainier was already up. She riffled through her purse, fished out an iPhone, and started tapping. "I won't be able to get free until eleven or so. Well, better than nothing."

I was calculating furiously. There was research to do in the Historical Society, but the pull, the *draw* I felt—this sixth sense that the baby's body was important—was very strong. "Can I come? You said it would be okay and Sarah . . ."

"Yeah, yeah, I checked, I didn't forget," said Uncle Hank. "The anthropologist—Nichols—said it would be fine. Just mind what she says. You want to call Sarah?"

"I'll let her know. Thanks." Then I had another thought. "If that's okay with you, Dr. Rainier. I mean, maybe you don't want me to see where you live or something. . . . Maybe there are some kind of, I dunno, *rules*."

"Thanks for asking. As it happens, there *are* rules." Then she grinned as she took up her wine glass. "I've already broken several. So what's one more?"

I didn't really have homework. I'd finished while waiting for my appointment with Dr. Rainier. I wanted to rethink my list and decide where next to go with it.

I never check for messages; who would e-mail me, after all? So when I fired up my computer, I was surprised when Sarah pinged me right away.

> sarah13: Where have you been? Did you get my message?
> ccage: I just finished dinner. I got home late, remember? I haven't checked my messages. What is it?
> sarah13: I found it. Stuff about the Nazis...well, the German PWs. Using my dad's account with the university. I was able to search a ton of databases. I can't believe I never thought of this before <eye roll>. I mean, who needs the Historical Society? Well, I guess for the microfiche, but when you've got the search terms, it gets a ton easier.

Of course, she couldn't know about what I'd discovered with Dr. Rainier. I started typing *Yeah, I found out stuff, too—* but then I erased it. I could feel Sarah's excitement vibrating through the screen. She'd done something for me, and I remembered what she'd said the other night about me making it hard for people to be nice to me. (Heck, if I were being Freudian, Dr. Rainier, I might start talking about self-fulfilling prophecy.) So, instead I typed:

> ccage: What? Tell me.

Sarah went on to detail pretty much all the stuff I already knew. She was so happy, though, that it gave me a good feeling to let her go on. Then she wrote something that made me sit up:

sarah13: . . . and the really weird thing was when people would open their doors and there would be like their long-lost brother or cousin or something.

What? I typed:

ccage: You're kidding. There were people in town who had *relatives* who were Nazis?
sarah13: Well, soldiers, yeah, DUH. A lot of Germans in the United States had relatives still overseas and a lot were in the war. If they got captured and sent here, they'd try to find their relatives. There are stories about long-lost cousins and brothers and things like that showing up.
ccage: Wow. So the prisoners could just walk around?
sarah13: Depended on where. Some towns, they were really nervous about having the prisoners there, couldn't wait to get rid of them. But other towns, like Sheboygan, places like that, people were sort of ambivalent. Some places, the guards wouldn't even bother with rifles. No one tried to escape because where would they go? They got fed, and they got money, and they were taken care of, and they had work. What would be the point?
ccage: What about Camp Winter?
sarah13: Like the newspaper said, Eisenmann—only he was real YOUNG—he donated his old dormitories. Some of the prisoners went to work in the fields, and others worked in the foundry. This pissed off the union, and they were going to strike, only there was a fire that killed a bunch of union officials, and then the strike just kind of

went away. This was after the murder too, so I guess the union didn't have much stomach left for fighting.

ccage: Who set the fire?

sarah13: No one knows. They said arson, but it was never solved. The fire was like a very big deal down in Milwaukee because of the union thing; there were a bunch of people saying that Eisenmann had broken the union's back, and some people said maybe he got his guys to set the fire. Only he was in the clear because he was in the hospital. The Milwaukee paper said Mr. Witek's father really cut him up pretty bad....That's where all his scars come from. Anyway, the papers said that maybe Eisenmann's people did it, but nothing was ever done.

ccage: What about church people? Remember the article? It said that some church groups were protesting.

Then I thought of something else.

Wait a second . . . when was the fire? Was it the Sunday that the union people were meeting?

sarah13: No, it was a week later, on a Saturday night. The union people were meeting after the end of their services— Jewish people have their Sabbath on Friday night and all day Saturday . . .

ccage: No kidding. That's weird.

sarah13: Well, not if you're Jewish. Anyway, there were a bunch of nonunion people there too and their families. The fire killed like fifteen people, and all but two were Jews.

I felt sick. Fifteen innocent people, and to the Jews, the symbolism of the fire and being burned alive, especially in light of the Nazi death camps, must've been devastating.

Sarah went on.

sarah13: Christian, your great-grandfather, he was one of the fifteen who died. The Milwaukee newspaper said that he got four people out and then went back in.

This was news. Uncle Hank had never mentioned this. All I knew was the dying-in-the-fire bit.

ccage: He went back to rescue someone else?
sarah13: No. That's what's so amazing. He went back for the Torah scrolls.
ccage: ?
sarah13: Parchment scrolls of the first five books of the Bible, Genesis thru Deuteronomy. The Jews call them the Five Books of Moses, and the whole Torah's done by hand. Hang on, I'll send you a picture. . . .

A link appeared, and I clicked on it.

sarah13: got it?
ccage: Yeah.

A window opened and a photo of a muscular man popped onto the screen. In either hand, he held one end of a large wooden dowel. His arms were spread to reveal a large section of inked parchment held tautly between the dowels. The scroll unrolled from side to side, not up and down as I expected—the way you see pictures of Romans reading scrolls, for example. Zooming in, I saw the same kind of stylized letters I'd seen on Mr. Witek's mezuzah. The scroll was very tall too, easily three to four feet high.

> ccage: Wow, that's big.
> sarah13: Yeah, they can weigh up to 40 pounds. I read that if someone drops a Torah scroll, the whole congregation has to fast for more than a month. Anyway, they're like these really holy objects and I guess they were still in the sanctuary. The reporter said that one of the synagogue members tried going back in, only your great-grandfather stopped him and went in himself. Then the roof caved.

Holy crap. I wondered if Uncle Hank knew this. Ten to one, he didn't. So never mind that this was a piece of Winter's past that no one ever talked about—which was kind of ironic, considering that our assignment had been to look at local history. Yet hadn't Dr. Rainier said history was written by the winners? In this case, the town's history had been completely whitewashed, obliterated, relegated to old newspapers.

Maybe I shouldn't have been surprised. I mean, I was a prime example of something people wanted to forget. Ignore me to death and eventually I'll go away. I could see that this might all be stuff people really wanted erased: the day the Germans came, the murder, the fire, all of it.

Perhaps the fire had been the final straw. After all that had happened, maybe it was just too much for the Jews of Winter to bear.

What would it be like to watch your community dissolve around you? Hell, that's what. Mr. Witek would already be cut off from the community because of his father. His friends would drop away one by one. Pavel wouldn't want to swing with him anymore. The other kids in school wouldn't talk to him, or they'd elbow one another as he walked by. Going to school must've been torture, the whispers swirling in his wake.

I knew all about that kind of life. I lived it. Only I hadn't left, not yet anyway. Planning on it, though. College never looked so good.

But here was what I didn't get: why had Mr. Witek come back?

—

sarah13: Helloooo? You okay?

I shook myself back to attention.

ccage: Yeah. Sorry. Just thinking. This is a lot to take in all at once.

Then I remembered.

Did you figure out where the synagogue was in town?
sarah13: 8th and North Lake Street. Here, I'll send you a picture.

I clicked on the link, and a scan of an old newspaper page appeared on my screen. The article, on page eight, was from the *Milwaukee Post-Dispatch* and was dated 5 November 1945. The story had been buried and took up one column along the lower right of the page. Above the headline—Fire Destroys Town Synagogue, Kills 15—was a black-and-white photograph of the synagogue as it had looked before being destroyed.

I took one look and thought: *Of course, it had to be.*

The White Lady was a synagogue.

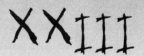

XXIII

We IMed a little more; I told Sarah about the forensic anthro-pologist, and that got her all excited. Before we logged off, Sarah said:

sarah13: Oh, I forgot. I searched for that woman, Catherine Bleverton. I mean, we ALL know about Mr. Eisenmann, but his wife's name was Judith, not Catherine.

She was right. That had flown right past me.

ccage: So tell me already.
sarah13: There wasn't much. She was the daughter of some brewer down in Milwaukee, not as big as Pabst but in the same league. All I found out was that she drowned in 1946.
ccage: The very next year? After the murder?

sarah13: Not even. More like six, seven months. Some kind of boating accident. The newspapers didn't say much, but if you read between the lines, I think she pulled a Natalie Wood.

ccage: What? Who?

sarah13: <eye roll> Natalie Wood was a famous actress who got drunk and slipped off her boat and drowned. Like in the early 1980s. Anyway, Eisenmann was there, and he said Catherine had like two bottles of wine with dinner or something. She didn't wash up until a week later about fifty miles down the coast.

ccage: Was there an autopsy?

sarah13: I don't know. I mean, it was an accident and this was 1946, so . . . What? You think this is connected? Like how?

I didn't know. I wasn't even sure I thought the murder and Catherine Bleverton's death were related, just that it seemed kind of bad karma for all that stuff to happen so close together.

I guess I was thinking like Uncle Hank. For a cop, there are no coincidences.

I told Sarah I'd see her tomorrow at Dr. Rainier's house and then turned off my computer. Tiptoeing to the top of the stairs—careful to avoid the creaky board dead center—I listened. I heard Uncle Hank's low growl and Dr. Rainier's soft, musical murmur, punctuated by the splash of water and clink of cutlery and glass. They were doing the dishes and talking. Just like . . . a couple.

That gave me a very complicated feeling.

I got ready for bed and then stretched out on top of my sheets. My entire body craved sleep; my brain felt sore, but I couldn't calm down. I had the sense that I had disparate bits and pieces of an important story and that I was very close to things falling into place. You know how trees and garbage get all jammed up in strainers sometimes? That's how my brain felt: like a logjam with white water roaring all around, only now things were moving, the strainer breaking up, and logs starting to float free and pick up speed.

After about a half hour of this—enough to hear the front door close and Dr. Rainier's truck rumble off and Uncle Hank's slow step up the stairs to his room—I flicked on a bedside lamp, padded to where I'd tossed my jeans, fished out my list, and then settled back against some pillows.

I'd inked in more information alongside some of the items—the White Lady as an old synagogue, for example—but there were now other things I knew, avenues to explore, and I felt as if I needed to order all this into some coherent narrative, if just for myself.

Flipping to a blank piece of paper, I wrote:

Mordecai Mendel Witek was a Polish artist who moved to Winter sometime after 1935. His wife's name was Chana; they had two children, Marta and David. Witek worked in Eisenmann's foundry as a ceramics artist, and during that time, he became involved with the labor unions. The unions must have had a lot of Jewish members because there was a large enough Jewish population to support a synagogue, Beth Tikva, which was nicknamed the White Lady, and the Jewish community let the unions use the synagogue for their meetings.

In June 1945, Eisenmann lent the dormitories on his foundry's grounds to the military to house German prisoners of war. This wouldn't be so hard because of all the Germans in town. The PWs were brought into Winter to work the fields and supply manpower for the foundry.

Something dinged in my head. Something important there, but I was missing it. I chased after the thought a couple seconds, staring at that last paragraph a moment, but nothing surfaced.

I continued: *There must've been problems with the unions before this because the PWs had been in the U.S. since 1942. Maybe Eisenmann had asked for them before, and maybe he had to wait his turn, but Eisenmann's a rich guy. He can get what he wants. Also, there are clearly enough workers in the foundry to support a union— so maybe the idea of getting the Germans to work here was to break the unions, not because Eisenmann really needed the help. This would be a way of rubbing the Jewish union members' noses in it, by threatening to give their jobs to Nazis if the union called a strike.*

Oh, I liked that. Eisenmann was ruthless enough to do that. I knew this was precisely the way other manufacturers had broken unions before: calling in scabs to work the jobs the union vacated. I knew from history class that there had been some well-known strikes in Wisconsin during the Great Depression.

I went back to my narrative:

The Germans arrive. Witek is a union official, and he's pissed and so are the other union members. But there's nothing they can do about it.

I stopped again. Here, my narrative started to break down. The Germans arrived in June or July; the murder happened in October. So what happened in between?

According to the newspapers, somewhere in that time period—or maybe before—Witek either had an affair or became obsessed with Charles Eisenmann's fiancée, Catherine Bleverton.

So what if Eisenmann decided to meet Witek and have it out with him, tell him to stay away from his fiancée or else? Witek went bonkers, attacked Eisenmann; Brotz was maybe someone Eisenmann brought along as a witness. Only Brotz gets killed; Eisenmann gets cut up; Witek panics and runs away. . . .

Leaving his wife and kids? That may have made sense, but it didn't feel right. But it *did* make sense because . . .

"Oh boy." I actually hit my head with my hand. "You are so stupid."

Katarina at Sunset. The painting of Catherine in Mr. Witek's room: the one of the woman in the red silk kimono.

And now that I was really thinking about it, that weird jumbled dream bubbled up in my brain—the one about a garden room and brook and Papa painting. . . .

I could fire up my computer again—but I didn't really need to. I didn't need to look up the various spellings of a particular name or figure out if one was the Russian or Eastern European variation. I knew it was. There were David's charged, horrified memories, after all. So I knew that this is what I would find: Katarina and Catherine Bleverton—Mr. Eisenmann's fiancée—were one and the same.

Well, that probably wasn't a good thing.

On the other hand, women posed for artists all the time. Except Catherine Bleverton was rich, an heiress. She'd have a position in society. I doubted she wanted just *anyone* to see her nude because she'd surely have been recognized. And where would Mordecai Witek and Catherine Bleverton have met, and how? He was an immigrant Jew, probably poor, and married. He had kids. It wasn't like they'd go to church and meet up with the Blevertons in the pews.

Milwaukee? Maybe. That's where she lived and where Witek was when he first came to Wisconsin. I remembered the numbers above and below the Star of David signature Witek favored: 3 and 9. The numbers on the kimono painting were 4 and 5. Dates. They probably referenced a *year*. Maybe Witek actually met and painted Catherine Bleverton in 1939, way before she knew Eisenmann. So she and Witek had known each other for nine years? Maybe ten?

Wow.

Well, why not? I didn't know what the rules of the Lakeside Arts Festival were, but I suspected an artist could enter anything he wanted, old or new. Entering *that* painting of a well-known woman would've been seen as either incredibly daring or sensationally scandalous. It certainly made people sit up and take notice—and it solidified Witek's reputation.

So was that when they started their affair? In 1939?

Even as I thought this, I realized there was another scenario. Catherine Bleverton might have commissioned the portrait herself. Witek might not have initiated a thing. Maybe she saw something he'd done and sought him out. Catherine could've said she wanted something scandalous for whatever reason. Then, years later, when Witek's star is rising, she commissions another portrait, just as sensual. I wondered where the kimono portrait had been done. By 1940, Witek was living in

Winter. So either they'd kept in touch or she contacted him in 1945 to paint her again. But by then, she'd have been engaged to Charles Eisenmann and . . .

Holy crap.

So an affair was discovered and a man was killed accidentally, and Witek went on the run—but then why the wolves? Why the swastikas?

It was so frustrating. The clues were there but jumbled up in David's mind. For example, those wolves . . . no, no, men— *Germans*—who turned into wolves.

Then I remembered what Pavel had said: Wolfsangels.

So I broke down, flicked on the computer, and looked them up.

Turned out that *Wolfsangel*—or "wolf's hook"—is an old German symbol that has two meanings. The upright version's called a *thunderbolt*; the horizontal variant means . . . *werewolf*. Men who turn into wolves.

And, the Wolfsangel was used as a symbol for the 8th Panzer Division, World War II.

Okay, then riddle number two: what was with the barn?

Yeah, yeah, I knew that was where his father had murdered a man and attacked Charles Eisenmann, who must've confronted Witek about the affair. The barn had tremendous significance to David, which made sense.

Only here was something: why mix up the *wolves* and the barn? Was that only because David knew that German prisoners had worked the bean fields? That might explain it. The Germans would've been traumatic enough for the Jewish population. Given David's history, the barn would be loaded. Only I wasn't quite sure I bought that. David had seen Germans at the train station and the foundry, but *I* had gone to the barn. I had painted the *barn*, not the train station and not the foundry.

Here was another thing: *I* had climbed up to the hayloft, dangled from a window, and spray-painted a pair of wolf's eyes and swastikas and the words *I SEE YOU.*

But David had seen his *father*, who wasn't German but Polish. Had Brotz been a prisoner? No, that didn't sound right; the paper said he was a local. I was missing something but what?

Okay, riddle number three: Could I time travel at will? Could I make it happen and do it while I was awake and not dreaming?

Only one way to find out.

Pen and pad in hand, I closed my eyes and imagined a simple blank canvas. I would jot things down as I went along; after all, I'd done this in my sleep. So maybe now.

XXIV

Well, the short answer was no. Not then, anyway.

The only thing new I had when I woke up was a crick in my neck from falling asleep sitting up. That and a nagging sense that something important had happened, but I couldn't put my finger on it. There were a couple of blue streaks of ink on my sheets from where I'd moved around during the night but nothing on the pad. Either David was off-line or I was just too exhausted. I suppose that was possible.

As I was brushing my teeth, though, the image of the White Lady—Beth Tikva—swam into my brain. There had to be someone who knew more about that place or the people who'd been here—because I was still having trouble wrapping my head around how a whole community just pulled up stakes and left.

After a few minutes' Googling, I found what I was looking for: the Wisconsin Jewish Museum. The museum's website said it had all kinds of archival material, which was good, but the museum was in Milwaukee, a three-hour drive from here. Also, the museum closed early every Friday and remained closed all day Saturday. The good news was they were open on Sundays, which was the only day I could get away anyway. I checked the hours and thought I'd call and say ... what? *Hi, I'm a stupid kid from Winter, and there used to be a synagogue here, only it burned down and everyone left, and do you have any idea why?*

I clicked on Contact Us and that took me to a page that talked about archival services and how to submit questions. What did I have to lose?

To: archivist@wjm.org
From: ccage@magna.com
Subject: Winter Synagogue

To Whom It May Concern:
    My name is Christian Cage, and I'm a junior at Winter High School in Winter, Wisconsin. As part of a local history project, I've discovered that there used to be a synagogue in our town called Beth Tikva. It also went by the nickname, the "White Lady." This synagogue burned down in November 1945 and was never rebuilt. I would like to understand why. I would also like to understand why the Jewish population here left the town. Is this because there was a German prisoner-of-war camp in town? I have since discovered that many German PWs, along with Italians and Japanese, worked the fields and factories in the United States during World War II. No one I have spoken to here seems to know much about this, and newspaper articles of the time don't have much information.

Okay, that was kind of a lie; I hadn't talked to *anyone* other than Sarah and Dr. Rainier, but . . . you know. Part of it was true.

> In addition, this synagogue is something that the town seems to have forgotten, probably because so many years have passed. On the other hand, I think this may also have something to do with a murder that occurred here only a month or so before the synagogue was destroyed. I refer to the murder of Walter Brotz by Mordecai Mendel Witek, a Jewish painter who was kind of a local celebrity. Witek was never caught. I have included the hypertext link to that article below.

I stopped typing. Should I mention David? What could I say about him? I resumed:

> I think that Mr. Witek's only living relative—and to the best of my knowledge, the last Jew in Winter—is a son named David. Mr. David Witek is suffering from terminal Alzheimer's, however, and can't communicate.

Okay, so that wasn't exactly the truth either, but I didn't want to sound completely insane.

> The only other contact person I can find in newspaper articles is a man named Albert Saltzman, Beth Tikva's president. In the one picture of him I found, he looked in his forties or fifties, so he's probably dead by now. I mention him because he might have relatives who could answer my questions.

That was going to be the end of my letter, but my busy fingers had a mind of their own:

> One more thing: If there was a synagogue here, wouldn't there also have been some kind of cemetery? Does anyone know where that is?

I reread that last part. Why did I want to know that? That was the second time in a day that thought had occurred to me.

> I would appreciate any information you might have about the murder and what happened after the fire. Thank you for your time. I would also be happy to speak with you if you'd like to call instead.

I typed out my number, agonized over the closing—should I write "sincerely" or "regards" or . . . ? I chose "*Sincerely*," typed my name, and hit Send. I didn't know if anyone would answer, but it was worth a shot.

My computer chimed. Sarah was online. I told her what I'd done.

> sarah13: Hey, that was a really good idea. You never know.
> ccage: Yeah. I don't think I'll get much, though. I mean, if we're having this much trouble and we *live* here. . . . The only other person would be the president, Mr. Saltzman, and he'd be ancient. Probably older than Eisenmann. He's probably dead.

sarah13: Maybe he has relatives. Maybe they know some-thing. On the other hand, what is it you want them to tell you that you don't already know?

ccage: Already know? I want to know why everyone left. I want to know why the synagogue burned down. I want to know

why I keep dreaming about wolves and blood and death

why *nobody* here seems to know anything. I mean, it's like you look around and there are lawns and houses and every-thing looks so normal, only things *weren't* normal.

sarah13: You're focusing way too much on this. I mean, bad things happen everywhere. Murders happen everywhere.

ccage: Yeah. Maybe. But isn't it weird? That nobody knows anything?

sarah13: <eye roll> How many people have we really asked?

ccage: Uh . . . a lot of people? I've even asked the *sheriff*, and all he knows are a couple facts.

sarah13: Maybe there's nothing more to find out. Not everything is a conspiracy. You're just way too paranoid.

ccage: You try spending your life with people looking at you.

sarah13: Are we starting that again? You need to get out more.

ccage: Hah-hah.

sarah13: Look, the reason the Jews left . . . hello . . . isn't it OBVIOUS? They were hated—maybe not by everybody, but Eisenmann broke the union and the union got burned out. They had church groups protesting their meetings. I wouldn't want to stay either.

We went back and forth like that a few minutes more, and then she said I was going in circles, and I told her I'd see her in about a half hour, and we logged off.

So here's the stupid thing.

Talking to Sarah like that . . . it was kind of fun.

Uncle Hank was in a good mood. He drove me and Sarah to Dr. Rainier's house and whistled all the way out. "You all are in for a real treat," he said over his shoulder. "Not many people see something like this up close and personal. TV makes everything look like movie stars do this stuff, and it all goes by real fast. But a lot of crime scene work is detailed and time-consuming and boring."

"Boring?" asked Sarah.

Uncle Hank nodded. "We're small enough that each of us knows how to process a scene if our main guy's busy. You can spend a couple hours sifting through trash, picking up cigarette butts, looking at footprints on a front door from where some idiot's kicked it in so he can do a smash and grab. Hours of work. Sometimes you solve a case that way, but more likely you catch the guy because he's stupid enough to talk to his buddies at the bar, and then word gets back to us. Most criminals are stupid."

I'd heard a lot of this before, and so I tuned out. Actually, I was kind of worried because of what I'd written, about the cemetery. I'd drawn a cemetery too, come to think of it. Sure, Dr. Rainier said that Mr. Witek was dying, and yeah, I'd seen Lucy die in my head and then for real, and so . . .

I knew Mr. Witek would die—and soon. I was running out of time.

Time for what? Well, for one thing, when Mr. Witek died, the past would be gone—at least, the one broadcasting in my dreams. I would no longer have access to it, not in my head and not through traveling back—which I really believed was happening. However I did it, I slipped into David's skin and his past. So it was possible to go back . . . maybe. . . .

And then I had a truly creepy thought. What if David and I were going to, I dunno, trade places or something? Like forever? I'd die in his body, and he'd get to live out my life in mine. What if all this was some kind of dress rehearsal for the main event?

A little voice, not David and certainly not me, sounded in my head: *Yeah, but aren't you the one who wants to go to the other side, to the sideways place and find your mom? Everyone says she's dead, so what if she is dead and this is your big chance, sort of a short cut?*

"Christian?" Uncle Hank's eyes were framed in the rear-view. "You all right? You look a little peaked."

"I'm fine." But I closed my eyes and pretended to sleep so he couldn't read the lie.

I'd never been to the old Ziegler place, mainly because it's off the main drag about a half mile up a winding dirt and gravel road to a bluff overlooking the lake, and I've never had a reason to go there.

As we rounded the last bend, Sarah said, "Wow, that's beautiful."

Framed by gnarly oak and maple, the house was silhouetted against the crystal blue of a crisp October morning. The front of the house, which Dr. Rainier said was a Queen Anne-style, faced east. The sun deepened the brownstone a ruddy blood color, accentuated by copper gutters that had weathered to a deep green. There was a large circle drive with a stone fountain in the center that was piled with colorful mums.

"How many rooms are there?" asked Sarah.

"About twenty, I think, counting the servants' rooms on the third floor." Uncle Hank grinned. "Wait until you see inside. There are two sets of stairs, back for the servants, front for everybody else. It's kind of interesting, and Helen's doing a real nice job in there."

Sarah picked up on that right away because she turned to me and raised her eyebrows and mouthed, *Helen?* I pretended not to know what she was going on about, and then she just gave me a look—like *DUH.*

There were several cars there already including a white panel van that Uncle Hank said belonged to the Madison crime scene people and a truck with the tailgate down and a big Coleman thermos perched on the bed. Off to the left of the house were two guys in coveralls with what looked like survey equipment shouting at each other. A third guy stood by the truck, a Styrofoam cup in one hand.

"Who are they?" I asked as we got out.

"Engineering people contracted by Madison." Uncle Hank slammed the driver's door shut and palmed on his Stetson. "They're marking the grid they'll use for ground-penetrating radar. Never know if there isn't something else out here."

"You mean, like someone buried?"

"Yup. Doubt it, but given what we *do* have . . . pays to be on the safe side."

The chief engineer's name was Mosby. He shook Uncle Hank's hand, held up his coffee cup, asked, "Want some? Got it in the thermos. Help yourself to crullers too. I already ate three of those suckers."

"You stopped at Gina's," said Uncle Hank. He handed the bag of crullers around. I fished one out and offered the bag to Sarah, who gave the crullers a longing look and then shook her head. Uncle Hank took a bite and then licked sugar flakes from his lips. "When I was a deputy, I musta gained twelve pounds before I learned to not stop in there for coffee." He nodded at the two men who were laying out yellow string across the sun side of the slope. "How big you going to make that thing?"

"The grid?" Mosby scratched his chin. "Well, if you *had* a grave, it'd be a lot easier because then we could use it as a central referent. Given you got nothing outside, I picked four points of a rectangle in a hundred-yard block. So figure . . ." Mosby screwed up his nose. "We can probably finish this side of the property in about two days, the back side and gardens in a couple more days. We're just lucky there aren't a lot of trees around the main house."

"Why is that?" asked Sarah.

"Roots'll sometimes chunk out something that looks like a grave, or maybe sometime in the past, someone started a well or dug out rocks, and then things got covered up. Back'll be a nightmare with that garden. Trees are the worst, but . . ." He squinted in the morning sun. "We'll walk the grids. If there's a grave out here, we'll find it."

Inside, the house opened up big with high ceilings, dark wood trim, hardwood floors, and a huge scrolling walnut staircase

213

to the left, just like a movie. Sarah made a lot of ooh and aah sounds, and it was kind of cool, especially later on when we saw the trim around the dining room ceiling, which was walnut carved into bunches of grapes and leaves and apples and barley. The house smelled like coffee and lemon wood polish.

Dr. Rainier met us at the door. She wore a peacock blue sweater that really set off her hair and eyes, and black jeans. Actually, she was beautiful. She showed smiles all around, though I think she held Uncle Hank's gaze a fraction of a second longer than anyone else's. "Come on up. Dr. Nichols is just getting started."

She led us up the back stairs, which were narrow and very plain. The paint in the stairwell was dingy, and there were fingerprint smudges on the corners. "It's going to take a year or more to get this thing into spec, much less any kind of shape," said Dr. Rainier. "I'll have to do it in stages, but that's okay. Gives me plenty of time to decide and change my mind a few times."

"A woman's prerogative," said Uncle Hank, and she gave a good-natured laugh. Sarah and I traded glances that might have been groans.

The stairway gave onto the end of a long hall on the third floor, the servants' quarters. The temperature was noticeably colder than the rest of the house. The wallpaper was faded, and a few sections sagged. The doors were plain wood, and there was no ornate wood trim. The light switches were the old push-button kind, and the wood floors up here were scuffed and worn.

"Which room is the body in? " asked Sarah.

"Servant's room." Dr. Rainier tilted her head toward the end of the hall. "This way."

The room was in the west corner with two shuttered, double-hung windows. Faded foam green striped wallpaper with tiny roses covered the walls. Directly across the door was the fireplace, its back wall blackened with soot, the brick and mortar hearth noticeably lopsided as if the house were listing to the right. Broken bricks and chunks of mortar littered a slate floor that then gave way to a threadbare carpet. The room smelled stale with a faint overlay of old rot.

As we entered the room, a compact woman with cropped brown hair and wearing white coveralls looked over her shoulder. "Ah." Cradling a tablet PC on which she'd been jotting notes, she pushed up from her crouch, her knees crackling. "Damn this chill." She came toward Uncle Hank, hand outstretched. "Dr. Denise Nichols, Sheriff. We spoke over the phone."

They shook hands, and after Uncle Hank introduced us, he said, "What do you think?"

"Come see for yourself." Dr. Nichols waited as we crowded around the half-dismantled hearth. I don't know exactly what I was expecting to see—probably something like out of an Indiana Jones movie.

This wasn't like that at all. If I had to pick something to compare it to, it would be like those reproductions of Neolithic graves in a natural history museum and not even half that interesting. Only the baby's head and the very top of its rib cage were visible; the rest was still encased in mortar. The leather flesh pulled tight over its skull, giving it the wizened appearance of a dried-up old man. Its thin lips peeled back in a death grin to reveal toothless gums. A thin tuft of brownish hair clung to its scalp. Its eyes were closed, but the flesh over the sockets was caved in, so I knew the eyeballs were gone. There was something wrong with the head, only I wasn't immediately sure what it was.

Sarah broke the silence first. "Where are the ears?" As soon as she said it, I realized that's what had bothered me.

"Yeah, that passed by me too, the first time around," remarked Uncle Hank.

"Good eyes," said Dr. Rainier.

"Yes, very." Dr. Nichols nodded her approval, and Sarah beamed. "I know graduate students who would miss that in their first pass. You might think they'd been sliced off, but you'd be wrong. In this case, the pinnae, the external part of the ears, are just tiny nubbins. See?" She pointed to what looked like a raisin on the side of the head. "When it's bilateral like this, you begin to wonder about a syndrome of some sort, such as Goldenhar or Treacher-Collins. I think it might be the latter. Look at the jaw. It's quite tiny for a newborn, and although it's tough to see because of the leathering effect of mummification on the skin, the eyes actually slant *down*. So, if it *is* Treacher-Collins, that might help us."

"How?" I asked.

"Well, with Treacher there's a fifty-fifty chance of passing on the abnormal gene to a child. So it's likely a parent would have the same problem or carry the gene but not express the disease. People with this syndrome have normal intelligence, so if they're only mildly affected, say, small or missing ears, they could get by quite well. They would be deaf, of course, but nowadays, with bone conduction hearing aids, that can be ameliorated."

Sarah got there way ahead of me. "So maybe whoever put the baby here didn't want anyone to connect the dots that he or she might be the parent."

Dr. Nichols nodded. "Another possibility, however, is that the parents or the birth mother interpreted the abnormality as a kind of curse. Killing such an infant wouldn't be abnormal at all, depending on the time period. Or this might mean nothing, just an incidental congenital abnormality. We'll know more, I hope, when we get the block back to our lab and can do a proper examination."

"You're not going to take the body out here?" asked Sarah. She sounded disappointed.

"We really can't. It's much better to do this in a controlled setting. Excavating a body from concrete or mortar is tedious and exacting. We'd be here quite a while. Also, X-rays we've taken indicate that the mummification doesn't extend all the way down. There are several toes missing, and one of the feet has disarticulated. There are many more bones in a child's skeleton than an adult's, so it will be a question of painstaking work with dental tools as well. This is more properly forensic archaeology, but we take all comers."

"Do you know how old the baby was?"

"Judging by the head circumference, about a month old. There is one interesting finding." Retrieving her tablet, she tapped her way to a photograph. It was an X-ray. The baby's arms and legs were drawn up toward its chest. The ribs were like the bars of a birdcage. There were several bright, tiny, circular dots over the baby's torso and another oblong object at the crook of a knee.

Dr. Nichols pointed to the circular objects. "I don't know what that other oblong thing is, though it might be a charm, but *these* are most likely metal snaps, and that already helps us date the body. We have no other way of doing so in this situation, and it's the same principle as if we discovered a grave at some archaeological site. You need artifacts to date things. In this case, metal snaps came into wide public use in the first decade of the 20th century, around 1910. So we know that this child has been here not longer than a hundred years but more likely closer to seventy."

"How do you know that?" I asked.

Dr. Nichols's eyes sparked. Without a word, she turned over one of the loosened bricks. Stamped into the brick were the words **GOLD & BRICK**. And a date: **1941**.

"Gold and Brick is a very famous company that's been around since the 1880s. Unlike many other brickmakers, they stamp all their bricks with a date. Even so, we'd be able to tell the approximate date the baby was walled up by looking at the bricks themselves—their composition, how they were made—and the mortar."

"So that's the *when*," I said. "But that doesn't answer the why, or how."

Dr. Nichols's smile was regretful. "Or who."

We left Dr. Nichols making preparations for cutting out the section containing the child's body. On the way downstairs, Dr. Rainier said, "It's almost noon. I made some sandwiches if you're all hungry."

"Starved," said Sarah. She was grinning from ear to ear. "This is going to be great for my paper. I'd like to hang around and watch them take out the brick block, if that's okay."

To tell you the truth, I didn't want to stay. I guess I'd hoped—expected—that seeing the baby's body would *do* something, maybe shake something loose in my head. I was still edgy, like there was something here I was meant to see, but I couldn't figure out what.

"We can eat in the garden room. There's a nice view," Dr. Rainier was saying as she led the way down a short hall toward the back of the house. "The stream is really strange, but I think the original idea was to bring the outdoors inside. Of course, you have to turn off the pump for the fountain as soon as it gets cold, but you can see the garden in the pattern of the stained . . ." Her voice died as she saw my face. "Christian? Christian, what's the matter?"

I could barely form the words. My heart sounded impossibly loud in my ears. I must have looked as shocked as I felt because Uncle Hank was by my side in an instant and took me by the arm. "Christian. What is it?"

No mistake: There was the empty stone streambed, and above the picture window was the patterned stained glass. Outside, the graceful figure of the stone woman emptied air from her urn into the dry fountain; and to the left, wind stirred the bare spindles of an ancient willow.

It was the garden room of my vision and the same room as in the painting.

The house had belonged to Catherine Bleverton.

XXV

"No." Sarah shook her head. All of us, including Dr. Nichols, were sitting around the kitchen table, a nearly empty platter of sandwiches between us. "Impossible. There was no deed transfer and no record of a sale. I know. I looked at everything. The Zieglers owned this forever. They *rented*, but they never sold it."

"So it's possible that Catherine Bleverton rented the house, right?" I'd only picked at my sandwich, and now I pushed the plate away. I couldn't really *tell* everybody why I'd reacted the way I had; not even Dr. Rainier knew about the time trip to the garden room. Thank God there'd been the painting in Mr. Witek's room. That, along with *Katarina at Sunset* (which Sarah knew about so I didn't look completely nutzoid), was enough to explain my reaction.

I said, "I mean, she lived in Milwaukee before. Eisenmann lived *here*, and he wouldn't move to Milwaukee if his foundry was in town. So they'd probably want to build a house or something, but she couldn't live with him. They didn't, you know, *do* things like that back then." Actually, I didn't know what people did in 1945, but I seemed to be in good company because everyone sort of looked at one another and nodded like they thought it was a good-enough explanation.

Then Dr. Rainier said what we all thought: "Makes you wonder if she was living here when that baby was walled up."

Sarah said, "Or if Catherine Bleverton was the mother. If she was, then the father . . . could it be Mr. Eisenmann's kid?"

Uncle Hank screwed up his face. "I don't see it. They were gonna get married. They could've gotten married earlier, if it came down to it, then go away somewhere, come back when the baby's been born, and people might talk, but so what?"

"Unless Eisenmann couldn't leave," I said. "He had a business to run. The war was just over, and there'd be a lot of rebuilding to do, tons of opportunities. I don't see how he could run his business by remote control. It's not like they had computers."

"Well, we're not talking the Dark Ages here. They did have telephones and telegrams, and people would direct their affairs from overseas all the time," Dr. Rainier said, with a smile. "But here's the other problem. We know that Catherine Bleverton died in 1946, and we know that they weren't married yet, and Mr. Eisenmann was on the boat with her. Maybe it's a question of digging deeper into the newspapers of the time, but I would think that a pregnancy would've been hard to hide. The illegitimate baby of an heiress would've made *all* the headlines."

"You said the engagement was announced in the spring of 1945. Given that the child's only a month old, Miss Bleverton would've been pregnant throughout the latter part of '45, early 1946. You could check the social columns, see if she dropped out of sight, but that's not the sense I get." Dr. Nichols took a big bite of her second sandwich, chewed, swallowed, and said: "I think this baby belonged to somebody else."

I could feel my theories doing a real flameout. "You'll do DNA on it, won't you?"

She nodded, chewed some more, followed that with a swig of water, and said, "We'll see what we can extract. The body appears to be in good condition, however, so that shouldn't be much of a problem. *Our* difficulty comes in knowing where to go next. If there *are* relatives of Miss Bleverton's still living—and assuming we can locate them—we will ask for samples. That's no guarantee we'll get them, however. There's been a crime committed here, certainly, but there's no hard evidence linking Miss Bleverton to this house. I know . . ." She held up a hand when I opened my mouth in protest. "I know. You say there's this painting of Miss Bleverton with this room as a backdrop. But consider this: This house is beautiful. I'm sure this room was known, and painters, as well as their subjects, look for exotic locations all the time. She might have suggested this as a backdrop for her portrait. That's very different from actually living in the house. In addition, we have no idea if Mordecai Witek didn't just paint this from memory. He might have seen the room, sketched it, and then filled it in when doing the portrait in a studio."

I knew this wasn't right, but I couldn't contradict her either. "So you can't force them."

Dr. Nichols shook her head. "Nor am I about to suggest to Mr. Eisenmann that he give us a swab either. There is, in fact, more to implicate the Zieglers, the original owners, and then renters than either Eisenmann or Bleverton. I'm sorry. I wish it were easier than it is, but . . ." She shrugged.

"She's right. I can't see how Eisenmann can be forced to provide DNA, with no evidence," said Uncle Hank. "Unless there's something else to date that baby, all we know is it was put there sometime after 1941. Coulda been anyone."

I nodded like I understood and agreed, but I was already thinking about what I'd experienced and thought: *Yeah, but what if it wasn't just anyone?*

And what if Charles Eisenmann's not the father?

We stayed until Dr. Nichols and her team had extracted the chunk of hearth with the mummified baby. That ended up being nearly half the hearth, something Dr. Nichols wanted to do for both comparison purposes—looking at the composition of the types of mortar and brick—and safety's sake: "And you never know if maybe we won't find something else embedded in the cement."

When they were done, Dr. Rainier looked at the ruined masonry and said wryly, "Well, I never much cared for brick anyway."

The message light was blinking when Uncle Hank and I got home. Uncle Hank punched up the recording:

Hello, I'm calling in reference to an e-mail sent by Mr. Christian Cage to the Wisconsin Jewish Museum in Milwaukee. Mr. Cage, my name is David Saltzman, and your message was forwarded to me by the archivist at the museum. I thought to call you because I wasn't sure when you'd look at your e-mail next. I am

Albert Saltzman's grandson, and I would be very happy to speak with you about what I know about Beth Tikva and the events surrounding the murder of Mr. Brotz and Mr. Witek's subsequent disappearance. It's about noon here; if you can call back before four thirty, we can talk. Otherwise, this will have to wait until Saturday night around eight or Sunday morning.

He rattled off his number, which I jotted down on a slip of paper. When I hung up, Uncle Hank said, "It's four fifteen now. You can just catch him, I'll bet."

I dialed, heard the phone ring at the other end, and then a woman picked up: "Hello?"

I identified myself and then asked, "May I speak to Mr. Saltzman?"

"Of course. One moment." She must have covered the phone because all I heard then were muffled voices and then the sound of someone putting down the phone, approaching footsteps, and then the man's voice that had been on our answering machine: "This is Rabbi Saltzman."

Rabbi? I hadn't been expecting this. "Uh ... Rabbi, this is ... ah ... Christian Cage? From Winter?" I heard my voice rising in a question at the end of each sentence—our English teacher hates that—and muscled back my nerves. "You called me back about Mr. Witek."

"Ah, Christian, yes, thank you. I'm sorry that there won't be much time for us to talk today. It will be Shabbos soon—our sabbath—and I can't speak on the phone until Saturday night."

"Okay."

"Anyway, I want to caution you that I know some of what happened from back then but not a lot. There are many things people want to forget, and I believe Winter is one of them. In fact, the community dispersed after Beth Tikva burned and the congregation decided to relocate. Then, too, there's been a lot of attrition over the years. More and more young people are choosing to settle somewhere other than Wisconsin, and most of the people from that time are dead."

"Except David—Mr. Witek."

"Yes, I was astonished to hear that. He's one person the community had lost all contact with. You said he has Alzheimer's? Where is he living?"

I told him and then added, "He's not doing very well."

There was a pause. "By not very well, you mean . . . what, exactly?"

I pulled in a breath. "He's dying. The doctor here said he probably has only a week or two at this point."

Rabbi Saltzman was quiet a few moments. Finally, he said, "I'm sorry to hear that." Another pause. "Look, I have to go. May I call you on Sunday?"

After we hung up, Uncle Hank said, "This keeps getting more and more interesting. You know, I finally located the old files on the murder, and there's barely anything there. Interviews with Witek's family, of course. . . ."

My ears pricked. "Interviews? What did the son say?"

"Nothing."

I couldn't believe my ears. "You mean, he said he didn't see anything?" That would be a lie, only I couldn't very well explain how I knew that. Not yet, anyway. I didn't have a clue why David would lie.

"No," Uncle Hank said. "He said *nothing*. Literally. My grandfather—your great-grandfather Jasper—saw the child, and that boy was totally mute. They sent him down to Madison finally, and the psychiatrist who saw him had spent time in England with the orphans there from the war. His report's in the record. He said the boy was suffering from some kind of extreme mental trauma, like you saw in kids who'd lived through the Blitz or having their towns bombed."

"Post-traumatic stress?"

"We'd call it that, yeah. They say *shell-shocked* in the record. Anyway, they never did figure out why. The boy stayed in the hospital for months, and when he finally quit being mute, the doctors said he had no memory for the night of the murder. The last thing the boy remembered was going to school two days before. Traumatic amnesia is what they said. Only here's the thing that stuck in my grandfather's mind." Uncle Hank gave me a significant look. "Trauma over *what*?"

Well, I knew the answer to that one.

Now if I could just figure out how to make sense of what David had seen before it was too late.

XXVI

That night I had no dreams. Saturday morning, I jerked awake early: no headache, no mutterings in my head, nothing from out of this world trying to send weird Christian Cage any kind of messages. The door, minus a knob, remained on my wall, but for once I had no creepy-crawly feelings or the sense that anything waited behind other than primer and drywall.

Why? That was the question. Was it because I was giving up on finding my mother? Searching my feelings, I decided this wasn't quite true. I loved my mother . . . no, that's not quite accurate. I mean, how can you love a three-year-old's *memory* of a mother?

As I lay there trying to imagine what Dr. Rainier might say, I realized one change in me. For once, I was interested in the world. There were things *happening* out here that were fascinating and new and very, very different.

I mean, well, for one thing, I kind of had a friend. Maybe Sarah had always been there—looking back on it now, I think that's probably true—but I either had never allowed myself to think of her that way or been so caught up in seeing through my mom's eyes that I was blind to what was right in front of me.

For another thing, Winter's forgotten past had a hold on me. I wanted to find out more. I mean, if you discovered that German PWs and maybe some Nazis had lived in your town and might be mixed up in a murder, wouldn't you be a little, well, obsessed too?

Most of all, I allowed myself to think that maybe all of this was happening along the lines of some hidden design. You want to say higher power, go ahead; I don't mind. I'm not sure where I come down on the subject of God and all that, but we were all connected in some way: me, Sarah, Uncle Hank and Dr. Rainier, and David Witek. I had always been different and had abilities I shied away from to protect the few people who cared about me—just Uncle Hank now. The guilt I lived with about Aunt Jean . . . I didn't know how it would help Uncle Hank to know what had really happened.

Perhaps David was the catalyst. Or maybe my life had been a journey to this point in time, a road I'd been traveling without understanding the destination.

Or it could just be a bunch of crap.

As freaked out as I was about what was happening, I wanted more. I wanted to find out what had happened in that barn. David was either trying to tell me or his brain had gotten just messed up enough that he'd somehow glommed on to me or our brains had meshed their wavelengths . . . something.

But here was the undeniable fact: David Witek was going to die. His brain was crapping out. . . . So I should be surprised that I'm not getting as many messages in the night? What if his brain had up and quit? So what I had could be all I was going to get from David?

That completely sucked.

⁓

For once, I won when it came to Uncle Hank. He wanted to drive me out to Dekker's or have Justin do it, but I flat-out told him that wasn't going to happen. I wouldn't bike out; the chop shop was way out of town, and the roads weren't that great, and yeah, yeah, I didn't want to get into any "accidents."

"I'm seventeen." We were at the table, and I splashed more coffee into my mug. "You can't protect me forever. I appreciate it, but I should drive myself out. You *know* where I'm going to be. Nothing's going to happen to me while I'm there."

Uncle Hank's face darkened. "Accidents happen in shops all the time. Pneumatic lifts fail, cars take a tumble. . . ."

"I won't be in the shop. They're not gonna want me painting the motorcycle in there." I didn't strictly know that, never having painted a motorcycle in my life. "It's important I do this on my own. Soon I'll be gone, either at college or . . . well, you know, at college. I'll have to manage on my own, and that means fighting my own fights, and there isn't going to *be* a fight anyway. Did your dad take you everywhere just because he was worried you'd be a target?"

"I was different."

"You mean, not everyone thought you were weird."

Uncle Hank held my gaze a long moment. "Damn it, you know what I'm saying. Don't twist this around to be my fault."

I was sorry, but I held my ground. "I'm not blaming you. I am who I am. I've got to live in my own skin. You can't live my life for me. When Aunt Jean was alive, you always said that the most important thing in life was growing into being the best man I could be." It was a cheap shot, and I knew it as soon as I saw the pain cross his face, but I pressed on: "Well, I'm trying and this is one step, and you got to let me take it, no one looking over my shoulder to make sure I don't scrape my knees if I fall."

The muscles in Uncle Hank's jaw jumped, and I thought he'd say no, but then something seemed to bleed out of him like the air whooshing out of a balloon. His shoulders sagged, and he sighed. "Oh Christian, believe me, when you fall, it's going to hurt a lot more than that."

But he let me go to Dekker's alone.

The morning was crisp and cold, with a glaze of frost icing the stubble in the fields and stretches of fog hanging in clouds over dips in the road. Dekker's dad's place was west of town about fifteen miles out on a county road with no name and dominated by fields and farms. On the way out, I spied wild turkey. A lone Cooper's hawk lifted from a speed limit sign as I shot past. No crows.

The shop was at the end of an old strip mall of about four stores, all of them out of business. Across the road was a combination gas station-country store that sold bait and fishing licenses. Next to that was a crummy little bar that did a pretty good business during the fishing and hunting seasons and served only the locals who live out this way the rest of the year. Actually, I heard that the bar did really well because it was one of those places you could do things you might not want other people to see. Fifteen miles is a long way from Winter.

There was a rusting pickup perched on blocks in the front of the shop and about ten other junkers scattered on dead weeds off to one side. A pile of tires was humped alongside, and I saw similar piles of just about any kind of car junk you could think of: rearviews, hubcaps. There was even a pile of door handles.

Dekker's father wandered out of the shop as I crunched in and parked the truck. He wore a grimy long-sleeved shirt and stained coveralls that had probably been blue but were now a splotchy steel gray. A soiled red kerchief was loosely knotted around his neck, and as I pushed out of the truck, he jerked off the kerchief and began wiping engine grease from his fingers.

"What, no escort?" He smiled through a wild growth of red beard going smudgy gray at the corners of his lips and revealed a mouthful of stained teeth going black at the gum line. "Sheriff let his little *neffyou* outta his sight?"

"Hello, Mr. Dekker." I didn't know what to do with my hands, and he didn't seem to be in the mood to shake, so I stuffed them into the front pockets of my jeans. My breath fogged in the cold morning air, but that wasn't why I shivered. Behind Mr. Dekker, I could see two other men in coveralls talking across the engine block of an old Chevrolet wagon, its hood yawning open. Then one said something to the other, and they turned to stare out at us too. I said to Mr. Dekker, "Uh, I'm here to take care of Karl's motorcycle. Is he, uh, is he here?"

"Nope. Still waiting on him to get done with his shift at the foundry. He'll be along soon."

"Okay. Well, I can get started."

"Yeah." Mr. Dekker didn't move, though. Just wiped his fingers and then threaded the kerchief back around his neck and knotted it in place. His hands were large as shovels. Then he jerked his head toward the shop. "Around back."

I followed him down a gravel path overgrown with weeds. At the back of the shop was a kind of shed that reminded me of a hiker's shelter: enclosed on three sides, open on one, with a slanting roof. Dekker's bike was there, and I was startled to see that the body had already been painted a bright glossy black. To the right of the bike, three boards had been set up between two sawhorses. On top of the boards was an array of small cans of acrylic paint, a set of aluminum four-ounce cups, and a spray gun that looked a little like the kind you used on a hose to water your garden. A face mask, like the kind you use for spraying pesticides, sat alongside a carton of latex gloves. On the ground was a boxy black metal air compressor and a hose snaking to the spray gun.

Dekker read my confusion. "Karl decided to paint the body hisself. What he wants you to do is some nice detail work, seeing as how you're such a good artist and all."

"Detail work? I don't . . ."

Mr. Dekker broke in. "Airbrushing. Don't tell me you never heard of it." He picked up the steel spray gun and rattled off the various parts, a dizzying array of jargon: air caps, fluid nozzles, fluid adjusting knob. Then he said, "The thing about this is it's gravity-fed; you put the paint in one of these cups that you've screwed on the side, and that means you can tilt the gun sideways and do detail work underneath if you need to. But once you get the hang of it, it's pretty much point and shoot."

He showed me how to mount the fluid cup, adjust the volume of fluid being fed into the spray gun, and how to manage the airflow. He finished by saying, "You're a smart boy, an artist, right? You'll get the hang of it."

I eyed the spray gun and paints dubiously. "What does he want me to paint?"

"Well, I don't think he knows. Flames, maybe, they're always nice." He laughed and up close, his breath smelled of rot and cigarette smoke. "Of course, he don't like it, you can always come back now, can't you?"

So then he left me to it.

I stood there a couple of seconds, staring at the airbrush and paints. I thought that he might be right; I did have a knack, and I knew the theory of airbrush painting, and it couldn't be that tough. But there was something, well, *soul-less* in a spray gun, like I was getting ready to do battle rather than create.

I cranked my head around to see if Mr. Dekker was watching. He wasn't. This shed or lean-to or whatever was a good forty yards away from the main shop, and I guess Mr. Dekker figured I wasn't going anywhere. Or maybe he wanted to save something for his kid to do—you know, beat the crap out of me or something.

My hand snaked around to my hip pocket, and I pulled out Mr. Witek's canvas roll of brushes. Yeah, I'd brought them. Why? Heck if I know. But that morning, just as I left my room, I pulled open the drawer where I'd been storing them ever since the night that door reappeared on my wall, and I fished them out. I just had this feeling that I ought to bring them along. Now I knew why.

The pouch of old brushes felt natural and right in my hands, and a weird little charge shivered up my arms and brought out the hackles on my neck, like an electric current. Like I was making some kind of connection.

But what to paint? I didn't know, and then I thought: *Draw, just think of Dekker and then draw....* I picked out a size 2 flat, thinking that I would use that to sketch a quick outline in white, then maybe yellow for the undercoat to make the top coat of colors really pop—and red.... There should be a lot of red because red was the color of blood, and Dekker was all about blood and violence and the stuff of darkness and nightmares and ...

The air smells of hay and horses, and it's dark outside and so cold the crickets don't chirp anymore, and I wonder if they see the wolves in the darkness, because I do. They've not seen me because I'm in the loft—no one knows I'm here, not even Papa because no one knows all my hiding places—and I saw them come, their eyes glowing and engines grumbling. Down the hill, I can see the solitary yellow rectangle that is Mama and Papa's room on the second story, and I wonder if Mama is there now, comforting Marta, waiting for Papa to return. I know she doesn't realize that I've squirmed out my window and down the trellis and run as fast as I could to the barn before the others could arrive.

Now, peering through gaps in the boards, I can just make out Mr. Eisenmann and another man and Papa. Papa is shouting; he's shaking his fist in Mr. Eisenmann's face. The other man is talking to Papa, trying to calm him down. He catches at Papa's arm: "Mordecai, stop, you don't want to cross him; this can only end badly if you ... "

Papa curses and the words sound ugly coming from his mouth. That's how I know Papa is beyond caring. I can't see his face well, only his body from the shoulders down because of the angle, but I know from his voice and the set of his feet and the way he bunches his fists. When the other man speaks, Papa shakes him off and then pushes him so he goes staggering back. I hear a cry and then a crash as the man smashes into the side of a stall. The horse inside snorts and whinnies in alarm; it gives the stall a stout BANG with its hooves. . . .

"There now, Witek, stop, you're upsetting the horses." It is Mr. Eisenmann, and his voice is abrupt, the way it is when he gives orders. "What's done is done. Now, of course, we can talk about a monetary settlement. . . ."

"Money?" The word explodes from Papa's mouth. "Do you think money matters? I hold you responsible for this. I warned you, but you wouldn't listen and now this. . . ."

"It's not as if she's innocent." Mr. Eisenmann's tone is colder than ice. "She's brought this on herself. I hate to be crude about it, but no one forced her to lift her skirts. *That* is the result of breeding and *your* responsibility, wouldn't you agree?"

Papa says nothing for a time. Through the gap, I see his hands unfurl, and I think: *No, Papa, no, don't give up, don't let him win.*

When Papa speaks again, his voice is ragged. "How much money?"

"A yearly stipend to pay for her needs and the . . . well, a yearly stipend. That's more than generous, considering that I've absolutely no legal obligation in this matter whatsoever."

It is the wrong thing to say. "Yes, you *would* think of that. Wait until they take your lives from you, just . . . *wait*. . . ."

Papa's voice breaks, and now I hear that he is weeping, and it is almost more than I can bear. "We pay and pay, the Jew *always* pays. . . ."

"Come now, Mordecai, you're being overly dramatic. I gave you your life, your job, your position. Is it my fault that I was taken advantage of?" Yet Mr. Eisenmann sounds almost bored. "It's not as if your family is the first to suffer from this kind of thing, and it won't be the last. *You're* just lucky that I have the means to help you."

"Only because you don't want the scandal."

"And you do?"

Papa says nothing.

"I thought not. That's wise. There is, after all, your boy to think of and your wife."

Papa's voice is tight as a string. "You don't own me."

"On the contrary, I own every inch of your flesh. You owe everything to me: your position, your job, your *life*. I gave you your chance; I discovered you in that cheap little flat in Milwaukee with the rats and the cockroaches. I got Anderson to rent that farmhouse to you dirt cheap so you could paint to your heart's content. I scraped you off the street, and I can throw you back just as easily. So you do not tell me what to do. I tell *you*. Is that clear?"

A pause. Then Papa comes back: "Perfectly."

"I am so glad. Now you *will* inform the union members of my final, nonnegotiable offer and count yourselves lucky I don't call the National Guard and throw you all in jail. Don't think I won't. There is plenty more labor to be had, and all I have to do is say the word."

"And you'd like that, wouldn't you? You're all alike, all you Germans," Papa says, bitterly. "You're all brothers under the skin."

"And the Jews aren't? Of course, we take care of our own. Don't you lecture me about brotherhood and morals."

"But the Jews aren't murderers."

"No, you're just thieves," says Mr. Eisenmann easily. "You think to cuckold men like me."

"What . . . *what*?"

"You heard me. You need a dictionary? You want me to draw you a pretty picture? Oh but of course, you do that so well, don't you . . . when you're not busy *screwing* what isn't yours."

No one says anything. My skin is icy with sweat. I didn't tell, Papa, I didn't.

Eisenmann barks a harsh laugh. "No wonder now where your daughter picked it up so well, eh? She must've learned from Daddy."

"I . . ." Papa sounds strangled, like he's choking on his own words. "I . . . I don't know what you're talking about."

"Oh come on. You think I'm a fool? You think I don't know? I'm talking about you and Catherine. I'm talking about you, my *employee*, and my little wife-to-be."

Oh, Papa. Oh, Papa. Below, there is silence. My heart thuds in my chest. Oh, Papa, leave now, leave these people, *leave*, just let the wolves go. . . .

Then the other man says, "I don't need to hear this."

"No," says Mr. Eisenmann. "Stay, Walter, I insist. I'll need a witness in case Mr. Witek here decides that violence is the answer to his particular problems."

Papa finally speaks: "Nothing happened."

Mr. Eisenmann lets go of a nasty laugh. "No? That's not what I heard."

"You couldn't have heard anything. Anything you've heard is a lie."

"Oh, I assure you: Catherine may be many things, but she doesn't lie to me. In fact, she told me about your boy spying on the two of you. In truth, I think she found it rather exciting. I know she couldn't get enough of me after she related her little tale of voyeuristic abandon. Tell me, is your boy all right? Not traumatized seeing Daddy in a rather compromising position?"

Papa says nothing. My face burns.

"Cat got your tongue? Oh stop pouting, Mordecai. Do you think it escaped my notice that she wanted you up at the house? Do you think *anything* escapes me? I *gave* you to her; I'm paying for the damn portrait after all. She's like a cat in heat that way. She fancied herself an artist, and I gave her one. Only a word of warning, Mordecai: She is rich and capricious and easily tires of a new toy, and that's exactly what you are. You're a novelty, and she will throw you away the moment you prove inconvenient. I'm doing you a vast favor, warning you about this.

"And tell the truth, you've been lusting after her since that sunset painting, haven't you? Oh yes, you're such a good married man, a man with principles . . . no wonder you jumped at the offer of a job in Winter. Take you far away from Milwaukee, yes? What must have gone through your mind when she arrived here and you found out that we were engaged? If anyone is the injured party, it is I."

At last, Papa has found his voice: "My family suffers in ways that yours will never. We are poor compared to you; we are Jews; and now my daughter . . ."

"And now your daughter has proven that even a Jewess makes some very bad choices. Given her . . . difficulties, I'm being generous, and you know it. Be thankful you still have a job." Mr. Eisenmann's voice turns brisk. "Now, are we done here? Brotz, if you'll bring around the car..."

"Wait." Papa's voice is urgent. "You can't mean that this is the end of it. You can't let them get off! They're *Nazis*, for God's sake! They've killed my people, my parents...!"

"I will do what I want when I want, and whom I choose to hold responsible is my choice, not yours and...Take your hands off...Mordecai! I'm warn..."

A shout and dull sounds, thuds, then scuffling below, and the snort of horses, the BANG-BANG-STAMP of their hooves, and then the other man—Walter—is shouting: "Stop, stop it, Mordecai, no, stop, you'll *kill* him...!"

Oh, Papa, no! I can't see what's happening; they've moved out of my line of sight, and so I creep to the stairs leading to the main floor of the barn, and I peer through the square. I see Papa and there's blood on his shirt and face and hands; only it's Mr. Eisenmann's blood that's spurting in great gouts from his nose. His face is coated with it; his chin is oily; the air stinks of rust. He's on his back, his arms crossed over his face for protection, and Papa is astride, pounding his fists into Mr. Eisenmann wherever he can land them. Then Walter is there, dragging back on Papa and screaming: "Help, help! We need help in here!"

Now there's the sound of running feet and a shout, and now there are two others.... They are men, but their faces are changing, and their eyes are yellow, and one darts to the right, out of sight and then... Papa, Papa, the pitchfork, the pitchfork... no, no

the air's screaming,
what the *fuck*

239

"What the *fuck* are you doing, what the fuck you put on my bike?"

I whirled around, paintbrush still in hand. High above, crows wheeled and cried, but that was not what froze my blood.

Karl Dekker loomed, squinting through curls of cigarette smoke. He was even grimier than before, and broad streaks of soot painted his neck and face and inked the hollows of his eyes. If you didn't know better, you'd think he might be a coal miner. He still wore his work coveralls, and a lunch pail dangled loosely from one filthy hand. He reeked of scorched metal. Tweezing the cigarette from his lips, he jabbed it at the bike. "I *said*, what the *fuck* you done to my bike? I sure as hell didn't ask for *that* shit."

"I . . ." I had no idea how long I'd been elsewhere—watching the past through David's eyes—and my first horrified thought was that I'd pulled a Jackson Pollock on Dekker's bike.

Then I got a good look at what I had done. At what I'd *drawn*.

I had painted over the fairing, and what I had painted there were the unmistakable features of a wolf's head: from its yellow eyes to a narrow streamlined muzzle. Fangs, long as scythes, glistened above and below the headlights and, as an added touch—and again, completely without my conscious mind getting into the act at all—I had painted a swastika dead center on the front fender.

I got slowly to my feet, my eyes bugging out of my head. I was still clutching Mordecai Witek's brush in one hand. "I . . ." I swallowed. "I . . ."

Dekker grabbed my neck and thrust his face toward mine. "Listen to me, you fucking asshole. I want some goddamned

Nazi shit on my bike, I'll ask for it. You think I need this? What you trying to do, hunh? You trying to say something?"

His breath stank of cigarettes and sour beer. I said, "I'm sorry . . . I . . . I wasn't thinking. . . ."

"Fucking got that right." He gave me another shake then thrust me to one side so hard I backpedaled, feet tangling. My hip butted one of the sawhorses, and the makeshift contraption toppled, slopping an open container of red paint onto the cold earth. "I want a fucking freak show on my bike, I'll ask for it. How'm I gonna ride that, hunh?" He aimed a kick at my midsection, but I rolled, got to my hands and knees, and scuttled back against the rough wood of the lean-to.

"Hey!" It was Dekker's father, trotting over from the chop shop. "Hey, Karl, back off, back off. . . . " I watched as Dekker's father collared his son and dragged him off. Dekker was arguing, his hands waving, until his father finally gave his son a shove in the direction of the shop. At the corner, Dekker screamed something else before disappearing, nothing good I was sure.

"I'd stay outta his way for a while, if I was you." Dekker's father planted his fists akimbo. "Not that this isn't a fine paint job. Ask me, it's pretty nice, good detail on that wolf and all— except that Nazi shit. What were you thinking, Cage? You are so thoroughly fucked, you know that? Now we got to paint that over and start again. . . ." Mr. Dekker shook his head, sucked on his teeth. "You sure do manage to land yourself in a world of hurt, don't you?"

Well, that was an understatement.

At least, I got out of there in one piece. Dekker's dad lectured me some more as I cleaned my brushes off as fast as I could. Yammered at my back all the way to the truck and then I hightailed it out of there, knowing that wasn't the last time I'd see that chop shop—or Karl Dekker.

Once the shop was out of sight, however, my mind returned to that time trip—if that's what it was. The experience had been vastly different from my dreams, of course, and the other time in the hayloft because, this time, I'd been awake and the transition was seamless. One minute here and the next there. This time, everything had been very clear. The narrative made sense. Sort of. I mean, it made sense to David, or David's mind was able to follow a story line of sorts.

Until it came to the end. When the wolves showed up. When everything had fallen apart.

I knew, instinctively, that the brushes had been the trigger this time. Before, I'd worked in my sleep, when my dreaming mind took over. But there was some special connection when I handled Mordecai Witek's brushes. Everything became clearer.

Or maybe this was how painters worked, the same way as writers put down words to construct sentences to make paragraphs to create a story. Only a painter builds a story stroke by stroke, color by color.

So clear. So *close*. I didn't know why Mr. Witek's brain had chosen that particular moment to establish a connection or why the images, even experienced through a young boy's mind, felt as if they'd been etched in acid. Yet the answer to what had happened, the trauma David had been unable to face all this time, wasn't on the tip of my tongue so much as begging for release from the tip of a brush. . . .

That's when I hit on an idea: if I could work in David's *presence*, that might be the final tumbler of a lock that needed to click into place. Hadn't he responded while I was there? His eyes opened; he saw me; his voice screamed in my head because he recognized we'd made a connection. All I had to do was get *close*. Surrounded by his father's work, I could draw on all that and really *draw* what had happened; I would see it in my head, and it would come out my fingers. Hadn't I been *drawing* the wolves? Wasn't I some sort of conduit for David's thoughts? So, yeah, twenty minutes, thirty, that's what it would take. I'd have to figure out a way to slip into Mr. Witek's room when they let me back to work in the home. If I could get Dr. Rainier to help.

I was maybe a mile out from the house, passing a field of pumpkins, when I noticed something really weird.

Along the road, on every fence post, was a crow.

There had to be, what, fifty? Sixty? At least. Not a single bird lifted off. They made no sound. But they were watching me, like soldiers at their posts. It was like I was some kind of general and they were troops for my review.

Me, I dropped my foot on the accelerator and sped past, but their eyes followed me all the way, and I got a really, really bad feeling.

Uncle Hank met me at the door as I bounded up the steps. My mind was so focused on planning my next move that I didn't hear Uncle Hank call my name until he'd said it twice and then stopped me with a hand on my arm. "Sorry," I said, and then my heart almost died in my chest when I got a good look at his face. *Oh no . . . was Dr. Rainier . . .* "Uncle Hank, what's happened?"

"That was Helen . . . Dr. Rainier just now," he said. "I'm sorry, Christian, but David Witek is dead."

XXVII

The news was a punch in the gut. I don't remember what I said to Uncle Hank, but I stumbled up to my room and fell onto my bed, facedown in the pillow, still in my paint-spattered clothes. Paint speckled my arms, drying in tight puckers, and I could smell myself despite the chill of the day, but I couldn't move, didn't want to see anyone, couldn't bear the thought of speaking to another soul.

Dead. I pressed my hot, dry face into the pillow. It was so *unfair*. How the hell could that have happened? I was so *close*, things were so *clear*. . . . I remembered what Dr. Rainier had said: *At the end, some of them display astonishing moments of clarity.* Now I knew what it was I'd experienced: David's death. I was some kind of weird death magnet.

Tears came, eventually, big wracking sobs, the kind where your chest is tearing itself apart. Maybe I could cry myself to death or at least to sleep. I kept my face pressed into my pillow so Uncle Hank wouldn't hear. I couldn't handle explaining myself to him.

Well, what the hell was there to think about? My parents were dead, and they were waiting. All I had to do was paint that knob, give it a turn . . .

A rap on my door. "Go away," I said.

"No."

Flipping onto my back, I propped myself up on my elbows. "Go away. I don't feel like talking."

I expected her to say something like, *oh okay, if that's what you want,* because she was a shrink and weren't shrinks supposed to, like—I don't know—*listen* to their patients? Just my luck I get the shrink who hasn't read the manual because the knob turned, my door swung open, and Dr. Rainier came through like something out of a dream.

Anger crowded into my throat. "Are you *deaf*? I don't want to *talk*! I don't want to see you! Get *out!*"

She didn't bat an eyelash. "No," she said and then closed the door behind her. Pulling out my desk chair, she sat, crossed one knee over the other, and laced her fingers in her lap: what you expect every shrink is going to look like and she never had, up until that moment. "It's unacceptable for you to hide. You've got to talk about this."

"No, I don't." I flopped back onto my bed. I threw an arm over my stinging, watery eyes. They felt like I'd scrubbed them with sandpaper. "I don't have to do a thing more. Talking hasn't *helped* and I'm *done*—with you and this town and everything."

"You haven't struck me as a quitter. If you were, you'd already have walked through that door there."

That got my attention. "How do you know about that? I haven't told . . ."

"I didn't get my degree out of a Cracker Jack box, thanks. I know a door when I see it and *you*," she jabbed a finger at me, "are a coward. You come this far, you hint that you've got these powers, and you're too freaked out to use them? People like you give me a headache. Always whining, complaining . . ."

If she was trying to piss me off, she succeeded. A flare of rage fired my chest, and I sat straight up, my fists bunched. "Coward? I'm not a coward. I *kill* people! I do something that brings out—that *draws*—death! Everything I touch, everyone I care about . . . they *die*! Don't you get it?"

"Really?" she drawled. Her tone was so dismissive, I wanted to break something, throw something across the room just to hear what destruction sounded like. How could I have been so stupid? I thought she cared about me, but she really thought I was just another idiot. "Oh, I get it, Christian. I get that *you* believe this. But I don't."

"Fine." I fell back onto the bed. "You don't believe me. Fine. Then get the hell out of my room."

"Or what? You going to hurt me if I don't leave? You going to draw me to death?"

*Yes, that's **precisely** what will happen.* But I didn't answer. An odd ringing filled my ears, the kind of high whine people say you can get from taking too much aspirin, but I knew better. The ringing resolved; it had been some kind of clarion call, and now the muttering started up in earnest: a gibbering crowd pressing against that unfinished door.

Her voice boiled up through the hubbub. "I don't believe you can do it. I don't think you've got the talent. You're nothing but a sponge, a conduit maybe, but you've got no power on your own. No way you can draw a scenario out of your own head and make it what you want. You're dependent on everyone else to feed you the emotion because you're too scared to use your own—"

"*Screw YOU!*" I shot to my feet so fast I knocked over my nightstand. My lamp smashed against the floor in a bright, gaudy explosion, like what you see in movies. I snatched Mordecai Witek's brushes from my back pocket and shook the pouch in her face. "You think I can't use these? Let's see how you like it when I do *you!*"

Her expression was utterly calm. Her dark eyes were bright as a crow's. "Yes, do that, Christian. Draw something out of your head. Draw me into something, and then make me experience it. Show me what you can do. Or are you really all talk and no action?"

I almost hit her. My fist, bunched around those brushes, was inches from her face, and it would've been easy, so easy. Then I thought: *Fine. Fine. You think you've crawled around private hells? You don't know the half of it, lady. I'm your worst fears realized. So you want this? You got it.*

I don't remember much. I do know that I unrolled Mordecai Witek's brushes and grabbed a fine; pawed through my desk and fumbled out paints; and then I started, not so much painting as filleting, slashing, cutting in a vicious fury on my walls. I could feel Dr. Rainier behind me, but I didn't need to see her face; I'd memorized those contours, and so I closed my eyes, and I reached down deep, and then I pulled, I *drew* as hard as I could. I reeled out the darkness from her gut, and I let myself go. That subtle click and then my mind detached;

and I was filled with the same floaty, helium-balloon feeling I'd experienced before with Miss Stefancyzk and Aunt Jean. And with Lucy—not the time I'd pulled the image of her as a happy girl in a white dress on a summer's day, but as I'd drawn her at the moment of her death, her gnarled fingers cramping around a chunk of charcoal, black streaks like tear-drenched mascara sliding across the page as she collapsed. From somewhere deep down, I drew up a foul, putrid blackness that not even Dr. Rainier suspected lived inside. Oh, I was floating all right, but I was a balloon caught up in a black funnel cloud, a tornado, and the roaring wind was my fury—all the hurts and losses, all the slights and whispers and evil thoughts of the people of Winter and all their secrets—

I worked fast, urgently, in broad strokes; my mind completely elsewhere; my muscles obeying some hidden reservoirs of thought of which I was unaware: my body as the vehicle for an unseen, ghastly puppeteer. I worked until my arm hurt and my shoulder throbbed; I worked until my fingers screamed. I don't know how long I painted, but the hours swept by in a blur, the way they do in dreams, and then finally, the energy vanished the way a storm cloud sweeps over the land and out to the lake.

Spent, panting, my chest going like bellows, I opened my eyes.

Behind me, Dr. Rainier made a harsh, guttural broken sound, the caw of a dying crow.

But I didn't turn around. I couldn't. Instead, I stared, riveted at the ugliness of what I had painted.

Dr. Rainier's deepest dread and worst fears, realized.

How to describe a nightmare?

Each is ultimately unique. Yes, there are universals. That's what Sarah said once—another nugget from her psychology class about the collective unconscious. But every dream requires a unique dreamer, every fear a person who feels the sharp sting of terror.

Think of the foul stink of an unused basement: dank and earthen, churning with slithery worms thick around as your wrist and fecund with the smell of decay. You know that if you take a single step into that muck, you're lost because the things that live there—not just the greedy worms but macerated corpses with ropes of bloated intestines and skeletal fingers and maggots boiling in eyeless sockets, and fat, mucus creatures with pinpoint eyes and jostling teeth—they'll reach up and grab your ankles and draw you down, screaming and thrashing until the muck flows down your throat and you drown.

But you're just a child; you're only six, and there's no power because of the storm raging beyond the house. You're miles from nowhere, and the monster's coming, and you have to do something because the animal's up there, shouting your name, axe in hand. It's already killed your mother, and now it's coming for you. So, whimpering, you slap the slimy moist wall, looking for the light switch, but there is none. You don't have a flashlight. But you have to go, and you have to get down there now and hide because the monster's coming; you can hear it moving through the house and smell its fetid drunk's breath and know without having to see that there are strings of fresh meat dangling from its teeth and your mother's blood on the blade of that axe. You know it is worse to stay aboveground than to go below.

So you take a step and then another, and then the darkness rushes forward and swallows you up, and you're in the basement, with no way out.

The basement is dark-dark-dark and smells bad: dust and dried-up rat poop and mildew. No muck at the bottom the way you thought, but that doesn't matter because this is just as bad. There are spiderwebs, big sticky ones that drag across little Helen's face as she pushes deeper into the basement, looking for a place to hide.

In the third room, she runs into a brick wall, and now there is nowhere else to go, only the furnace to hide behind, and she does just that, huddling down, the grit digging into her knees. Her heart is going *puh-boom-puh-boom-puh-boom*, and she's trying not to cry. But she's so scared, she lets out little eepy sounds, just like Cookie. (Whenever Cookie slept, she had nice hamster dreams, only sometimes she went *eep-eep-eep*. But that was okay because even if Cookie was scared, she could wake up. Then the bad dreams would be gone and the monsters too, and everything would be all right.)

But nothing will ever be all right again, not ever-ever. Because Helen knows that the bad thing living in her daddy is awake; it always wakes up when he drinks, but now the drinking's gone too far. IT just took over: all the way, exploding behind her daddy's eyes like a volcano.

That's when Helen's momma ran up the stairs. *Run!* Momma shouted. *Run, Helen, run!*

But it was already way, way, way too late.

The thing in Helen's daddy hit Momma real hard, and Momma crashed against the wall like Raggedy Ann. All Helen's books went *bang*, and then there was blood trickling down Momma's chin, and Momma's teeth were orange, but she was still shouting: *Run, Helen, run, baby, run, **run**!*

Only Helen couldn't. Helen was so, so scared: for Momma and Cookie and especially for Daddy, lost somewhere in the monster. Her daddy's teeth were all spiky, and his eyes were yellow and green with black slits up and down, snake eyes, lizard eyes. IT scooped Cookie out of her cage. Helen started screaming, but the thing in her daddy just laughed: not a funny laugh or one when you're happy because there are butterflies or dandelion fluff or because Cookie's stuffed her cheeks with so many seeds they look like furry balloons. It was the kind of laugh only a monster with a daddy mask makes.

IT threw Cookie to the floor. Poor little Cookie bounced and went *eep-eep-eep* and tried to get away. Helen screamed, *No, Daddy, No, Daddy, NONO!* But IT didn't care; IT didn't listen. IT just stomped real hard—again and again and again until Cookie was nothing but blood-jelly hair and squiggly pink guts.

That's when Helen ran as fast as she could to the basement and where she hides, waiting to die. . . .

And now, there's a sudden flare of yellow light as the thing with the daddy mask pushes open the basement door. "Helen?" ITS voice is bloody. "I know you're there. Come out, Helen. Don't make this worse than it has to be."

Nononono . . . There's a dull bang, the scraping sound of metal, and she knows that the monster's in the first room, heaving the washer to one side, to see if she's hiding there.

Oh please. Please. She isn't praying. God has a bunch of better things to do than help her, especially since she's made such a mess. But Momma always said Helen should call on God to help if things got bad, and Helen thinks things probably can't get much worse.

Another light, brighter now: the second room. The thing keeps calling, saying he won't hurt her, he just wants her to come out, and he needs to explain. Meanwhile, jars go bang-*crash* and boxes go bump-*thump*. She doesn't move because she knows: he is IT.

And then a crisp SNAP! Two bare bulbs burn hot yellow-orange because IT is in the third room, the furnace room. There's the stink of sweat like her daddy's been mowing the lawn on a hot day but also a sharper stink like gasoline. She smells ITS fury, too: the odor of a bloated raccoon by the side of the road. ITS boots scrape concrete. She can just see the tip of ITS shadow inking the near wall to her left. More bangs on top of the furnace ductwork and something heavy makes the metal go boom-boom-boom and she thinks: *Axe.*

She knows IT will look behind the gas furnace next and then . . .

Save her.

The thought is like a jag of lightning across a starless sky. Behind me, Dr. Rainier is making that broken sound, and I know that this is what's killing her, this nightmare come to life that I made happen: that she somehow survived once but will not live through again—without my help.

Save her.

For once, I don't hesitate. I step forward, into the painting, or maybe *her* world rushes to meet me, I don't know. But suddenly I am there, in that basement, at the entrance to the furnace room. I smell her father's insanity and the iron stink of her mother's blood. Her father is a muscled giant, with a lizard's eyes, rounding the far corner of a furnace. IT grips an axe, smeary with red blood, and the thing that had been her father stares down at a frightened little girl, and then IT reaches down—

"NO!" In two strides, I've crossed the basement. Her father half turns, but I spring, arms outstretched. I crash into him; off-balance, he reels, the axe clattering to the cement, and we go down in a heap. I have the advantage of surprise, but he is older, bigger, and much stronger. Bellowing, he slams a fist into my head. It's like a bomb going off; my vision sheets white and then red, and then his fist slashes the air again and catches me in the stomach. Gagging, I topple back as vomit spews from my mouth, and then I'm rolling onto the cement, unable to breathe.

Get up. I'm trying to pull in air; I hear her father drunk-staggering, lurching for the axe, which is actually closer to me, and my brain is screaming: *Get up get up or you're dead, get up or you're going to die here in her nightmare get up get up get up . . .*

I lunge for the axe a split second ahead of him. My desperate fingers close around the handle, which is slick with blood, and then his fist hammers between my shoulder blades. My face smashes against the hard concrete; I actually bounce and my head snaps back. Blood spurts from my nose, and there is blood in my eyes because my scalp has split, but I still have the axe; the axe is in my hands, and I roll to one side, and then I'm swinging—the axe hurtling, whickering the air—and I am screaming in a voice I no longer recognize as I heave the axe in its murderous arc with all my might—

"Christian!"

Screaming, I thrashed awake in a tangle of bedding. I'd thudded to the floor at some point in my nightmare, and now

I lay in a halo of splintery glass. My nightstand was on its side; the base of my lamp was cracked in two at the same time the bulb burst. My face was still wet and hot from tears and snot, and drool smeared my chin.

"Christian?" Dr. Rainier's voice rose in alarm. I heard her say something, and then Uncle Hank was banging on my door, bawling: "Christian, what's going on in there? Christian, open the door!"

A dream. I was shuddering. A nightmare, but it had been my own. I'd fallen onto my bed and cried myself to sleep and dreamt that Dr. Rainier found me, goaded and taunted me into action, and the rest was . . .

"Coming." My throat was raw, the act of talking like swallowing a razor blade. I coughed; smeared snot from my face with a sheet; and then half-crawled, half-staggered to the door.

Uncle Hank's eyes went wide when he saw my room. "Christian, what in God's name . . . ?"

Dr. Rainier took one look—at me, the room, and the ruin of bedclothes on the floor—and her skin went paper white. "My God." She took me by the shoulders and peered up into my face. "Christian, what is it? What did you see?"

"What?" asked Uncle Hank. "Helen, what are you—?"

"The answer," I croaked. I was limp as a rag doll, wobbly-weak as a baby. I tottered, and my head, so light in my nightmare, swam with vertigo. "I . . . I saw . . . I . . ."

My knees buckled, but then Dr. Rainier had me by one arm and Uncle Hank moved in to take me by the other.

"Easy," he said. "We got you, Christian, we got you."

"Oh . . ." Then my throat clogged and I couldn't speak. We three stood in the wreckage of my room, as the sideways place pressed in and my head whirled, but they wouldn't let me go, they would not let me fall.

"Christian?" Dr. Rainier. "Tell us. What did you see?"

My tongue flicked over my parched lips. I was desperately thirsty.

"The answer," I said finally. "I saw how to paint the answer."

XXVIII

"That's insane." Uncle Hank thrust his jaw out at a stubborn angle. "*Paint* yourself into another man's past? It would all be in your head, your imagination. Just like what happened upstairs. You had a bad dream was all."

I shook my head, just as stubbornly. "I was angry. You've never been there to see what I can do, but Dr. Rainier has. She *knows* I'm telling the truth." I glanced across the kitchen table. "Tell him. Tell him about your father."

Staring at the table, Dr. Rainier hunched in her chair, cradling a mug of coffee she hadn't drunk. She'd said nothing when I told my story, but now her eyes crawled from the table to my face. I was shocked to see how drawn and pinched her features were, and a pang of guilt tugged my heart. I realized—too late—that I had violated a private hell, revealing it at a time that had not been her choosing. I remembered her strange choice of words in our very first meeting: *I don't have to be an axe murderer to know how to deal with one.*

Actually, I doubt she'd ever told anyone the whole story. For that matter, I'm not sure what the real story was because I had intervened. For the first time, I had taken an active role in someone else's nightmare—

And that was the answer, you see? That's what I had been meant to discover. All this time, I'd thought my only recourse was to be an onlooker, a spectator to some private horror. Yes, I *drew* and then made pictures of what came out of my fingers, and I'd always thought the power came from elsewhere, that I was just the messenger. That was wrong. I'd had the power to get involved, probably from the start. After all, hadn't my anger dredged up Miss Stefancyzk's nightmare and Aunt Jean's?

My dream had been only that: smoke and mirrors. Yet the one thing Dr. Rainier had said during one of our sessions was that houses were the body of the dreamer, each room revealing a different facet of the personality. Well, I'd descended to the basement where the nightmares are. In the nightmares, I had dared to get involved.

Now, awake, I could act. I had to because that's where the truth lay: in a waking dream that was not my own but which I could visit because I'd been there before.

She cleared her throat, and when she spoke, her tone was measured and distinct. "I am not prepared to talk a lot about my past. It would be . . . inappropriate. But I can tell you, Hank, that Christian is right. My father was a drunk, and he did murder my mother. He would've killed me if I hadn't managed to hide in the coal chute back of the furnace. That's where the police found me." Her eyes squeezed shut, and she pressed her knuckles against her lips. "You don't know how many times I've gone over it in my mind. If I'd just been able to get to the axe first. . . ." She opened her eyes and said, "That's what you did. You lived out the fantasy for me, I think. Or maybe the impulse to save a life just . . . overwhelmed your good sense, and you stepped into what you created. It wouldn't have done any good."

"No," I said, "because what's past is past."

Her head moved in a slow nod. "Yet that means you *can* slip in alongside . . . although I'm not sure if this means the person has to be alive for it to happen."

"I've thought about that. I think I've been in David's skin enough to . . . *draw* myself in and follow it through. I think that's why he wanted me to find his father's brushes . . . like what they say about automatic writing."

"Well, I haven't considered it, but I don't see why there can't be automatic drawing too."

Uncle Hank burst in: "Oh for chrissake, listen to the two of you. Christian has a nightmare, and now you two want a séance."

"It wasn't *just* a nightmare, Hank. I've never told anyone about my father, and I certainly wouldn't tell a patient. Anyway, where's the harm?"

Uncle Hank goggled at her. "The *harm* lies in fueling some poor kid's fantasy. . . ."

I cut in, getting hot. "I'm not a kid and it's not a fantasy, don't you get it? This is exactly what I did to Miss Stefancyzk and Lucy; I didn't intervene, but I drew their futures, and I did the same thing to Aunt Jean. . . ." Too late, I clamped my mouth shut, but the damage was done.

Uncle Hank's features went slack a little at a time. It was like watching a building crumble brick by brick. When he spoke, his voice was low and deadly. "What are you talking about?"

Dr. Rainier tried to step in. "Hank, that's not important right now."

He ignored her. "Tell me what you mean, Christian."

So I did. It didn't take long. After all, I'd been ten and angry at some slight: angry enough to reach down and *draw* out of Aunt Jean a picture of *her* worst fears realized, only of the future not the past.

In Aunt Jean's case, I drew, in meticulous living detail, what it would be like to be trapped in a car slowly sinking into an icy lake, without even the mercy of unconsciousness to ease her way. Oh no, in my ten-year-old's rage, I made sure she saw and felt every agonizing, panicky second as the water crept to her chest and inched to her neck and slid past her nose. How it would feel as her lungs burned and her throat convulsed and then that moment when she had no choice and must expel her life in great glittery, silver bubbles, each rising to the surface to release screams no one ever heard. . . .

It hurt just to remember. It was worse to say it out loud.

When I was done, there was a very long, very dense silence so quiet that when I swallowed, it was like thunder in my ears. Then I dared to look at Uncle Hank.

His face was a ruin. There was such searing horror in his eyes that his tears must have burned away before they could fall. He was so still he looked made of wax.

"Uncle Hank," I began.

Without a word, he scraped back his chair and strode from the room. He did not look back. A moment later, I heard the bang of the kitchen door, and then his truck growling to life, tires crunching over gravel as he backed down the driveway and then roared away.

Dr. Rainier spoke first. "Give him time."

I shook my head. "He'll never forgive me. We'll never be the same."

She was quiet. She didn't try to stop me from crying. When I'd cried myself to hiccups, she went to the sink, wet a paper towel with cool water, and brought it and a dry towel back for me to wipe my face. "Listen to me: Things stopped being the same the moment you spray-painted that barn. Things are never meant to stay the same, Christian. You're seventeen. This is your time now, and you have work to do. And I think it's got to be *now*." She paused and looked at me for a moment, measuring her words. "I think that's what your dream was trying to tell you too: not to wait too long or else this might all fade. Almost all religions believe that the soul hovers for a time after death, and I'll bet Judaism's no different." When I looked at her in surprise, her shoulders moved in a small shrug. "Why not? Many superstitions have some basis in fact, and I'm out of my depth here. I don't pretend to understand this, but I believe you, and I'm willing to follow you wherever this leads. Don't forget: you saw my nightmare. So . . . you got my vote."

"What if it *is* God?" I blew my nose. "I mean, what if I have some kind of mission or something?"

"Then you better get cracking," she said.

XXIX

Dr. Rainier drove. It had turned cold again, and the sky was hard and glittery with stars. There was no moon, and once we'd past the last of the houses, the sky looked like someone had upended a bowl of diamonds over the earth. The village was a faint gray smudge on the eastern horizon.

I said to Dr. Rainier, "Can I ask you a question?"

Dr. Rainier's skin was bottle green from the dash. She kept her eyes on the road. "Can I answer it?"

"Maybe. Well, sure, you could . . . if you want to."

"So what's the question?"

"Do you wish you had killed him?"

The question hung there, and I was feeling stupid for asking when she said, "For years afterward, yes, I did. I wish I'd been older and stronger. In a way, I wished that I'd been you, the way you were in the dream. Maybe you picked up on that because the emotion is so bound up with rage, I don't know."

I wanted to ask why rage and anger and death were things that my mind snagged on, but I didn't. Now I'm pretty sure I didn't want to know the answer. I mean, what could she say, right?

She continued, "He got forty years for second-degree intentional homicide, no possibility of parole. Looking at it now, I think that forty years in a cage is just as good as being put to death—maybe better, because if you ever get out, your life is pretty much done."

"So he's still in prison."

"Yes, he is and, no, I've never gone to see him. We don't even have the same last name anymore. Rainier is my mother's maiden name. Anyway, that doesn't exactly answer your question, does it? I guess I try not to think about it anymore because I can't change the past. What's done is done. I was just a little girl, and there was no way I could've saved my mother—or me, for that matter."

"Is that why you became a shrink?" The question was out of my mouth an instant before I wished I could call it back. "Sorry, that was stupid."

"No, that's okay." She flicked a glance at me and then returned to the road. There were no streetlights out this far, and it looked like we were following the shaft of her headlights off a cliff—which, maybe, we were. "It's a question to which I've given a lot of thought. The quick answer is . . . sure. I want to understand how my mother could've loved a man like that. I want to know how a little girl considers a monster like that her father—because he was, once. I think the drinking started up after they'd been married a while, and I'll bet he tried controlling it. Did you know, he was a doctor? A surgeon, if you can believe it. His patients worshipped him. He held it together in the operating room, I guess, but I really don't know what ultimately happened. I suppose you could say that I've never cared to find out."

"Why not?"

"Because then I would be making him the most important person in my life. My past would revolve around him, and he doesn't deserve that kind of energy. Sounds counterintuitive, I guess. Psychiatrists are supposed to want to understand all the minutiae. But I've decided that he's not worth my time. He's a focal point in my past, sure. Otherwise, my guess is you'd never have had that dream—but he's only one point, and you can get trapped that way, endlessly looping to the past. You have to let go, or you'll burn up in the past, simple as that."

Like David Witek, I thought. Maybe his waking life hadn't always returned to that horrible moment in the barn when his father murdered one man and maimed another. In the end, though, that's what his thoughts fixed on, orbiting that moment like doomed satellites.

I said, "I'm . . . I'm afraid to let my mom go. It's not only being, you know, obsessed. You know what happens to me, what I can do. You saw my walls."

"I did." A pause. "I also saw that door." Another pause. "Do you have any ideas about why there's no knob?"

Sure I did. "What do you think?"

"Careful, you're picking up bad habits." Her lips made a small smile, there and gone in an instant in the darkling shadows. "Fear is a healthy emotion, Christian. You haven't failed your mother or abandoned her by not opening that door."

"You sound like you think there's a real place behind it."

"Isn't there?" She gave a little laugh. "Heavens, Christian, there's been a lot of stuff happening ever since I met you. I don't understand it all. So . . . which is it? Is that what you imagine is beyond the door, or is this a place you're thinking about going to?"

"I . . . I honestly don't know which. I try to imagine where my mother might be and what things look like through her eyes. I guess I kind of graduated from doing just her eyes and doing . . . the . . . you know, the sideways place. That's what I call it because I think my mom just slid a little too far. . . ."

"I see." She was quiet a moment. "You know, Christian, what you've done is, yeah, obsessive, but it also takes courage."

"Yeah? Actually, looking at it now . . . it kind of gives me the creeps. I'm scared for my mom and dad, and I'm freaked about *where* they might be, and now I'm not sure I really want to go there. I guess it would be like revisiting the past over and over again."

"Has it occurred to you that they might both be dead?"

That didn't hurt the way I thought it might. "Sure. I mean, does that look like any place on this earth?"

"Good point. But what if you've reached in, the way you did with Lucy, and pulled out your own destiny?"

That hadn't occurred to me. "I . . . I don't know. You mean, my own death?"

"I don't know. I don't understand what you can do. But if that is the case, . . . would you really want to go there?"

"Not right now," I said, truthfully.

"But you've been tempted."

"Yes." That was the truth. The next wasn't. "But I wouldn't know how to do it."

She didn't say anything. I don't think she believed me; after all, she was the one who'd noticed there wasn't a knob. Uncle Hank, he never said anything at all about the door.

We rode in silence a few moments, and then she said, "Promise me one thing: if you ever decide to try, tell me first. Okay?"

"Why?"

"Because," she said, "you might want someone there to pull you back out."

The stone base of the barn winked in and out of the headlights as Dr. Rainier's truck ground up the western approach road. The building seemed much more massive at night, and when we rolled to a stop and Dr. Rainier killed the engine and lights, the darkness slammed down like a black wave.

Dr. Rainier dug two flashlights from her glove box and handed one to me. Her face was unreadable in the dark. "You're sure you're ready for this."

I nodded, remembered she couldn't see me, hooked my hand around the strap of my backpack, and said, "Yeah. I've got to."

Stones squealed and popped under our shoes as we climbed the last hundred yards. The scaffolding was still in place; the grass was chill, and I could feel the damp through my Chucks. I played my light over the barn, sliding the fuzzy silver blue beam along the northwest face. The ghostly outlines of a swastika were still visible.

"Oh my God." Dr. Rainier's voice was barely a whisper. "Christian, look. On the roof."

Crows. Hundreds. The roof was black with them. Their bodies blanketed the old shingles. As our lights caught them, they stirred with a rustle like dead cornstalks. Their eyes sparkled like green glass in our flashlights.

"They won't bother us. Come on," I said. "We can go in through the basement."

Dr. Rainier followed my lead. "Is that where it happened? In the basement?"

"I think so. I remember hearing the horses, and I thought I saw the slats of the stalls. I just don't remember the floor. . . ."

The basement floor was brick laid on edge. My light picked out a crumpled, half bag of concrete mix in a corner, next to an empty horse stall. Our footfalls echoed, bouncing against brick and wood. I had not been down here before, and I was surprised to see that the iron rods of each horse stall, as well as the screen doors, were still in place. The air smelled more strongly of rust here. In the center of the basement was a flight of stairs that I knew led to the haymow and from there to the enclosed cupola. The remains of two long ladders were visible both in the right and left corners on a north-south diagonal and led to a square-cut opening in the wooden ceiling.

We walked the length of the basement from south to north. My skin started to prickle as I approached the south end, and I swung my light to the left. A door sagged on wrought-iron hinges, and when I grasped the handle, it swung open only grudgingly, the bottom edge scraping brick. I threw my light over the empty interior. There were iron studs and pegs hammered into the brick, and in one corner, I saw the disintegrating remains of a wood-handled rake.

Dr. Rainier was at my elbow. "Some kind of place to keep tools?"

"Maybe." My body was itchy now, with a familiar electric tingle that told me this place was important. Then I thought: *pitchfork*.

Backing out, I turned left and walked to the north end of the barn. My skin, now alive with what felt like an army of ants, almost writhed. I swung my light right and left, trying to understand the source of my discomfort. But I saw nothing except more brick and empty stalls, and I eventually retraced my steps until I stood right of center. Then I stabbed my light straight up to probe the darkness above our heads.

"What are you looking for?" asked Dr. Rainier.

"David was watching from the haymow. I remember the stairs. . . . Got it." My light fixed on a wide gap in the ceiling where the boards had pulled apart. "That's it."

So from where I stood now, David had seen his father and Mr. Eisenmann and Walter Brotz quarrel. On this precise spot, Mordecai Witek had thrown himself on his boss, had snatched up a pitchfork, and . . .

My head was starting to buzz. I felt the familiar ballooning sensation like I was filling up with helium, my head going hollow, and I knew the time was on me, the moment was now.

Hurry.

Clicking off my flashlight, I stuffed it into my backpack and then pulled out the packet of drawing pencils and sketch pad I'd brought from the house. The leather roll containing Mordecai Witek's paintbrushes was in my hip pocket. I wouldn't be using the brushes, but I wanted them there.

"What do we do now?" Dr. Rainier's voice sounded a little small coming from the darkness behind her flashlight. "What's going to happen?"

"I don't know." How could I possibly draw what David himself either had not seen or could not bear to remember? Or was I here now to be a silent witness? Because I could not participate: this would not be like my nightmare of Dr. Rainier's father. This would be like immersing myself in Aunt Jean's death and Miss Stefancyzk's madness; I could watch; I could witness.

Could I take David's place?

You'll never know if you don't try, I thought. *Stop dicking around and do it!*

I snatched up a pencil, more out of panic than because of any other emotion. Certainly, there was no thought involved. My hands were itching, my skin on fire, and then I was falling, the darkness swallowing me up and

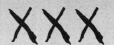

The hayloft is dusty, but the air is crisp and bites my nose. Light seeps through gaps and seams in the wooden floor, and there is a bigger, brighter bolt of light shooting from the throat of the stairs leading from the basement. Beside me, David crouches, his brown eyes huge with terror, his skin paper white with fear. Does he see me; does he sense me? I don't think so; I'm not there, after all, and even David is what I imagine him to be from this vantage point.

Angry voices boil from below, and now I move, noiselessly, to the stairs. The floor should creak, but it doesn't; David should notice what I'm doing, but he can't. I throw one last look back, and he has not moved; he is frozen in his fear, like a mouse cowering in a corner, hoping that the cat won't smell or sense him.

As I descend, I smell horses' sweat, nutty feed, and the scent of freshly churned earth. Along the north side of the barn, I see that the floor is incomplete: a rectangle running the width of the barn and easily ten feet wide. Bags of concrete and mounds of brick hunch in one corner.

A mound of fresh hay is neatly heaped before two stalls near the stairs. The long hickory handle of a pitchfork that would have made Grant Wood proud protrudes from the hay.

The ladder's rungs have worn smooth over the years, and I slip and for a crazy instant, I think, *Oh no, now they'll see me, I've blown it.* . . . But that won't happen; all those men below—Charles Eisenmann, Mordecai Witek, and another man I instinctively know is Walter Brotz—they could run right through me. They will stare right at me, and I still won't be there.

I am a ghost in a land of phantoms and remembered nightmares.

"And tell the truth, you've been lusting after her since that sunset painting, haven't you?" said Charles Eisenmann, resplendent in the sulfur glow of the bare bulbs hanging from the barn's ceiling. This evening, his suit is dark, the trousers neatly pressed, and when he gestures, the light winks off the thick gold of a monogrammed pinkie ring. He hooks his thumbs in his vest, and the gold links of his watch chain with their fobs gleam and sparkle. "Oh yes, you're such a good married man, a man with principles . . . no wonder you jumped at the offer of a job in Winter. Take you far away from Milwaukee, yes? What must have gone through your mind when she arrived here and you found out that we were engaged? If anyone is the injured party, it is I."

By contrast, Mordecai Witek is small and brown in his plain coarse trousers and white workman's shirt. Still, his eyes are bright with defiance and his cheeks are hectic with color. "My family suffers. We're poor, we're Jews . . . and now my daughter, she is already marked and now . . ." His face twists with anguish, and now tears start in his eyes. His fists bunch, and his lips are trembling. "She is my *daughter*. . . ."

Charles Eisenmann shows his teeth in a laugh. "And now your daughter has proven that even a Jewess makes some very bad choices."

"She was *forced*. . . ."

"*Forced?*" Eisenmann sneers. "That's not what I heard. You think I missed how she hung around the gates every day with all the other girls? She wanted it, and you know it. The only difference between her and a whore is she thinks she's in love. She just decided on a . . . well, *universal* language."

Witek flinches back as if he's been struck. Even Brotz—goggle-eyed and slack-jawed—is surprised and shoots a worried look at Witek and then over his shoulder, toward the basement doors that open into the west barnyard.

"Now be thankful you still have a job and a roof over your head. You're lucky I don't get Anderson to turn the lot of you onto the streets. If you'll take my advice, Witek, you'll go down the hill to your family and lay it out for them."

"Lay it . . . She'll be ruined," says Witek.

"She's already spoiled goods. But don't worry. These are modern times. If you want my advice, afterward you can send her away. Doesn't she want to be an interpreter? So send her to one of those special schools in Chicago or New York or maybe San Francisco where no one knows her and she can start fresh . . . if not exactly virginal." Mr. Eisenmann's voice turns brisk. "But we are *done* here."

"No." Witek takes a step forward, hesitates. "Please. Wait."

Eisenmann's not listening. He gives an imperious snap of his fingers. "Brotz, have them bring the car around. . . ."

"Wait." The urgency in Witek's voice cracks like a whip, and Brotz stops dead in his tracks. "This isn't the end of anything. They're *Nazis*, for God's sake!"

"So?" Eisenmann regards Witek with a coolly contemptuous expression. "Get a hold of yourself. They are soldiers. True, they are German soldiers, but they are not Nazis. None of them were members of the Party. . . ."

"You think they'll *admit* that?"

"And if they were, they would certainly not be *here*. Most of these men were conscripted into the military just as our soldiers were. You can't hold them responsible for the actions of their superiors."

"But they've killed my people, my *parents*. . . . !" Witek's voice balls with fury. His tears are ones of rage now.

"And that didn't seem to stop your daughter, did it? Think of it, Witek: she opened her legs for the enemy, and you're about to be the proud grandfather of a German bastard. Fitting, don't you think?"

Brotz is taken aback. "Mr. Eisenmann . . ."

Eisenmann whirls on the smaller man. "What?" He bites the word off. "You have something to add? Why are you still here? Get the damn car!"

"Ye-yes, yes, uh-uh-of course, s-s-sir," Brotz stammers, "b-b-but I really, *really* don't think it's wise . . ."

Charles Eisenmann's face is wine-colored and glistens with rage. "I am not *interested* in what you or anyone else thinks! Now get the damn *car*!"

The air has grown thick and poisonous. In their stalls, the horses are stamping and nickering their alarm. The mood is so charged, I can practically *hear* the crackle of Eisenmann's hatred and disdain and of Witek's shame. And I can only stand, rigid, shaking. I am helpless to do anything but watch and witness, and yet I feel every word as the blow Eisenmann intends. I think of the old man I know now—that gargoyle with his gold watch fobs—but what I see now is far, far uglier.

Witek says again, "Someone has to be responsible!"

"And who that someone is remains within my purview, not yours," says Eisenmann. "Go ahead. Make a fuss, create a scandal. You'll accomplish nothing, and your reputation will be ruined. I will win, and I will do what I want when I want. Whom I choose to hold responsible is my choice, not yours and . . ."

With a wild cry, Witek uncoils like a panther, hurling himself at Eisenmann. The other man is caught completely off-guard, and then Witek has him by the neck. Witek's fist is a blur as he smashes Eisenmann's face. There's a smart crackling sound like the crunching of eggshells under a boot, and the other man's head snaps back. Blood spews in a brilliant claret curtain from Eisenmann's nose. He staggers back, but Witek goes with him, his blood-smeared fist cocked for another blow. The horses are going berserk, whinnying and bashing their hooves into their stalls. Eisenmann sputters and blows a bloody froth, choking: "Brotz . . . Br-Brotz, help . . . hel . . ."

With a snarl, Witek hammers Eisenmann again. This time, the sound of his fist is sodden, and he lets Eisenmann drunk-stagger backward, his arms windmilling, until Eisenmann smacks up against a stall. The horse inside brays and snorts, and there is another sharp BANG of hooves against wood, accompanied by the squeal of overstressed wood.

Brotz breaks out of his paralysis. He scurries for the open basement doors: "Help, *help!*"

Gory fists still bunched, Witek stands over Eisenmann as if he can't quite believe what's just happened. Moaning, barely conscious, the foundry owner's face is a mask of blood; blood oils his clothes. Eisenmann begins to choke, and Witek jerks free of his paralysis.

"My God." Witek bends over the fallen man. "Oh Marta . . . Mr. Eisenmann, Mr. . . . ." He hooks his arms over Eisenmann's body and rolls the fallen man toward him as Eisenmann makes a gargling sound. A moment later, Eisenmann vomits onto the brick floor—

And I think: *Mordecai Witek—David's father—just saved his life. Eisenmann would've choked to death on his own vomit. . . .*

There's a commotion of voices and men running, and Witek looks up as Brotz reappears with two other men in tow. One carries a crowbar; the other, a flashlight.

I gasp. I recognize them at once. I even know one man's name because I've seen it written in a sketchbook in Witek's very own hand.

"My God, you've killed him!" cries Brotz. He takes a short step back. "What have you done?"

With all the blood and now lying so still, Eisenmann *does* look dead, but Witek says, patiently, "No, but we need to get him to a hospital. Come on, if you'll help me, we can load him into your car. Then we need to see Sheriff Cage. . . . " He frowns at the other men who haven't moved at all. "Did you hear me? Mr. Eisenmann needs medical attention. Here, Brotz, come help me."

Reluctantly, Brotz shoots a glance at the other men and then moves to squat behind Eisenmann. The other two are still as statues; they only look at each other, and then the one whose name I don't know—but that face, now that I've seen him, I understand why David kept calling him *Gemini*—says in his flawless English, "So, he's still alive?"

Witek gives a curt nod, and I see how he struggles against his next impulse—and fails because, above all else, he is an honorable man. He pushes to his feet and says, quietly, "This is, ultimately, at your doorstep. I won't say that it's your fault because I did strike that man. I will bear the consequences. But you compromised my daughter, a girl so easy to take advantage of, and this is the result. I should never have gone to Eisenmann but directly to your camp commander, and I still intend to do so. I will go to jail, but I'll see that you are punished. . . ."

"I wish you hadn't said that," says the other man, too easily, and I see what he's about to do an instant too late.

"Look out!" I take a step forward. "Mr. Witek, the crowbar . . . !"

Of course, no one hears me. I'm not there.

The air whistles as the crowbar whips around in a vicious cut. Witek has no chance, and I try to console myself with the thought that he probably never saw it coming.

The crowbar hits with a meaty *kunk*, the metal smashing Witek's skull just below the left ear. Witek grunts: *Guh!* Then he simply drops in a loose-limbed tumble, dead before he hits the bloody, vomit-spattered brick.

I scream.

This time, the men's backs go ramrod straight. For a crazy instant, I freeze with fear. Are they reacting to *me*? But no, their heads jerk up toward the ceiling. I follow their gaze, and then my heart stutters: *God, no. . . .*

There, perfectly framed in the stairwell, is the twisted, horrified face of David Witek.

"Papa!" he screams again, a child's high cry. "*Papa!*"

The one who's killed Mordecai Witek barks a short command in German, and the second man—one with a crescent scar over his left cheek and a bit of a lazy eye—sprints for the stairs.

"Run!" I shout, even though it's no use. "Run, David, *run!*"

As if he's heard, David's face disappears. I hear his feet scurrying across the haymow, heading for the north ladder and then the heavier thuds of the man—of *Daecher*—as he chases him down.

"What are you doing?" Brotz has been kneeling by Eisenmann, but now he's on his feet, backing away. "What have you done?"

"Relax, Brotz," says the other man. As he takes a step, Brotz backs up, and the other man laughs. "What, the crowbar makes you nervous? There." He tosses the crowbar aside to clatter against the bricks. "I'm just taking care of a few problems for the boss."

"But . . . But you killed . . ."

The other man spreads his hands. "And he would've killed our boss, no?" He looks toward the stairs as Daecher reappears. Daecher has David, who is kicking and flailing, tucked under one massive arm like a sack of wheat. The other man turns back to Brotz. "Anyway, so sorry you had to see this."

Blinking, Brotz runs a hand through his hair. "I—" he begins, but that is all he manages.

The other man moves just as fast as before. Without taking his eyes from Brotz, his right hand shoots out, wraps around the pitchfork, and then he has the pitchfork in both hands. He charges, driving forward like a jousting knight with a lance.

The tines spear Brotz right through his breastbone. Brotz gets out one sharp scream, and then the tines are all the way through, and the other man is grunting, still driving forward. His momentum propels Brotz back. The tines dig into the horse stall behind Brotz with a solid *thunk*, tacking the man to the wood slats like a bug on cardboard.

Brotz is still alive, his eyes bulging, his hands wrapped around two of the tines. His mouth opens, and a fountain of blood pours out, and then he twitches a few seconds. Then he dies.

The other man lets go of the pitchfork. He's breathing hard. The stink of blood is very strong, and the horses are snorting. Daecher's standing behind David, hanging onto the boy's arms. The boy weeps; moans dribble from his lips, but he's not fighting anymore.

On the floor, Eisenmann lets go of a long groan.

The sound is startling, almost unearthly, and makes the other man snap to. He looks over at Daecher, then flicks a finger at David. "He's the only one?"

Daecher nods. "We should . . ."

"No." The other man shakes his head. "A little boy, we would have a hard time explaining."

"But the women in the house, all this commotion, they'll hear . . ."

"No, they won't. They can't." The Gemini squats before David. Reaching forward, he grabs the child by the chin. "Look at me," he commands. "Look at me and stop that crying."

David does. He goes absolutely still. Huge tears roll down his cheeks, but not a single sound bleeds through his lips.

"This is how it will be," says the second man. "If you ever say one word of what you've seen here to anyone, then I will kill your mother, and I will make you watch. I will kill your sister, and I will make you watch. And then I will gouge out your eyes and cut off your ears and slice out your tongue, and then I will kill you too. Do you understand me? Not . . . one. . . . *word*."

(*. . . don't take my mouth . . .*)

And that, I think, is precisely when David went mute. Still weeping, the boy nods.

Daecher growls, "I think it's a mistake."

"No." The other man straightens. "The mistake will be if we don't seize the opportunity."

I know then, at that instant and a blaze of intuition, what that opportunity is. Even if I had not seen what happened next, I could have guessed because David had seen it himself: the Gemini twins, one immortal and the other not.

The second man bends over Eisenmann, who is coming around; I see that in the feeble movements of his arms and legs.

"Be quick," says Daecher.

"Of course," says the second man. He stands, strides to the tool closet I'd seen earlier, steps inside and then, after a few moments, reappears.

And he has a corn knife.

The blade is a good foot and a half long, like a machete, but with a squared end. The wood handle is dark from skin oils after years of being used to chop stalks.

David freezes when he sees the second man come toward him with the knife. But the second man smiles, almost beatifically. He actually reaches out and tousles David's hair.

"Don't you worry," he says, with a chuckle. "This isn't for you."

Turning his back on the boy, the second man squats over Eisenmann and goes to work.

I can't do anything but watch. I watch it all happen, and then I feel the earth moving beneath my feet, as if a chasm's opening. I remember what Dr. Rainier has said about private hells, and I think, surely, that if this is David's private hell, the torment he is fated to relive for the rest of his life, I share it.

Then the earth yawns open, the ground splits, and I fall; the blackness rises up and closes around, and I am falling.

Mercifully, I pass out.

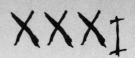

XXXI

After what seemed like a long time but must be only minutes, I became aware of something cold and hard along my back. Then someone was shaking me: "Christian, Christian, come on, wake up."

I cracked open my eyes, squinting against the glare of flashlights. My right shoulder throbbed, and my right hand was cramped. My face felt sticky, and I put my left hand up. The fingers came away glistening with blood, and my cheeks felt wet, my eyes gritty like I'd been crying. "Wh-what . . . what ha-happened?"

"You fainted," said Dr. Rainier, sounding immensely relieved. "You were drawing like there was no tomorrow, and then you started screaming, and you got a nosebleed, and then, well, it looked almost as if you'd had a seizure. . . ."

"Can you sit up?" A gruff voice, deeper, male. A hand reached from behind a glare of flashlight and cradled the back of my head. "You took quite a tumble there. You need to go slow."

I hung onto Uncle Hank's arm as he and Dr. Rainier helped me sit up. Uncle Hank handed me a kerchief to wipe my face. I smeared away blood; my head felt as if someone had taken a hammer to it. "When did *you* get here?"

"About ten minutes ago. Hel . . . Dr. Rainier called soon as you went into some kind of trance, and I got here fast as I could." He turned to Dr. Rainier. "What were you thinking? Taking a chance like that with my boy, what were you *thinking*?"

"No," I said, "I was the one who came up with the idea."

"That doesn't excuse it. You're just a *boy*. . . ."

"I'm not a boy. I know what I'm doing." I looked at Dr. Rainier. "I was there. I saw it. I know what happened."

Dr. Rainier had gathered up the hasty drawings I'd made. Her face registered first disbelief, then astonishment and, finally, horror. She looked up quickly. "These two men," she said. "Christian, I've seen them before."

"What?" Uncle Hank took the drawing from her. "One of them's a walleye."

"A strabismus," Dr. Rainier corrected. "But I've seen them both."

"I've only seen one of them before." I pointed to the one with the strabismus; I'd rendered in a few quick strokes, the man grasping a small struggling boy. "His name's Daecher, and there's some kind of serial number after his name. I think . . . I think they're both German PWs from the camp. Mr. Witek's father must've drawn a lot of them."

Dr. Rainier was nodding. "That's where. In that sketchbook by Mr. Witek's bed . . . this one." She tapped the paper. "He's there too."

I said, "He's more than just here on paper."

"What?" Uncle Hank and Dr. Rainier said at the same moment. "What do you mean?" asked Dr. Rainier.

I turned to Uncle Hank. "Is Mr. Mosby still here? The guy with the ground penetrating radar?"

"Yes. He said they wouldn't finish with the old Ziegler place for a couple of days yet. Why?"

I pointed to the north side of the barn—and then I showed them one of my drawings: two men, shovels in hand, shoulders hunched, bent to their task. "We need him."

So that's how I discovered how a grave looks on GPR: a rectangular, dark gray lozenge, because even though bodies have no corners, for some reason, every gravedigger cuts four. It wasn't possible to see how many bodies were in there. Mosby said all we'd get was the grave itself.

"But it's down there," he said. "Right under the concrete and that brick. Bet my company on it."

That was close to midnight. No one felt much like sleeping. So after rousting the relevant people and applying jackhammers and crowbars and then spades, we'd opened that grave by seven, first light. By that time, someone had gotten through to Dr. Nichols, who'd pulled up at six thirty, hair mussed and eyes red-rimmed. She was jazzed.

Not one skeleton but two: both men, laid out alongside each other, possibly because it had been easier to make the grave wider than deep. After over sixty years, the tissues holding the bones together had disintegrated, and the skeletons were disarticulated, in pieces but still clumped into two distinct shapes.

One wore a tattered set of work trousers, and I could see where the crowbar had smashed into Mordecai Witek's skull. Dr. Nichols felt along the legs and hips and then fished around with her fingers beneath the body—and withdrew a frayed, gnawed-looking leather wallet. Dr. Nichols carefully unfolded the wallet and tweezed out a ten-dollar bill, two fives—and a photograph: four people, discolored with age and faded. One was barely recognizable as Mordecai Witek.

Even though they were photographic ghosts, I was reasonably sure who the other three were. I'd even seen them before, without knowing it: the family portrait in Mr. Witek's room. Looking at Marta, I thought I knew something else too.

"The lab might be able to do something with that," Dr. Nichols said, carefully slipping the photo into an evidence bag. "But this." She held up a thick rectangle, about the size of a Social Security card. "This is good."

The card had once been pink. On one side was a black seal, what looked like some kind of bridge span against a backdrop of mountains and the letters, **IABSOIW**. On the reverse, the card read:

THIS IS TO CERTIFY THAT:
Mr. M. M. WITEK
is a member in good standing of the
International Association of Bridge,
Structural, and Ornamental Iron Workers
of WINTER, WI
Local No. 119
This card good until Dec. 31st, 1945.

"My Lord," said Uncle Hank. "He never left."

"Looks that way. Of course, we'll do DNA and get a comparison sample from his son's body," said Dr. Nichols. "I'm sure his executor will have no objections. But I'd say this card is pretty persuasive, wouldn't you?"

The other skeleton would be a problem. The man's nose was broken, but that was the only bony injury visible on Dr. Nichols's cursory exam. She didn't find a wallet, though she thought that he might have been some kind of farmhand. "Look at the clothes, how rough they are. Very coarse weave and I think there's some kind of logo here on this remnant of a sleeve. Bleached, I'm afraid; I can't read it, but you can see where this part of the cloth is quite a bit paler than the rest. The lab people might be able to clean it up. But we might never know who he is."

I knew better. I'd seen and drawn what the two Germans, Woolfe and Daecher, had missed because there's a big gush of blood when you cut a man's throat with a corn knife, especially when he's still alive, and blood can hide a lot.

I said, "If you can find the left pinkie finger . . . that would help."

After ten minutes of careful sifting of trowels of dirt through wire mesh, Dr. Rainier said, "Hey, I thought I saw something metal. . . ."

Dr. Nichols's gloved fingers carefully picked out a length of bone she called a metacarpal—and then, a man's gold pinkie ring. On the ring was a set of initials in fancy, curlicue script.

"*C-R-E*," I said. "Charles Randall Eisenmann."

"But that's impossible." Uncle Hank looked from me to the ring and then to Dr. Rainier before saying again, "It's not possible. Eisenmann's alive."

284

"Then how do you explain the ring? Look at pictures from the time period. He always wore this ring, always. He's still got the gold watch chain and fobs; they're in the pictures too. But I'll bet that if you compare a picture from 1944 to one in 1946, the ring's gone." I pointed to the ring in Dr. Nichols's gloved fingers. "That's because the real Charles Eisenmann was still wearing it when he died, and the guy who took his place forgot about it. He changed out of his clothes and made sure he had the pocket watch. But he missed the ring."

Uncle Hank still wasn't convinced. "How do you fake something like that?"

I knew the truth because I'd seen it happen. "Because there were the scars. All we know is he got them on the night of the murder, right? He got attacked? But what if the guy who took his place did them to himself? What if someone *helped*?"

"It's possible," Dr. Nichols put in, "especially if the damage is extensive and people are primed to accept it because there would be other cues—the clothes and the watch chain and the fobs. Close enough is all that's required."

Uncle Hank screwed up his face. "I still don't buy it."

I turned to Dr. Rainier. "You recognized those guys in my pictures, right?" When she nodded, I said, "Can you get Mr. Witek's sketchbook?"

"I don't see why not. It's locked up with his personal effects, but—" She turned to Uncle Hank. "A request from you would probably do it. A warrant, if you need it. You certainly have enough presumptive evidence right here for one."

"Sure," Uncle Hank agreed. "But what would I be looking for?"

"The Gemini twin." I riffled through my stack of drawings and tugged out the one with the second man, corn knife in hand, bent over Eisenmann. "That guy."

"Any jury would say you saw the drawing and it hung around in your subconscious," Uncle Hank objected. "Heck, that's what *I'm* saying."

"Ah . . . not bloody likely," interrupted Dr. Nichols. Her capable fingers crawled through the debris on that mesh screen, and then she was thumbing dirt away from an oval disk made of thin metal.

Dr. Rainier's eyebrows knit. "What is that, a machine tag?"

Dr. Nichols's eyes actually twinkled. "Oh, it's a tag all right, just not for a machine." She extended her hand.

In the center was an aluminum oval as big as her palm. A single, deeply incised line bisected the tag along its long axis. There were also three round perforations in the aluminum, two above and one below, and a remnant of what looked like a shoelace was threaded between the two holes along the top of the oval. Above and below the line were a series of numbers and letters that read: *9356 Pz. Gen. Rgt. 26.* A large *O* had been stamped along the lower left-hand edge.

"I have no idea what those abbreviations mean," said Dr. Nichols, "but I'll bet that this is some kind of dog tag. That number corresponds to identification, a serial number."

"The Wolfsangels were a Panzer division," I said. "So the *P* and the *Z* could be an abbreviation for Panzer, right? So maybe this is for Soldier 9356."

"With an O blood type," Dr. Rainier chimed in. "That does make the most sense in terms of the *O*, right?"

"Maybe. We bag this, send it on, and see what comes up, but I've got a very good feeling about this. Artifacts are the most helpful element in terms of dates and identities. But let's talk DNA for a second. If this man is the real Charles Eisenmann, then we can match his DNA to the relatives buried in your town cemetery, specifically to his parents. Fifty percent of his DNA will match his mother, and fifty percent will match his father. Those numbers can't and don't lie. You get a sample from the man who claims he's Charles Eisenmann, and the DNA will expose him." Dr. Nichols practically preened. "Sheriff, I'd say that you have more than enough evidence for an exhumation."

Someone had brought coffee and doughnuts, but I passed. The night was finally catching up to me. All I wanted was to get home and fall into bed. I stumbled out of that place of horrors and into a gorgeous Sunday morning in late October. A fine mist veiled the pond to my left and floated above dips in the meadows. I pulled in a lungful of air, but my head didn't clear. Something nagged at me, and I couldn't put my finger on it. But what more was I supposed to do?

As I stood there, Dr. Rainier and Uncle Hank came to flank me on either side. They looked tired too, but I knew that Uncle Hank still had a long day ahead. He said, "Dr. Rainier will drive you home. You look done in."

"I am," I said, "only..."

"What?"

I craned my head to peer back into the barn's dank shadows. "I don't know, it's just . . . I don't know." They followed me as I trudged around to the barn's northwest face. The scaffolding was still in place. I'd be lying if I said I was sad to never lay eyes on that again. The ghostly remnant of that last swastika was still visible, and I thought about that for a second. I had never thought about this before, but now I wondered: why had I been compelled to spray-paint *this* side of the barn? *Nothing* was co-incidental here, not the dreams I'd had or meeting Mr. Witek or gazing out from the haymow . . . nothing. So *this* side was important. But why?

That's when I noticed something else: all those crows were gone. Yet I sensed they were still somewhere close. . . .

"I'll be right back." Before either of them could say anything, I was monkeying my way up the scaffolding to the precise spot where I'd first felt that icy wash of dread weeks ago now. Maybe I shouldn't have been surprised when that turned out to be level with that swastika. Then I stepped away from the ladder and turned to scan the fields and hills.

"Christian?" Uncle Hank called. "What is it, son?"

I didn't reply. My eyes picked out the ruined house— David's house, I knew now, and I wondered who or what had burned it down—and then, closer in, the pond with the copse of aspens at the southern tip. My breath hitched.

There were the crows. The aspens were black with them. There were so many crows that the branches of those aspens were actually bent.

And then I had it. Even if the crows hadn't been there to point the way, I realized that there was something in the aspens *now* that had not been there when I'd gone to David's time that first go-round—and as I thought about it, there was something *missing* from the basement of the barn that had been there the night of the murder.

288

In my mind, I heard Mr. Eisenmann sneering at Mordecai Witek: *She's already spoiled goods. . . .*

"Christian?" Uncle Hank called again.

"Oh my God." I half slid, half shimmied down the ladder to the ground. "I know what it is. I know *why!*"

I took off at a run, throwing myself down the hill toward the pond. I must've looked pretty crazy: my clothes still stained from my bloody nose, my hair wild. I heard them calling after me, but I didn't slow down. My legs thrashed through damp meadow grass that grabbed at my jeans and sucked at my Chucks. As I reached the aspens, the crows screamed and lifted in a black cloud for the sky. I plunged through weedy snarls, sweeping tangles away with my hands, until I found what I was looking for.

Yes, there they were, as real as I was.

Uncle Hank and Dr. Rainier came gasping up. "What the *hell*," Uncle Hank began.

I held one up for them to see. The stamp on the brick read: **GOLD & BRICK 1941**.

"They used them in the barn. So when they needed them again, they knew exactly where to go," I said.

"But why?" asked Dr. Rainier. "Why do that to a baby? Who would really have cared or connected them? Marta was just a servant."

"That's easy. That little baby was evidence *and* a reminder, and so the killer made sure, one way or the other, that *all* the Witeks were silenced," said Uncle Hank. "Every last one."

XXXII

I wish I could've been there when Uncle Hank and a deputy went to see Eisenmann. I had to wait to get the story second-hand.

Uncle Hank thought it would be better to wait until after church—not the least of which was because he could be sure where Eisenmann was and not run the risk of the old man getting wind of anything. So he and Justin stationed themselves across the street from St. Luke's Lutheran. At the stroke of eleven—the minister at St. Luke's is a stickler for punctuality—people started filing out of the old Lutheran *Kirke*. A few glanced at Uncle Hank and Justin, curious that the sheriff and a deputy were cooling their heels outside of church.

Eisenmann finally shuffled out in his finely tailored three-piece suit. The sun winked from the gold watch chain and fobs dangled from his vest pocket. He was chatting with the minister, using his gold wolf's-head cane to make some point. He turned when Uncle Hank mounted the steps and said, "Sheriff, what brings you to the Lutherans this fine Sunday? Here, I always thought you were a UCC man. Now, don't you go asking for favors for that nephew of yours. Even a Sunday dinner won't change my mind, no matter what the Lord tells us about Christian charity." I guess he thought that was pretty funny because that seamed and scarred gargoyle's face of his pruned up as he laughed, the lopsided lips peeling back to show his teeth.

Uncle Hank allowed this was so and then said, "Thing is, Mr. Eisenmann, I've got something of yours you're going to want to see, something I think you lost a while back."

Eisenmann stopped laughing and frowned. "Lost? I can't for the life of me think what you mean, Hank."

"I think for the life of me is quite apt, sir," said Uncle Hank, and then he held up two evidence bags. One contained Charles Eisenmann's gold pinkie ring. The other held that old aluminum dog tag from World War II—because that's what it was. The Germans even incised that line down the middle so one half could stay with the body, while the other was collected to keep track of the dead. It's the reason our soldiers have two sets of tags—except during World War II, when metal was scarce.

Justin said what happened next was pretty amazing. Eisenmann's laughter dried up. That ruined face went slack with astonishment, though the crocodile tears still flowed. For that instant, the facade of the man calling himself Charles Eisenmann crumbled away, and in his eyes, Justin saw a flare first of disbelief, then fear—and then something else not quite human.

Eisenmann tried to recover. He gave a weird little giggle, though his skin had gone milk white except for the two flaming spots of scarlet in his cheeks. "I'm sure I don't understand, Sheriff."

"No," said Uncle Hank, and then he put his hand on Eisenmann's arm, "I'm sure you do. Shall we, sir? We don't really want to do this here, with all these people around. Let's go in my car."

Eisenmann seemed to become aware of the silent, staring people on the church steps—men and women who thought they knew exactly who this was—and then he said to no one in particular, "No, I don't believe I shall. I have Sunday dinner waiting—"

"It can wait," Uncle Hank cut in. "Please come with us—Herr Woolfe."

Justin said that did it. A kind of groan dripped out of the old man's misshapen mouth, and his knees buckled. He would've fallen if it hadn't been for Uncle Hank and then Justin rushing up to brace him on the opposite side. A ripple of whispers ran through the crowd as Uncle Hank and Justin led the stumbling old man to a cruiser.

"Watch your head, sir," said Uncle Hank as they helped fold the old man into the backseat. "Here." He gently took the wolf's-head cane from Woolfe's slack fingers. (Yeah, talk about irony: that must've tickled him, taunting people with a symbol only he understood, not only a stand-in for his real name but the 8th Panzers.) "I'll hang onto that, if you don't mind."

Eisenmann—or, according to Mordecai Witek's sketchbook, Hermann Woolfe, serial number 31G-3945—turned a pleading look to Uncle Hank. His lips were trembling, and Justin said real tears splashed in the crevices and valleys of those ruined cheeks.

"They can't kill me." Woolfe's eyes swam with fear. "Not after all this time . . . who cares? Besides, Witek was nothing but a Jew. . . ."

"Sir, I don't think you should say anything else." Uncle Hank leaned in and buckled the old man's seat belt. "But for the record: He was a man, with a family. They all were."

Like I said, I wish I could've been there. But here's something else I think about when I consider all those good men and women watching that cruiser pull away:

How many suspected? Or knew?

Instead, I slept like the dead the whole day through. Uncle Hank finally trudged in sometime after five, but I was still asleep and didn't hear. For once, my sleep was dark and deep and if I dreamt, I don't remember.

I awoke well after dark. The house was the only thing that was quiet. I lay there a moment, listening, hoping I was wrong. But I wasn't.

Crap. I didn't know how to feel about that.

My bedside clock read 8:15, and I was hungry. So still a little sleep-fogged, I stumbled downstairs. I dumped cereal—yeah, Cocoa Puffs—into a bowl along with some milk and ate standing up at the kitchen sink. Feeling almost human again, I rinsed out my bowl, rummaged around in the fridge until I found a carton of orange juice, and then downed a glass.

I held myself very still and listened. Food hadn't really helped either. Not that I expected that it would. I thought I'd probably have to do something about this, and then I thought that, maybe, this was something Dr. Rainier and I should talk about.

That's about when I noticed that the message light of our answering machine was having fits. The box said we had eight messages, but the first five were hang-ups, probably people in town calling to find out what happened. (Uncle Hank says they never seem to learn that law enforcement people do not have the affirmative duty to gossip.)

The sixth was from Sarah: "Hey, Christian, I heard what went down at the barn . . . well, some of it. I guess the GPR guys were talking in Gina's or something. Anyway, that was way cool, and I hope you're okay and don't forget my party on Halloween, okay? That's this week, just in case you forgot. . . . Saturday night about seven. We'll do all sorts of stupid stuff, you know, bobbing for apples. Anyway, it'll be fun. So . . . see you in school? . . . Yeah, well . . . okay. Bye."

The voice that delivered the second message was a man's and one I also recognized: "Christian, this is Rabbi Saltzman. We spoke on Friday? I was going to get back to you, but a Dr. Rainier beat me to it. She called earlier today, right after I'd finished with my Sunday school classes. I should back up. . . . I called the home on Friday right after we hung up, and so I know about David. I've been in touch with his executor, a lawyer and . . . oh, I'm going to run out of time here, aren't I? Anyway, I gather from Dr. Rainier that there might be more remains of other family members? If so, I'll be coming up to Winter soon to make arrangements, probably in the next week or so. Why don't we meet then? Call me and we'll set something up when I know with more certainty when I'll be there." He left his cell number and hung up.

Dr. Rainier's message was to the point: "Christian, I'll expect to see you in my office on Tuesday. We'll talk about where we go from there." A longish pause. "That was . . . remarkable. You're very brave. Don't let anyone tell you otherwise." Another pause. "But do me a favor. Don't make any decision, not yet, and for God's sake, don't do anything stupid out of guilt, you got that?"

I stood there as the machine told me there were no more messages. I was stunned down to my toes.

How could Dr. Rainier have possibly known that the muttering of those voices from the sideways place was back?

I kept my word. I didn't do anything stupid. But I didn't do anything about the door on my wall one way or the other either.

School was pretty much the same, sort of. Everyone still stared, and they were back to huddling in groups, throwing looks my way, and then whispering excitedly. A couple of people surprised me, though. Said hi, how's it going . . . that kind of thing.

I bypassed the cafeteria at lunch like I always do and made my way to the art studio. Man, it felt like I hadn't been there for a hundred years. *I* felt different, like someone I barely recognized. The charcoal of my mom was still on its easel, but I hesitated a good minute before drawing the canvas away from her many faces.

I stood, studying those eyes I knew so well, that face I'd imagined in waking dreams. Mordecai Witek's brushes burned a hole in my hip pocket. Obviously, I wouldn't use them on a charcoal drawing, but I felt this compulsion to hang onto them the way a drowning person grabs onto a twig.

So was I drowning? Was I about to be swept over the falls? Because I knew I could be, if I wanted. I sensed that the power lay within me. Yes, David had found me, but I had always had the power to use. Even in death, I'd been able to touch his spirit or soul—whatever you want to call it.

But David was gone now, forever. I felt that the way you know when you've dropped a quarter down a sewer grate and it's gone for good.

But my mother—she was still out there, somewhere. All I had to do was dare to touch her soul. . . .

I replaced the canvas without making a single mark.

I ate my sandwich, alone, sitting on the school's back steps. The concrete was cold, and my sandwich tasted like sand.

Dr. Rainier said, "So tell me what you're thinking."

"I'm thinking I don't need to be here. It's not that I'm angry or pissed off or tired of you . . . that's not it. But I think we've pretty much established that this isn't in my head, and I'm not some maniac kid who's going to go all homicidal. This is a real ability with real consequences, and only I can figure out what to do with it."

"Do you know what that is? What you want to do, I mean?"

I shook my head. As crazy as it sounded, I had toyed with the idea of being kind of a psychic ghostbuster. I mean, here I'd helped to solve a real-life crime and expose Mr. Eisenmann as an imposter. And there was that baby in the hearth. . . .

I said, "Were you able to get it?"

She nodded and brought up a picture on her computer. "I snapped it with my cell phone, but I think I got enough detail."

She had. "You see it, don't you?" I pointed to the girl's red hair band. "It's the same as the photograph in Mordecai Witek's wallet. And look at how tiny her jaw is. She and her mom look a lot alike."

Dr. Rainier thought about it, then nodded. "So they both had Treacher-Collins? Possible. The hair band would hide that

296

Marta didn't have any ears, and her mother's hair is styled to hide hers. Either or both would be deaf, of course."

Both, I thought. Hadn't Woolfe told Daecher not to worry about the noise?

And I knew that Marta had wanted to be an interpreter—not of something like German or Polish but *sign* language. That's why she'd *cawed* in David's memories; that's why her hands were always moving.

Dr. Nichols said they could establish who the father was by comparing the baby's DNA with David and *his* father. I was also betting that Eisenmann—Hermann Woolfe—was the father. But what happened to Marta or how she'd allowed her child to be taken by Woolfe, I'd never know because David clearly hadn't. I was reasonably certain that Uncle Hank's prediction had come true—that a servant was the mother—because I remembered what I'd learned in one of my visions: that Marta worked for Catherine Bleverton. (Of course, I couldn't tell Sarah that, but the DNA would go a long way.)

There was also a lot I didn't know and probably would never find out: why the Witeks' house burned to the ground; why Daecher had never ratted Woolfe out (though maybe as Eisenmann, Woolfe had made Daecher's silence very worthwhile); whether Catherine Bleverton had been murdered out on the lake because she suspected or guessed the truth.

I said all this to Dr. Rainier and added, "And don't forget the synagogue. We have no idea what happened there either."

"Some things will always remain hidden, no matter how much you dig. The question for you now is what to do with the mysteries *you* really care about."

"My mom, you mean." I eyed her curiously. "When did you figure it out? That I was hearing the muttering again?"

"I didn't really . . . figure it out, I mean. I just had this . . . *feeling*. I guess you'd call it a premonition."

I thought about her willingness to believe *in* me and suspend her own disbelief. So maybe she had empathy—and a little bit more.

"So what are you going to do?" she asked.

"I don't know," I answered truthfully. "She's out there. *They're* calling me. If it was your mom and she needed help, what would you do?"

She was silent a few long moments. "I would have to think long and hard. We're not talking about dragging someone from a burning building. This isn't the same as driving to the next city and giving her a place to live. You don't even know if being in the sideways place hasn't resulted in some fundamental change in who she is. She won't be the mother you remember, not after all this time. No one's mother ever is, not only because a mother changes but because a *child* does. Yes, you'll always be her *child*, but that doesn't mean you're frozen in time. A parent's job is to be left."

"What does that mean?"

"The minute you leave home, things change. You can't and shouldn't want to go home again, and Hank would be doing a bad job of raising you if he insisted that you should."

"I don't know if you've noticed this, but he seems to have a hard time letting me do things on my own." I told her about the thing with the barn and Dekker. "By your definition, he's doing a lousy job."

"Don't confuse ambivalence and regret with incompetence. Of course, he's got mixed feelings. What parent wouldn't?

You're his only blood relative, and his job means that he sees all the ugliness in life, all the things that can go wrong. I haven't known a single cop who doesn't worry more the longer he stays on the job. Remember: he's alive. He's right *here*. All you have to do is reach out and take his hand."

We moved on to other things after that, like whether I would return to Aspen Lake. Dr. Rainier wanted me to; she really felt as if I was gaining some control over my . . . well, we just called it a gift, and she thought I could free up some of those other people, help them rediscover themselves the way I had with Lucy. The limiting factor was in my ability to protect myself from getting sucked into those maelstroms of rage and death. Or sucking them *out*.

"Otherwise, what are your options? Live like a hermit? Be by yourself so no one can touch you and vice versa?" She shook her head emphatically. "That's not a life. So I want you to try as hard as you can to be present, and that means staying engaged, here, with us."

I told her I'd try. I wasn't sure I meant it.

Then, at the door, she said the weirdest thing.

"I know this is a dark time for you. I know you want to escape all this; that all you see right now is evil and what you feel most is regret and loss. Believe me, the world's filled with dark places and the armies of the night are just waiting their chance. But remember this." She took hold of my shoulders and squeezed them hard. "There's also the light. Call it soul, call it God's light, call it the human spirit, call it hope. It doesn't matter what you call it. The only thing that matters is this. The light is here." She bunched a fist over my heart. "The light is power, and that power is love, and love is strong."

I gave a breathy laugh. "All you need is love?"

"You're smart, so don't act so dumb. You need a lot more than love, and you know it. What I was going to say is that love can also kill. Love, especially one that is so all-consuming that it overcomes reason, can be as destructive as any evil you can imagine. So be careful. You *will* beat back this darkness, Christian, I know you will. Follow your heart. Just don't get lost."

XXXIII

And *then* it was Halloween.

Uncle Hank always works on Halloween. Trick-or-treating is limited to the hours between six and nine, and the town has a big bonfire at the school at nine thirty. Curfew is ten o'clock. A little harsh for a Saturday night, but doing things this way really cut down on all kinds of vandalism.

So I biked over to Sarah's at five to help set up. The Schoenbergs live out a ways on about fifteen wooded acres, but I enjoyed the ride. Her father wasn't home; he'd gone to some kind of conference down near Madison and wouldn't be back until Monday night. Mrs. Schoenberg had things pretty organized: a big tub out back for apple bobbing, about a million bales of hay and bunches of cornstalks all set up near a big steel fire pit and more near the house for people to sit on, a piñata chock-full of candy and coins, and stuff like that. It was kind of old-fashioned, yeah, but there was also a karaoke set up in the basement and a stack of scary DVDs for anyone who just wanted to stuff his face with candy and popcorn and gork out.

Sarah opened the door to my knock, and for a second, I thought I had the wrong house. She wasn't just dressed up. She was beautiful. I mean, really beautiful. She wore this poufy, off-the-shoulder yellow dress with a very BIG skirt—like big enough to hide under—and a red rose in her hair, which she wore swept up in curls. A pair of white gloves reached all the way to her elbows.

"Wow." I looked her up and down. "You really look nice."

"Yeah?" She did a little twirl so her skirt poofed out like an umbrella. "I've always wanted to be Belle."

Yeah, I knew that. Back when we were little, she had this thing for Disney, and I guess it hadn't stopped even after she got popular. Or maybe Disney was something popular kids liked, I don't know.

She stopped twirling. "You're not dressed up."

"Uh . . ." I looked down at my black jeans, black T-shirt, and black Chucks. Touching the black beret perched on my head, I said, "I'm a starving artist. See?" I withdrew Witek's pouch from my hip pocket with a flourish. "I even brought my brushes. Hey, that reminds me. Didn't you want me to paint something, like a mural, for the party?"

Her neck flushed with color. "Well, I got to thinking about what you'd said, and I didn't want you to think that the only reason anyone would want to hang with you is for what they can get out of you, like, you know . . . work. You're here to have fun and be with people."

I didn't know what to say. "Thank you. That's really nice."

"Yeah, well, don't let it go to your head." Then she grabbed my hand and pulled. "Come on and help me set up chairs."

"I thought I wasn't supposed to work."

"Christian . . ."

So everything started out okay. Pretty soon there were about twenty, thirty kids, all doing different things. Everyone had dressed up, though a lot of them, like me, dressed down: hobos, gangbangers, things like that. I was the only starving artist, surprise, surprise.

Some of us made cookies with Mrs. Schoenberg—yeah, I know, it sounds lame, but it's really fun, and I really like chocolate chips. We drifted on to karaoke. I didn't sing, but Sarah's got a beautiful voice, and I liked listening to her. She sang something about kissing in barley and swing, swing . . . something like that, and I got this warm feeling in my chest. It was nice, like she was singing to *me*. In between, we took turns answering the door for trick-or-treaters, who came in waves of cars with their parents because of where the Schoenbergs live. I had fun watching the little kids see how much they could grab with one hand.

So, yeah, it was good.

Night came on fast, and a couple of guys—football jocks but playing it cool—started a fire in the big steel fire pit the Schoenbergs had in the backyard well away from the house and about fifty yards from the woods. The air had been cool before but now turned chilly enough for our breath to fog. I was prepared and pulled on a thick black sweatshirt. Sarah changed out of her princess outfit into jeans and a navy blue sweatshirt, which was kind of a shame, although she kept the hair, which was classy and cute at the same time. Mrs. Schoenberg brought out platters of graham crackers, bags of marshmallows, and those humongous Hershey bars for s'mores, which I haven't had since I was, like . . . well, I don't remember.

Anyway, does this sound really lame? Yeah, I guess. But there was something about hanging around the fire, toasting marshmallows, getting a little queasy with all that sugar, and listening to the sputter of wood send red sparks flaring into the night like fireflies that made me start thinking about how eager I'd been to get away and what I'd leave behind when I did. I tried to imagine what it would be like next year come May and June when I'd know about college—and I felt a little sad.

Right around then, I realized I was thinking about what it was like to fit in, if only a little bit. I mean, it wasn't like a bunch of guys were elbowing one another to be my best friend or anything. I wasn't the center of attention, either in a good way or bad. After people got over the novelty of seeing me there, I was just . . . there. I did some things. A couple of people talked to me. I was on the periphery, yeah, but there was this tiny opening I could see—because of Sarah. Like I wasn't getting all mushy or anything, but I kept thinking about us growing up, being close, and talking, and I thought that before you could grow to love somebody, you need to know how to be best friends.

Weird, I know.

I should've realized all that was too good to last.

Around nine, we did the piñata. Big mistake.

The voices started in, loud, like cranking up the volume. Had they been there all along? Sure, but low, like white noise, you know? You stop hearing certain things after a while because you get used to them. Anyway, the muttering suddenly got clearer and louder. I had practice not showing much in the way of how I'm feeling, but I felt like crying. It was so unfair; I felt, like, leave me alone; I'm trying to be normal for a change . . . but that was too much to hope for.

I think it was because of the piñata. Watching people wind up and then let 'er rip, I had this, well, *flashback*, I guess, to the moment when Woolfe whipped that crowbar around and smashed in Mordecai Witek's skull. I heard the crunch, I smelled the blood, my heart ramped up, and my palms were sweaty.

"Come on, Christian." Sarah was laughing. She held the baseball bat in one hand, and now she trotted over and gave my arm a tug. "Your turn. Give it a whack."

I tried begging off. "I'm really not very good at that kind of thing."

"Come on," she said, but her eyes were pleading and angry at the same time: *Don't be such a jerk, you were doing so well.*

I shot a quick glance at the other kids waiting for me to get on with it already. Something Dr. Rainier said—or had it been Sarah—came back to me: *Have you ever considered that you exclude yourself?*

"Sure. Hand it over." I let myself be blindfolded and then started taking shots at that piñata with the bat. At first people were egging me on, but then all the talk suddenly dried up, and I felt the air change. In the silence, I could hear the distant singsong of Mrs. Schoenberg talking to someone in the kitchen, a girl doing a breathy, very bad Mariah Carey imitation on the karaoke—and the sudden surge of the muttering in my head.

Oh no . . . I tugged off the blindfold and saw that everyone was staring at something behind me. I turned—and all the feeling in my body puddled at my ankles.

Karl Dekker was there. Curly and Larry or *whoever* flanked him. All three wore that weird mask and cape like that guy in *Scream*, only the glow-in-the-dark masks were pushed up on top of their heads. Trust me, the view wasn't any better or less scary. Silhouetted against the orange flames from the fire, Dekker was a demon straight out of hell.

Dekker's lips split in a wolfish grin. "Hey, Killer. Trick or treat."

And, right then, I knew something else.

Daecher.

Dekker.

XXXIV

No one said anything. I just stood there, baseball bat in hand, my brain totally frozen. I felt like every bad thing I imagined might ever happen was standing right there, like a chemistry experiment where you distilled away all the crap and ended up with only one element. In this case, the element was Evil, and Evil was Dekker.

How hadn't we heard them coming? This far out of town, they'd have to had ridden their motorcycles. Of course, none of that mattered now.

I became aware of a general shuffling. A quick glance over either shoulder and I saw that everyone else was edging away, trying to move to the relative safety of the house. Leaving me alone. . . .

Except for Sarah. She moved up, a little behind and to my left. Shadows danced across her face. She said, "What do you want, Karl?"

"Not anything you haven't given up before, but..."
Dekker's grin widened. "I just want to talk to Killer here."

"Stop calling him that."

"Oooh." Dekker mimed fear, and I flashed to that moment
at the school when I'd seen how his eyes slid over Sarah's body,
to the day he'd come to the barn and cut me with his knife.
Really, it was all the same, a ghastly replay. I'd been here before, and I'd lost every time, and this was the third time. The
last time.

Dekker said, "We got business, Killer and me. He ruined
my bike, not once but twice. This is the first time I got a chance
to talk to him."

No, this was the first time in a long while I'd been away
from town. Away from Uncle Hank. Away from the law. Every
time he'd *really* come after me—not the garbage in the school
yard, there would be too many witnesses—he'd done so where
it would take time for anyone to show up and help. So he must
already know that all these other people were no threat.

You want to be a man? This is the time.

I'd faced him down once before, at the school. I could do
it again. I had to. There was no one who could do this for me.

I found my voice. "So . . . talk. I told you I'd fix it."

"I know that. So how about right now? We go to my place,
you get started; that way I can supervise."

"I'm not going anywhere with you right now."

"Whatsa matter? You afraid?"

I said nothing.

Dekker took a step closer. "Come on. I know you got a
mouth on you. Come on, Killer, show off for Sarah the way you
did before."

"Leave her out of this," I said.

"I don't need protecting," said Sarah, heatedly.

Dekker laughed. "Yeah, you're a regular spitfire, aren't you? Let me tell you, Killer, I know what Sarah's like when she gets her blood up and she's like a cat in he—"

Darting forward, Sarah slapped Dekker across the face with a sound like a pistol shot. "Shut up!" She was screaming and crying at the same time. "Just shut up, shut up, shut *up!*"

We were too stunned to say or do anything. A couple of Sarah's friends took a few tentative steps toward her and then stopped.

Dekker said, "Sarah, you do that again, I'll set your fucking house on fire."

"Hey, come on." Out of the group, one of the jocks said, "Come on, Dekker, leave them alone."

"Okay, who's the brave guy?" Dekker turned to glare at the group. His cape flowed around his body like black oil. "Come on, brave guy, you want to come out where I can see you? You want to say that to my face?"

No one volunteered. Gliding forward, Curly touched Dekker on the arm. "Easy, man."

I said, "Listen, I'll come tomorrow, first thing."

"Tomorrow, I got to work. Someone's got to work, right? Because of your old man, I ain't got the luxury of worrying about homework or school or going to some fancy-ass college."

In the house, the karaoke singing had stopped. The fire crackled. Sarah had stopped crying, though her face glistened.

Of course, the voices were still there.

Before I could respond, a pair of floodlights snapped on above the kitchen door, spilling a harsh yellow glare over the yard. The group of other kids suddenly reappeared, as if the house lights had come up in a dark theater, and then Mrs. Schoenberg was pushing out of the kitchen, onto the stoop, and then down the stairs.

"You boys get out of here now, you hear me?" She was still pretty far away, but I could see that she had a phone in hand. She strode across the yard, and then she was toe-to-toe, right in his face: "All I got to do is hit Talk and this'll go to the sheriff, and you don't want that, Karl. I'm not fooling. I am truly sorry if you think life has been unfair to you, but you reap as you sow. Now get off our property, and get out of my sight."

Okay, I was impressed. This was one mom against three very bad guys.

There was a long moment where no one said anything—well, all except the muttering. Dekker stared down hard at Mrs. Schoenberg, who did not look away and most certainly didn't back down.

He said, "Let me tell you something, Mama. You think your little girl is so wonderful? You think she's so innocent?"

Sarah made a kind of broken sound, but Mrs. Schoenberg didn't turn around. Instead, she said, very distinctly, "Karl, I am sorry you've been so hurt by life, but that's no excuse to spread ruin wherever you go. Have mercy on others, and you might be surprised to find that they will have mercy on you."

If she meant to shame him, I think she succeeded—maybe a little too well, in retrospect. People like Karl Dekker don't bear shame well.

But at that moment, she seemed to have gotten through to him because Dekker suddenly turned to Curly and then Larry and then jerked his head. "Come on, let's get the fuck out of here."

They faded quickly into the darkness, moving fast for the front of the house, their black capes snapping behind. They rounded the far corner of the house, and a few moments later, I heard the roar of motorcycles growling to life. I remembered to take a breath.

"All right, everyone." Mrs. Schoenberg turned to the rest of us. "I don't see why this should break things up. You go—"

A sudden blast of engine roar split the air in a chain saw of sound, a racket that ruptured the night and rebounded off the trees as if the world were cracking apart at the seams. Someone just had time to scream, "HEY!"

I whirled.

Dekker and the others were on their bikes, racing over the yard, in a wedge like fighter pilots.

No one moved.

We were all stunned, immobilized for a split second too long as they bore down, and I realized they weren't going to swerve. In the lead, the tip of the arrow, Dekker's bike wasn't just a machine. With those glowing lupine eyes and snarling teeth, Dekker's bike was an engine of doom, a creature pulled from a nightmare . . . from the sideways place, and I had done that. I had given him the power. My fault, this was *my* fault. . . .

That was also the moment I saw two things.

Dekker and the others had pulled those masks over their faces, maybe for effect, but mostly because they *were* from hell. Their faces glowed as if drawing fire from within. They were gleaming latex gargoyles as hideous as the ruin Hermann Woolfe had made of his own flesh.

And Dekker had something in his left hand.

A pipe, maybe, or a crowbar, I couldn't tell. But I saw what he was going to do just as I had known what Woolfe would do an instant before he did. I knew, I saw . . . God help me, I saw, and I was as helpless in the flesh, in the here and now, as I'd been as a phantom in the past.

The voices were trying to claw their way out of my head. I didn't know which was louder: the screams of the other kids or the gibberings of the things living in my head.

"No," I whispered. "No, no. Stop. Please."

Mrs. Schoenberg was closer to the house, standing where Dekker and his boys had been, and separated from the rest of us by a good thirty feet—and they went right for her.

"No, no, look out!" Now I started forward, but I was too far away and much too late. "Mrs. Schoenberg, look out, get out of the way, *look out!*"

"*MOM!!*" Sarah screamed at the same instant.

Mrs. Schoenberg reacted, but she was too late. Maybe she saw it coming, maybe not, or maybe she only sensed that something very, very bad was about to happen. She took a few stumbling steps to the left, toward the house, but Dekker anticipated her, and then he whizzed past. I never saw where the pipe hit her, but there was that awful unforgettable sound from the past—of metal smacking meat and bone—and then a hollow popping sound, like what you'd expect from a cantaloupe if you smash it against concrete. The impact lifted her a foot in the air as a fan of blood exploded in the harsh backlight from the house floods. Mrs. Schoenberg made a sound—UNGH!—and then she crashed to the ground. She lay on the grass, her arms and legs jittering, and I could see that her head . . . oh, her face . . .

"NO!" Sarah was running for her mother. "Mom, MOM!!"

The other kids started screaming and shouting, and they broke apart, scattering like sheep as Dekker and the other two swooped and turned, pivoting sharply, tearing up clods of earth. I just stood there, and why they never mowed me down in that first pass, I'll never know. Maybe they were just too focused on the chaos, or perhaps Dekker decided he needed to get rid of Mrs. Schoenberg first. I mean, you get right down to it, how better to shock the hell out of kids—even grown kids like us—than to show them that adults can't protect them?

Dekker shot for the fire pit. Burning logs tumbled to the grass, some rolling to those dry hay bales, which caught fire almost at once. Sweeping up a flaming log, Dekker held it high as a torch and then sent it spinning and sailing toward the house—and the bales of hay and cornstalks heaped near the patio. The log buried itself in a square of hay, and an instant later, I smelled the sweet char of scorched alfalfa.

Sarah had reached her mother, who wasn't moving anymore. "Help!" She was almost drowned out by the engine roar. "Help, someone, help!"

The fires were going in earnest now. Dekker's two friends crisscrossed before the flames, their capes billowing, but I saw them pull up and turn at Sarah's scream. Their headlights glared out of the darkness like eyes, and I knew they were looking at Mrs. Schoenberg because in the next second, they'd wheeled around and were streaking back for the road, fast.

Leaving only Dekker—who was more than bad enough.

I don't know if anyone had the good sense to pull out a cell and call 911. I didn't have a phone, but I *did* see what

Sarah didn't. Ten feet from her mother's body, the phone Mrs. Schoenberg had been carrying gleamed orange in the grass.

To my left, I saw Dekker coming around for another pass and then the beam of Dekker's headlight speared Sarah, and his motorcycle sprang forward. Pinned in a bubble of silver-white glare, Sarah's skin was a ghastly, washed-out gray. Her shocked, uncomprehending eyes bulged, but she didn't move.

But I finally, finally did.

"Sarah!" With a wild yell, I rushed forward, cocking the piñata bat I still held with my right hand. As Dekker screamed up, I chopped the bat with everything I had. I'd been aiming for that horrible mask, but either he'd seen me or some preternatural sixth sense warned him. He ducked, hunched up his shoulders, and suddenly decelerated, trying to plant a boot and spin away, but he was going too fast. In the next instant, the bat connected. The blow was solid, and Dekker screamed as he and the bike went crashing sideways, wiping out, skidding along the ground.

A white blaze of pain shuddered all the way to my shoulder. I screamed, lost my grip on the bat, and then it was a choice: the bat or . . .

No, not the bat. Instead, I scrambled for the phone, prayed that Mrs. Schoenberg hadn't been bluffing like Sarah, and then heard the musical notes of the three numbers dialing and then a voice, the dispatcher: "Winter Sheriff's Department 911, what—"

"Fire! The Schoenbergs! Send help, send an ambulance *now*!" Then I dropped the phone but left the connection open, hooked my hand under Sarah's arm and hauled her to her feet. "Sarah, Sarah, come on, we got to go, we got to go *now*!"

"Wh-what?" Sarah was in shock. Closer to the house, there were screams and shouts, and she turned, saw the fire, and would've started that way if I hadn't yanked her back. "What, what are you . . . No! Mom, Mom, I can't leave . . ."

"*FUCK!*" It was Dekker, and I jerked around, saw him crawling out from under his bike, his hideous mask swinging in our direction, and then he was pointing, screaming: "You're dead, you're fucking DEAD . . . !"

"Come *on!*" And then I was running as fast as I could, dragging Sarah behind, sprinting for the woods. "Sarah, hurry, hurry, go, *go!*"

We plunged into the forest.

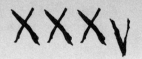

XXXV

The flames devoured the hay, releasing pulsing orange light that throbbed against the forest dark. In a way, that helped us because there was no moon, no other way for me to see where we were going. But the fact that I *could* see something meant that we could be *seen* too. We wore dark clothing and that would help, but we had to get out of the light.

"This way." I pulled Sarah to the left, angling us away from the fire. Here, the darkness was denser, thicker, and soon the woods swallowed us up. Branches whipped the bare skin of my face; snarls of brush clawed at my waist and legs.

"Cover your face," I said to Sarah. I put my arm up to shield my eyes. The trees pressed around us, but I had only the vaguest sense of where they were and when they were coming up, the sense of something really solid hurtling out of the dark for my face.

My idea had been that Dekker couldn't follow us in the woods, not on his bike anyway. He'd have to come on foot. If we could just get in far enough, then duck down and wait until the dispatcher got the fire department and Uncle Hank and the others out here, then we'd get out of this. We got maybe a hundred, two hundred yards farther in, and then I veered around a wide chunk of roots and clotted dirt and pulled Sarah down into a soft earthen bowl created when the tree had toppled. I had a fleeting thought back to Mosby and what he'd said about the difference between a depression made by felled trees and a grave, and I shivered.

The things you think about when you're a hair's breadth away from getting yourself killed.

"We'll wait here." I barely heard myself over the cacophony in my head—those voices that still clawed—but I forced myself to pitch my voice to a whisper. "Uncle Hank'll get here soon. It'll be okay."

"N-noooo," Sarah moaned. She was shaking. "Nooo, Mom . . . Mom's dead; they killed Mom. . . ."

"Hey." I wrapped her up, though my arms had begun to itch and burn with a familiar fire. Right, a lot of good that would do me now. Yeah, I had Witek's brushes but nothing to really draw with, nothing to paint on, no *paints* . . . and what would I draw anyway? Sarah felt small, fragile as a baby bird as she huddled in my arms. "We don't know that. . . . It'll be okay, Sarah, it'll be okay."

God, I hated how I felt: helpless and scared, waiting for a rescue. Why couldn't I *do* something? *Anything?* What good was I to anyone when it really counted? It was Mrs. Schoenberg who'd been the brave one, and when it mattered—when

I'd had the chance to warn her—my stupid, stupid brain hadn't registered the danger until too late. And what if Uncle Hank got here too late? What if Mrs. Schoenberg was already dead?

My arms were killing me. I tried clamping down on the itch. Useless, useless, useless, what could I possibly draw . . . ?

"Oh!" Sarah gasped. "Oh my God."

Startled, I looked up. "Wha . . ." And then I thought: *Oh no.*

A shaft of blue-white light lanced the woods directly in front of us. The light swept right and then left, then right again in a search pattern: skimming the floor, sweeping up to the trees on either side.

"Killer." Dekker's voice was almost a singsong. "Hey, Killer, I know you're out here. Come on out. Don't make it worse on yourself now. Come out and I won't hurt you."

Sarah was trembling now, a bone-deep visceral shudder. I said nothing. I barely breathed. The inside of my head was going ape shit. My arms were on fire.

"You killed my bike." Dekker's voice was closer, the bob of his light was brighter, and I knew he would find us soon. Even as quiet as we were, it would be a miracle if he didn't find us. Somehow he *would* know exactly where to look.

"I said, you killed my fucking bike." Dekker pitched his voice louder, and now I could hear the dragging lurch in his steps and then the rhythmic rasp of metal against metal as his knife opened, closed, opened, snick-snick-snick. . . . "My fucking leg hurts like hell. I'm going to find you, you cocksucker, and I'm going to mess you up so bad it'll be a miracle they figure out how to put you back together."

We remained silent, crouching behind that massive root ball, watching as the light stabbed and probed and got closer.

Maybe fifty yards now and there was no way we could get away, go deeper into the woods without being heard.

"Oh, and one more thing, Killer," Dekker sang out. "You remember your aunt? Aunt *Jean*? My daddy got drunk a couple of nights ago, and guess what he comes out with? The night your aunt drowned, he said he saw her car right before it went under. Said she went off the road and crashed through the ice and when he got to the bank, she was screaming, hollering her head off. Only he saw she was sinking, and so it wasn't any use going to get anyone. So he just had himself another drink and waited for the hollering to stop. Said it took a long, long time because he near about finished that bottle. Said she squealed like a pig before it was all over. *Wee-wee-wee.*" He giggled. "*Wee-wee-wee-wee*, help me, help me, I don't want to die, *wee-wee-wee . . .*"

I closed my eyes. Remembered the empty fifth found in that gulley. Maybe black ice had started the skid, but Dekker's father had put the period on my aunt's life.

And did it make a difference, really? Her death was fated. I had *drawn* it: pulled that horrible moment from the well of my rage and her secret hell. I couldn't remember if I'd drawn a drunk in there, and it didn't matter.

The voices, beckoning, clamoring . . .

And from Dekker: "*Wee-wee-wee . . .*"

I let go of Sarah.

She grabbed my arm. "Christian," she hissed in my ear. "He's baiting you . . . no!"

I didn't reply. My questing fingers closed around the pouch with Witek's brushes, and I pulled one out at random. It didn't matter which one, and I wouldn't need to see for this. Even if

319

I had decided on something more complex, I doubted I would need my eyes. I drew in the dark, after all.

Scrambling quickly to the deepest point in the bowl, I upended the brush, grasping it like a knife. Then I cut four sharp strokes into the dirt with the tip of the wooden handle: a rectangle. Then I visualized where the knob needed to be and quickly sketched a circle.

Now or never . . .

"Stay down." I swarmed to Sarah and pressed her back, out of the way. "Stay away from the door. Don't come down here or near it or me, no matter what happens."

"Door? What? Christian, no, no!" Sarah's terrified whisper thinned to a wheeze as I pushed to my feet. "What are you *doing?*"

"What I should have done a long time ago," I said and turned as Dekker's flashlight found me, firing my body in a silvery blaze. He was so close I could see he still wore that stupid mask.

"There you are, Killer," said Dekker.

"That's right," I said. "Here I am."

Then I bent, grabbed the knob—and turned.

For an instant, as my fingers scraped dirt, I thought, *You idiot, this isn't going to work.* But then it was as if the *idea* of the knob drew on substance from the air and my intent because I felt the hard metal solidify beneath my palm and against my fingers. The margins of the door began to shimmer and glow, and then I yanked back as hard as I could, and then I *drew.* . . .

I don't know what I expected.

No, I'm lying. I know what I wanted.

You know what I wanted? I wanted black wraiths and goblins, things with jostling teeth and bloody tentacles. What I wanted from the sideways place—if that's what lay behind this door—was death and destruction and vengeance. I embraced the blackness welling in my heart. My mouth was coppery with the imagined taste of blood. I wanted Dekker to feel every inch of pain and terror I was certain my aunt felt as she drowned, alone, in that freezing dark. *That's* what I wanted.

But that was not what I drew.

In the next instant, a great bolt of stunning purple light and sound blew apart the night.

Imagine looking down an elevator shaft that is infinitely deep and think of the brightest day that can exist on this earth—and then multiple that by a thousand. Ten thousand. The planet Mercury at high noon—so bright that the light is solid, it has a punch and heft, and now imagine that it is also sound that smashes the night, splintering trees with a great guttering roar. . . .

The Armies of the Light. That's what Dr. Rainier said.

Light thrust from the sideways place with a moaning, screaming, cracking sound like the rupture of the earth. The concussive force was so great it hammered my chest, palming my body, flinging me from the bowl. I slammed the tangle of roots, and for a second, my vision swirled as the air was driven out of my chest in a sickening whoosh.

The voices in my head were churning, a maelstrom of sound echoing the greater cataclysm I'd unleashed. But then, dimly, I heard Sarah, shrieking. . . .

No, God no, please, not Sarah! Clawing my way to hands and knees, I shook my head like a dog and looked up—and froze.

The forest was alive with streamers of purple and then lava and then gold and then scarlet. The light swirled in a dizzying vortex around the trees, spiraled up trunks, and spilled in a flood along the forest floor. It was spreading fast, wider and wider, and then I realized: the light *was* the voices, the voices *were* the light, and they were alive and hungry. Light unfurled in tentacles and spidery fingers, swarming over the earth with a rustling, rasping, clacking chitter like the mandibles of a million locusts.

I spotted Sarah, backed up against a tree. She was screaming; her hands were clasped over her ears, and her eyes were shut tight—and then my heart nearly died in my chest.

Because the light had her. It twined in her hair, tasted her eyes and ears, fingered her mouth, spun in twists up her legs—

"No!" I struggled to my feet. I screamed into the night: "No, no! Not her! She's an innocent! She's not what you're after! Leave her alone, stop . . . stop!"

I don't know if the light heard me; I may never know if the light is mine to command. But something *did* happen.

That awful purple light shuddered as it tasted Sarah's face and her tears—not a blow, a *caress*—and then it retreated like water from the shore, leaving Sarah moaning and shivering, huddled in a ball, her arms over her head. Heart in my mouth, I took a step toward her, and the light at my feet parted. It eddied and flowed; tendrils plucked at my skin and hair.

And then as quickly as thought, the light blistered the air, hurling itself past me, and then Dekker screamed. . . .

Light funneled around and around Dekker in a tornado that ripped branches from the trees and drew up dead leaves and debris into an ever-widening spiral. The light spun itself into a shimmering purple cobweb around his body and wherever the individual filaments touched, his clothes began to smoke. His black cape curled and burned; and then it was his skin that began bubbling; and Dekker's screaming mask was melting away; and then his mouth was wide, wide open; and the scalding light was pouring down his throat, boiling away his voice, eating his flesh like acid.

I didn't want to look, but I knew I had to. This Army of Light was mine. I had summoned it. I had *drawn* it.

Could I have stopped it? I don't know.

The truth is, I didn't want to.

Then that nacreous purple light convulsed, gathering itself into a veil so dense I couldn't see through it, as if *it* had become a darkness all its own. If Dekker was still there, I couldn't see him. The forest was thick with the stench of burning meat and molten latex and scorched wood and an unnatural fire.

And then it was done. I don't know how the light knew, but maybe it's like any other fight. When the enemy's dead, you know it.

The light pulled away in a quickening stream, rushing for the door. It did so with a sibilant whisper and in a rush—in that nearly silent way that a serpent slithers into the dark of its burrow. Muttering, the light spilled back, into the sideways place, and I followed, stumbling, because I had to see. . . .

Tottering to the very brink, I peered past the lip of the open door and down into all that bizarre radiance. Yes, I could see it all, and it was as I'd imagined: the rugged mountains, the clawing trees, and that queer spiked mountain. . . .

And something else: *my* face, shining, pulling together as if I peered into a mirror made from the sun.

Come. The light wavered and whispered, and now I could smell it, an intoxicating fragrance not of this earth and so rich I wanted to fall into it, into that mask of myself. *All you have to do is step through the door.*

Yes, all I would have to do is fall . . .

Then, cutting through the darkness, I heard Uncle Hank: "Christian! *CHRISTIAN!*"

There was no mistaking the panic in that voice. Or the love. He called again, but I didn't answer. I couldn't, not just yet.

Because here was the hell of it: I loved my mother. Didn't I? Or did I only love a mirage? A memory?

I couldn't decide. I didn't know. I balanced on the brink of two worlds, each with its claim and the promise that love waited as a reward. . . .

"Christian?" I could tell from his voice that he was moving off in the wrong direction, farther away. If I wanted to be found, I would have to guide him.

All you have to do is reach out and take his hand. That's another thing Dr. Rainier had said.

Then I heard something else above the call of the light and my uncle's shouts. I heard Sarah.

She was still curled in on herself, but she was moaning, and I knew she would never get out of these woods without help.

I couldn't do that to her, not to Sarah, who was kind to me and good.

So I turned away from the door.

Wait, whispered the light, though it seemed to scream in my head. *Wait*, my double sighed.

"Mom." Sarah was crying and rocking. "Oh Mom, Mommy . . ."

Wait . . .

I knew what I had to do.

I closed that door. I erased it, scuffing the dirt with my shoes, but I was crying as I did it. The light dissolved and splintered through my tears, and then it was gone.

Then I went to Sarah and held her and shouted for my uncle. And I didn't let her go until we were found.

XXXVI

Uncle Hank insisted that I get checked out at the hospital, even though I told him I didn't need it. Mrs. Schoenberg was already in emergency surgery, but Uncle Hank said they were talking about calling in a helicopter and flying her to Milwaukee.

"Is she going to be all right?" I asked. We were in the waiting room by then because Reverend Schoenberg was still a couple of hours away, and I wanted to stay until he got there. I hadn't seen Sarah since they loaded her into a second ambulance, but Uncle Hank said that Dr. Rainier was with her.

"If Mrs. Schoenberg pulls through, I don't think she's going to be the same woman," Uncle Hank said, heavily. "We'll just have to wait and see. What I don't understand is where Dekker got himself to. You say he followed you into the woods?" When I only nodded, he continued, "Then there ought to be some trace. A trail, something, but there's nothing. We got his bike, so I know he didn't use that to get away. Of course, his two buddies aren't saying anything." He checked his watch. "It'll be light in another couple hours. Maybe then, with dogs . . ."

"Maybe," I said. But I knew this world had seen the last of Karl Dekker.

I spotted Dr. Rainier pushing out of the elevator, and we stood as she came down the hall. "How is Sarah?" I asked.

"Sleeping. They've sedated her. Between the medication and the shock, she'll probably sleep until this afternoon. Physically, she's fine, but her memory's pretty foggy right now. We've ruled out trauma. Her CT and neuro exam are clean. So we'll just have to wait, see if this psychogenic amnesia clears," said Dr. Rainier.

"She said nothing?" asked Uncle Hank. "She can't remember *anything*?"

"Oh, I didn't say that. She remembers, I think, but what she says doesn't make sense."

"What did she say?" I asked.

"She said that the light ate him . . . ate Dekker." Dr. Rainier's eyes never left my face. "She said the light destroyed the darkness."

I couldn't speak.

"You're right. That doesn't make sense," said Uncle Hank.

"Well," said Dr. Rainier, "not to you or me."

———

Dr. Rainier and Uncle Hank went to get coffee and an early breakfast in the hospital cafeteria, but I stayed behind.

Maybe twenty minutes later, Justin came by and said that the guy with the dogs was maybe a half hour away from the Schoenbergs' place. "Fire chief says the house is gonna be okay. They'll need to build a new porch, though." He went off to find

Uncle Hank, and I thought about maybe settling in for a nap. I was so keyed up, I was sure I wouldn't get any sleep.

I woke when someone touched my shoulder. "Are you Christian Cage?"

"What?" Blinking, I pushed out of my slump. My neck hurt and drool slicked my chin. A lean man with clear brown eyes and a well-trimmed beard stood over me. "Yeah, yeah, I'm Christian."

He stuck out his hand. "Rabbi Saltzman. We spoke?"

"Yeah, yeah, sure." Dazed, I grasped his hand. His grip was firm, but his skin was warm. We shook, and I said, "What time is it? What are you doing here?"

"It's around nine. May I sit with you?"

"Hunh? Sure." I scrubbed my face with my hands as he dropped into the chair next to mine, and I noticed he wore a small crocheted cap with a Star of David.

He said, "I had already arranged to come up for David Witek's body today, but then I heard about Mrs. Schoenberg."

"How did you—?"

"Steve Schoenberg and I were at the same conference. I didn't think he should be alone, so we drove up together. He's with his wife now."

"She's out of surgery?" I *had* slept soundly. "How is she?"

"She's alive. That's all anyone can say. They'll move her to Milwaukee this afternoon. You want to maybe wash up and then get some breakfast? I'll bet we can scrounge up toiletries for you somewhere."

Well yeah, my mouth *did* taste like the bottom of a car. An ER nurse brought me a little packet of stuff they give to patients and a clean scrub shirt. Then she let me into a doctors' on-call room, which had its own bathroom and shower. After I got cleaned up, Rabbi Saltzman and I went to the cafeteria. The food was lousy—pancakes like Frisbees—but I was starved, and I ate every scrap.

Rabbi Saltzman had coffee. He waited until I slowed down and then said, "I hear you've had quite a night. Actually, speaking with Dr. Rainier, it seems to me that you've had quite the month."

The pancakes turned to lead in my stomach. "What did she say?"

He must've read my mind because he said, "Nothing personal, if that's what you're worried about. She told me about what happened last week, you figuring out about the bodies in the barn. She was a little . . . vague about how you did that. I gather that you've had some pretty strange experiences." He paused, as if expecting that I might respond. It seemed best to keep my mouth shut, so I did.

He waited another moment and then changed the subject. "Do you still want to know what happened to the Jews of Winter? There aren't many records. So much is . . ." He thought about it. "Well, not gone, but it is history, and if there's one thing we Jews need to remember is that life isn't lived in the past. So many Jews define their Jewishness only around the Holocaust, but our history stretches for thousands of years. So we should *remember*, we shouldn't forget, and we should abide by the past's lessons, but we can't remain there."

I mulled that one over and was surprised that I even had to think about what I wanted to know, if anything. In a way, I was still curious, but I felt as if I'd reached some sort of personal closure. There was much I'd already solved, more that I would never know—and while I did not believe that ignorance was bliss, I was pretty clear I could fill in the gaps.

So what popped out of my mouth was kind of surprising, even to me. "I would like to know what happened to the cemetery. You had to have one."

Rabbi Saltzman pushed back from the table. "Would you like to see it?"

"This is it?" I asked.

"What's left of it," said Rabbi Saltzman. "Not very impressive, I'm afraid."

Well, not exactly true. We stood by the edge of that grove of white pines, the ones everyone had always said were planted by shipbuilders. I told Rabbi Saltzman that, and he just shrugged.

"People remember what they want to remember. Say something enough times, and people will start to believe it. But the truth is that when the Jews left, they took their dead with them and planted these trees. The only things they left *here* were their sacred books." At my questioning look, he said, "Jews believe that God's name must never be destroyed. So any worn-out prayer book or Torah scroll or any book with God's name or written in Hebrew is placed in a special storeroom, a *genizah*. Every seven years, the genizah's contents are buried in a Jewish cemetery."

"So the books and Torahs are still out here? In the *ground*?"

"Yes. By this time, though, they're the trees, don't you think?"

I *had* always felt that this grove was different. I thought of the hours I had lain on this sacred ground and the intense peace that would seep into my body. "Why did they take everyone with them?"

Rabbi Saltzman didn't answer at first. He stared into the grove's shadows as a breath of wind whispered through the high branches. Then he said, "Because of Joseph's bones. You know the story? In Genesis?"

"No."

"Right before he died, Joseph made the children of Israel promise to take his bones when they left Egypt: *God will surely visit you, and you shall carry up my bones from here.* At the time, they probably thought he was crazy because life was good for them in Goshen, so why should they leave? But they promised. Eventually, of course, they became slaves. When God sent Moses and Aaron to lead them to freedom, Moses kept the promise and gathered up Joseph's bones to take with them."

"So Moses buried him?"

"No, Moses was not allowed into the Promised Land. It was up to Joshua, finally, to give Joseph a proper burial in Shechem, in a plot of land that Jacob, Joseph's father, had bought centuries before."

"And that's why you're here for Mr. Witek."

"To take him back, yes. I've also made arrangements for his father's remains when the pathologist releases them." Rabbi Saltzman hesitated and then said, "And the baby, even if it turns out not to be related to the Witeks."

I didn't think there was much chance of that, but I said, "Why would you do that? If it's not a Jew?"

"It seems the right thing to do. Who else will mourn that child?"

No one, I thought. No one but me.

"We Jews don't like leaving anyone behind," Rabbi Saltzman continued, and then he gave me a small grin. "I guess you could say that we're like God's Marines that way."

I don't know why I did what I did next. Maybe I was just so tired. Or maybe because of the presence in that grove, I don't know.

But I told Rabbi Saltzman everything. Pretty much. Not about Aunt Jean or Miss Stefancyzk or anything like that. That was part of a story that had nothing to do with David Witek.

Instead, I told the rabbi about the barn, meeting Mr. Witek in the home, my nightmares, the paintings. Drawing that final confrontation and then knowing where to look for David's father. I thought about telling him about the light and Dekker, but I didn't.

He listened and didn't interrupt. When I was done, he was silent a few moments longer and then said, simply, "I believe you."

"You do?" I searched his face for a lie, but his eyes were gentle and clear. "It sounds nuts . . . I mean, when you think about it."

"Oh, I suppose there were a few people who thought Moses had gone off the deep end when he claimed to have seen a burning bush that wasn't destroyed. Or Jacob when he dreamt his ladder of angels."

"You're saying it was . . . God?"

"I don't know. I'm not sure it matters. If you want to get scriptural about it, there are passages in Genesis and Deuteronomy, where it seems that people on the verge of death gain tremendous prophetic or clairvoyant powers. So maybe that happened to David. His mind had fixed on the one thing he could not leave behind, but he could no longer act for himself. Either he chose you or your mind found his, and then you acted because he couldn't. You did a great mitzvah."

"A . . . what? Is that like a good deed?"

He laughed. "Let me put it to you this way: In our religion, we have what is called the *chevra kadisha*, a holy society. These are men and women who give of themselves to the dead, preparing the body according to our laws and protecting the body until burial. To do so is a *chesed shel emet*, a good deed of truth. It is a kindness done without ulterior motive because the dead can never repay the favor." He put a gentle hand on my shoulder. "That is what you have done for David. I don't know what you believe, personally, but remember this: What you did was a great kindness, and God will not forget."

NOVEMBER 1: NIGHT

WINTER, WISCONSIN

So . . . that's it, I guess. Pretty much.

They took Sarah's mom to Milwaukee this afternoon. The doctors still don't know what's going to happen. Right now, Reverend Schoenberg's still in Winter because Sarah has to stay in the hospital for another day. Sarah's aunt is on her way to Milwaukee, though, so Mrs. Schoenberg won't be alone.

In a way, I think I ought to stay until everything's sorted out, but it might be a long time and I need to do this now, while I've got things square in my head. While I'm still brave enough to try. Because, of course, the muttering hasn't gone away.

You know what day this is? Yeah, yeah, the day after Halloween, hah-hah. It's All Saints' Day. I looked it up. It's supposed to honor those who've had visions of heaven—and not just any visions, but beatific ones: direct communion with God.

So is that irony or what?

I think Dr. Rainier knows. We don't have what I did with David, but I'm not sure that matters. I think she can accept this because it's like she said: parents are there to be left. I'm glad she'll be here for Uncle Hank when I'm gone, though. I've seen the way they look at each other. You don't have to be a telepath for that one.

It's important for me to say this, so there's no doubt. Most of all, I don't want any of you to feel bad or be sad because I don't and I'm not. Well, not much.

I love you, Uncle Hank. I wish we could go together, but we can't because I don't think that where I'm going is safe for you. You've kept me safe all these years. Now it's my turn to return the favor. But I love you.

So, please understand that you haven't failed. I *need* to do this. I need to see for myself what's possible. I need to see what that mountain's all about. I need to find out who's there. I've got a pretty good idea already.

If it's Mom, then I have to figure out why she can't get back. She might be trapped. Or maybe she won't leave Dad. Or—maybe—she doesn't want to come back because she thinks that what she's found there is better than anything this world can offer.

If she thinks that, she's wrong.

On the other hand, who knows? Maybe once I'm there, I won't want to come back either. But I don't know, and I won't until I see through her eyes, and let her see through mine: so she knows what's possible in *this* world.

Because this world is a good one. Because love is powerful and love is strong, strong enough to bridge time and space . . . and worlds.

—

Mordecai's brush feels right in my hand.

So does the knob that I've painted.

I take the knob in my hand and it turns—

And then there is light, that brilliant purple light so bright I have to close my eyes. But I still hear them, these Armies of Light.

I step toward them and whisper: "Mom?"

THE END

AUTHOR'S NOTE

The tiny village of Winter, Wisconsin, really exists, nestled in the only somewhat larger *town* of Winter—which seems to be a Wisconsin thing. Although I've never visited either, I'm sure they're lovely and as different from *my* Winter as night is to day. The only thing I know for sure is that neither the real town nor village maintained a prisoner of war camp during World War II. The same cannot be said for thirty-nine other Wisconsin towns that were part of a network of more than five hundred PW camps scattered across the United States and home to more than half a million German, Italian, and Japanese PWs from 1942 until 1945. Anyone interested in reading more about this can do no better than *Nazi Prisoners of War in America* by Arnold Krammer (Scarborough House, 1996). For Wisconsin history buffs, there's *Stalag Wisconsin* by Betty Cowley (Badger Books, 2002).

ACKNOWLEDGMENTS

Babying a book, like bringing up a child, takes a village, and I need to take a moment to gush about the folks who helped bring up this book by hand.

First off, to my indefatigable editor, Andrew Karre, who popped into my e-mail one glorious April afternoon and has since proven to be as insightful and thoughtful a reader and advocate as one could ever have the great good fortune to meet. Thank you so much, Andrew, for your support, patience, enthusiasm, and gentle humor. Never has a birth been so painless.

A big shout-out to everyone at Carolrhoda who worked on this book, and especially Lindsay Matvick, who—despite having several hundred clamoring authors—always saw me in the back whenever I raised my hand.

To my no-nonsense, straight-shooter, level-headed agent, Jennifer Laughran: every author needs such an advocate and anchor.

Big hugs and sloppy kisses to Louisa Swann, Jo Ann Dent, and Bev Schroeder, who helped chase away the book-birthing blues. Thanks also to my fellow writers from the Oregon Writers Workshop who critiqued the original proposal; and to Kristine Kathryn Rusch, who hinted, ever so gently, that I should just write already.

I am indebted beyond words to Dean Wesley Smith—friend, colleague, mentor, my very first editor. Thank you, Dean, for your wisdom, ever-available shoulder and the occasional, well-placed boot in the rear.

Finally, for David: Thank you, dear, for riding the roller coaster and not eating a single cat.